Love IS MAJESTIC

A NOVEL

CEDERICK STEWART

nyreepress

This book is dedicated to my wife,
Latresha and my daughters, Cedra and Eden.
God has shown me true love through you all. I
love you guys dearly and I pray that you will continue to experience God's love in all you do.

ALPHA

"I think I have everything," Majestic said, as she looked over the list in her hand. She had double-checked the list and her items in her luggage over and over. She was very detail-oriented and now was no different. Even though she was only packing to go on vacation, she still wanted to make sure that she had everything she needed. She was going to be gone for four weeks and she had a lot of items to be accounted for. She was so excited, and was looking forward to going on vacation. This is her first vacation since she opened her photography gallery, "Majestically Captured" seven years ago. She had put in so much time into it that she had little time for anything else. Opening up your own gallery is one thing, but doing it in Las Vegas is another thing; everything had to be bigger and better there. Through her ups and downs, she survived the tough times and now she was doing very well. She was well beyond her expectations financially, and she knew that was a blessing within itself. Majestic had certain aspects of her life within spiritual balance, which was very comforting. She only wished her love life was the same way. In the midst of all her accomplishments and achievements, the one thing that was closest to the heart was something she couldn't grasp. She came real close thirteen years ago. She had known a guy named Ryan and he was everything she wanted a man to be. A Christian man that was kind, caring, handsome and very respectful. Although they were just friends, they had hopes of getting married one day. They had actually loved each other deeply, and their actions showed it even without the title. They were actually more than friends because they crossed the fine line between friends and dating. They had in fact become intimate a few times. The only thing that stopped them from being together was that she went off to college, and he was leaving the country.

She had a plan that she didn't want to deviate from. Her goal was to finish college, move to Las Vegas and open up her gallery, which she did. Ryan wanted to leave the country with his parents to do volunteer work on a Caribbean island. Majestic had heard nothing but horror stories about long distance relationships so she never pursued one with Ryan. Many times she had been told that no long distance relationship ever worked out. There was too much time apart and too much space. You had to be able to trust someone 100% and without a doubt.

Majestic felt that she could trust Ryan but she let the whispers of others cloud her better judgment. Everyone kept telling her that Ryan was going to a Caribbean island full of women on vacation. Plenty of women that were going there for a good time and probably would stop at nothing to have one. She has heard people talk about their vacations and how wild some of them were. They spoke of the temptation that he would experience and possibly give in. Everyone told her that no man would be faithful in that situation. No man was that good and she believed them. She couldn't picture herself being in Las Vegas and falling in love with Ryan while he was on an island getaway. It really didn't make sense to her to put herself in that situation, so she felt like she should pursue her dream. She knew she was letting a good one go, but she chose her dream over love. Majestic just figured that she would eventually find someone new. No one ever thinks that they will stay unlucky in love, and in that aspect, Majestic was no different. She tried to move on and began to date. Every relationship she entered never truly got off the ground, which she considered as failure. She didn't want to believe that she failed at love, because she didn't think that she was the problem. The problem, she felt, was with all the men from her previous relationships. That may seem like finger pointing or passing the blame, but it was always the same reoccurring theme.

She reflected on when she was in high school, and the first time she had her eyes opened to "Proverbs 31:10." From that moment on she wanted to be a virtuous woman. Just the sound of that made her feel like it was a title worth having. Virtuous woman had a very unique and self-respecting ring to it. She had ranked it up there with other adjectives like beautiful, intelligent, respectful and trustworthy. She could think of nothing better for her to do than to be virtuous. She put her petty desires aside and promised God that day that she would be what he wanted her to be. She wanted to be good and wait until she was married before she became intimate. Of course, that was a goal that she wasn't able to keep. In this day and age, she never thought twice about it. She went with the flow with her relationships and intimacy became a part of her relationships.

Every time a relationship ended, she looked back over it and wondered where it went wrong. Majestic kept on thinking about what else she could have done. She knew there was nothing else to give and nothing else to expect in the future. Being intimate left nothing else to gain and so the relationship became stagnant if there was no true connection with the other person. So now she was tired of having no luck in relationships and she was tired of giving herself away and getting nothing in return but rejection and failure. So she just dusted herself off and told herself that she would never give in to lust again. Five years ago she decided that she was going to change. So she made a new goal of waiting until she was married. She couldn't take back the fact that she was intimate with past boyfriends, but she could make sure that it didn't happen again. That was her new goal. That goal is also a hindrance when it comes to dating. Even the most Christified man, which was Majestic's word for a man that swore he lived out the Bible but never showed it, ran when he found out. The first moment that things got going in the relationship direction, she had to be open and honest with whom she was dating. She would inform her mate that under no circumstances would she compromise her Christian walk. So in layman's terms, there was no chance of them being intimate unless they were married. Every man that was talking a good game in the beginning realized that Majestic was dead serious so they would decide to end the relationship with any excuse imaginable, instead of just coming out and saying that they were the type of Christian that would do everything else except abstaining from intimacy. Majestic couldn't understand why every man ran when they found out she did not want intimacy outside of marriage. What was so hard about waiting on someone you love and to show the love you have for your Heavenly Father? She knew the reason was because they could easily date someone else who wouldn't mind being intimate once the relationship got to a certain point. That point came sooner for some women and later for others, and Majestic knew what she was up against. She wanted to be respected above all. All she asked was that her man be respectful of who he was with, and take the time to enjoy the relationship and focus on getting to know each other. Majestic did not want to give away freely something that she felt needed to be earned. She felt Ryan earned it because she had high hopes of marrying him. She didn't become intimate with him to keep him but because she was blinded by temptation. She knew she cared deeply for him so she listened to her body instead of listening to the word of God. She knew the consequences of being intimate with someone and what takes place in the spiritual realm. No one thinks about how the spirits come together as well as the body. Majestic knew that to be intimate with someone was to let your guard down and let them have a piece of your very essence. To her that was your very personal essence and that is not something that she wanted to share freely any longer. Sharing an intimate act with someone else meant that person was worthy above all the rest, but how can that be shown to many men over the course of a lifetime? Are ten men worthy of such an act? Are twenty-five men worthy of such an act? Are fifty men worthy of such an act? God forbid that there are one hundred men that should be allowed such access. Is that person considered the worthy person of the moment since you are not married and the relationship could end at any time? Majestic thought over these questions carefully because she noticed it time and again where women complained of men that are non-committal. It is the same old sad story with the same formula; date, intimacy, then maybe marriage. If there were a formula for true happiness in dating, wouldn't the greatest prize of it all be at the end and not the beginning or the middle? What is there to look forward to if all you have left is a marriage certificate? You only get married for the first time, once. You can only have intimacy for the first time, once, and shouldn't that be your special gift to be given on your wedding night? Majestic still believed that it should be. She didn't care how many men didn't think so. Why would she date someone that didn't think that being intimate with her was the greatest gift she could give? She didn't short-change her thought of them and she wasn't going to let them short-change the thought of her. Majestic knew in her heart that they were missing out because in a non-conceited way, she knew she was worthy of the wait. After all, being of mixed heritage was a definite plus for her. She was Puerto Rican and African American, and her long, brown curly hair was a true testament to that. She was the average height for a woman but her slender, athletic build was a sight to see. She had some dark brown eyes that were accented by her semi-thick eyebrows. Most women would thin theirs out but she knew it complimented her eyes so she left them alone. Then to top it all off, she had some gorgeous, full lips that were just perfect. She felt that with the way she looked and the way she was morally that any man would beat down her door to be with her. Of course they did, but for all the wrong reasons. They want all the intimacy but none of the relationship, so she grew tired of dating. It has been a few years since she went out on a date, and it was no longer a problem for her. She is at a point in her life where she has refocused her goals, so love was on the back burner for a while. At the tender age of thirty-four, she still had a few years to hold out on things. She firmly believes that through her patience and her faith that she would in time find someone.

"Ok, I pretty much have everything I need," Majestic said, as she closed up her luggage and made her way towards the living room. She wanted to get on the computer and look up the island she was going to visit one more time. The name of the island was called "Velacious", and it was turning into a great tourist spot. She was looking over the pictures of where they were going to be. She was excited for the trip because this was going to be the first time she has seen Ryan since he left. Although they have exchanged pictures online, she hadn't seen him in person; she was looking forward to it.

"Man, I am going to be able to get some nice pictures for my new exhibit. This island is unbelievable." Majestic said as her heart started to race. It happened every time she was in the planning stage for a new exhibit. At "Majestically Captured", the place was a collection of exhibits. Each wall was a different exhibit. The gallery would display twenty to twenty-five pictures of any given exhibit on each wall. Her gallery was very long so there was plenty of room to put up movable walls to accommodate the pictures as needed. The pictures would be blown up to a size of two feet wide and three feet long, so they were a large enough size so you could capture a lot in each picture. They were big enough to put in a large frame and could be hung like a piece of art. Majestic would have her pictures done in a way that they looked like they were done in 3D, so the focus of her pictures stood out from the rest of the photo. Everyone knew the exhibits stayed up for a period of time, and they knew that if they wanted any picture for themselves that they can purchase them. Her photos usually ranged from hundreds of dollars all the way to the thousands. She hasn't entered the tens of thousand ranges, but she wasn't worried because she was doing quite well in her current range. Her clients knew that the exhibits were always different, so they were always coming in to get the first peek at what was new. Majestic was always thrilled; each time she would put out a red carpet and make it a black suit and white dress attire. Clients would come and it would have a feel of a movie premiere or awards show. It was truly a spectacle, and Majestic loved the attention her gallery would receive in the midst of it all. Other galleries had tried to duplicate what she does, but there was nothing better than the original.

"I'd better double the amount of film I was planning on bringing. I don't want to miss any shots." Majestic said as she continued to look over photos of the island. Majestic still used the old method of dark room film developing. She felt digital photos was fast food and she loved the time and effort put into developing her pictures. She was definitely intrigued by the island. The beautiful scenery is such an attraction and photos of the scenery alone were enough to make Majestic want to go.

"Ok, time for me to go to bed." Majestic said to herself as she logged off the computer. She had been packing for a few hours. She could not make up her mind on what she wanted to wear. She wanted her vacation to be perfect and that she looked her best all the time. She shut her computer down and walked over to her bed. She plopped down on the bed and closed her eyes. At that moment her home phone began to ring.

"Who could this be?" Majestic asked, as she grabbed the phone next to her bed. She didn't normally answer the home phone because most people called her cell phone as she was hardly ever home.

"Mom, I should have known that this was you," Majestic said as she smiled.

She knew her mom and dad always called her home phone first because they had that number memorized.

"Hey baby. How are you doing tonight?"

"I am good, Mom. I just got through packing my last suitcase. I am about to get a decent nights rest, finally."

"Good for you. You deserve it. John and I cannot tell you enough how proud we are of you. You have done so well with your gallery." Her mom had a strong hint of pride in her voice.

"Thank you Mom, but it wasn't easy. I know you remember all the days I would call you crying about how I wasn't making any money and how I was second guessing my ideas."

"Baby, all I remember is you crying. It took us a minute before we could make out what you said, and yes it was always money."

Majestic couldn't help but laugh at that statement. She definitely remembered those days well. It was hard for her to ask for help. She had taught herself to be so independent that it tore her up on the inside to ask for assistance. She wanted the whole process to be something that she accomplished on her own. That was how strong her will was to see her gallery flourish. The prospect of it being hers and only hers was a driving factor in her long hours and endless desire to have the best exhibits.

"I know Mom. Thank God for you and Dad."

"Thank God for God. Majestic you have shown me that God has given your Dad and me favor. You and your sister have been such a blessing to us."

Majestic knows that they have been good to their parents. It was real easy for them. Most children that grow up in the church, more often than not, find their way out of the church. Majestic and her sister made sure they didn't disappoint their parents. They didn't care about their friends acting like normal teenagers that were sleeping around, drinking and dabbling in drugs. They never paid any attention to any of the pressures that came with growing up. They stayed focused on their parents' rules and God's guidelines for life.

"Are you ready for your first vacation in years?" Her mom asked while yawning.

"I am ready. I was worried everyday before today. I have never been away from the gallery this long but I plan on checking in everyday so I think I will be good. Besides, I hooked up a camera system in the gallery that will show me a live feed of the gallery. I can just log in to the gallery's website and see what is going on anyway."

"What?" Her mom asked.

Majestic laughed because she knew her mom knew so little about technology that it was probably as if she was speaking a foreign language.

"I will be able to keep tabs on the gallery at all times. I have a great staff and I trust them to be on their best behavior. I just want to focus on sitting on the beach and taking in the sights. Of course I will have plenty of cameras and a ton of film."

"Always trying to get your next exhibit huh?"

"Yes ma'am. The competition is not going to be on vacation so I need to stay sharp and busy at all times. Besides, no one has the same eye for photos that I have." Majestic said matter-of-factly.

"I talked to Tracee and Patrick and they are ready to go."

"Of course they are. They are looking for the next spot to enhance the passion in their marriage. They is all they ever do, is look for the next opportunity."

"They can though Majestic. They are married and nothing is off limits including the frequency of the passion."

"Believe me they let it be known every chance they get."

"Majestic, does that bother you? You know their relationship?" Her mom asks as if she didn't really want to know the answer.

"Not really. I focus so much on the gallery that I don't get caught up in thoughts like that. I am happy for them. One day, I will have me someone who will be right for me. I can't wait for that day. I will not rush it though. I love the freedom I have with focusing on the gallery. I don't feel like sharing time with anyone else but God."

"I know that, but you are going to see your friend Ryan. I know how you really liked him and wished that things were different."

"I am ok. We both moved on. We have sent each other emails from time to time. Last time I heard from him was about four years ago and I believe at the time he was dating an island girl or something. It will still be good to see him again though."

"Did I ever meet him?"

"No you didn't. We were just good friends but we never got around to meeting each other's parents. We both knew that the relationship was going to be strictly a friendship so we didn't pursue getting to know each other's families. Ryan has met Tracee but that is about the extent of it."

"So he moved out to the islands to do volunteer work? Sounds like an honorable thing to do."

"He is definitely a Christian. He has a heart for the less fortunate and when he found out about an opportunity to do that, he jumped at the chance."

"Ok, a guy that great and you only wanted to be his friend? After hearing all of your shortcomings with your relationships, do you ever wish things were different?"

"We liked each other but I wanted to finish college and move to Las Vegas and he wanted to leave the country so we never pursued anything. We just left it as friends so that neither one of us would get hurt."

"Ok baby, well get some sleep and we will see you at the airfield in the morning."

"Good night Mom, and tell Dad that I love him. See you guys tomorrow." Majestic said, as she hung up. She thought for a second. It was kind of strange that her mom mentioned her being jealous of her younger sister's relationship. Majestic had never been the jealous type, and definitely not of anyone's relationship. She wanted a true loving relationship but she also knew that with any relationship she would have to sacrifice much to see it grow. Deep down inside, she didn't feel like she wanted to give up anything. She loved the way her schedule was and she didn't want to change a thing. She could still understand why her mom would ask her that question. They are going on a family vacation to a Caribbean island, and everyone had a mate except for her. Mom has Dad, Tracee has Patrick and Majestic has her cameras. What kind of pairing is that? She is the one with the non-living companion. They will be on a beautiful island getaway and she will be alone, but she was so used to it. Majestic knew that she will not be lonely or sad. She has always found a way to handle being by herself and this vacation trip will be no different. She turned off her night-light, and then her cell phone rang.

"Ok, this is crazy." Majestic said as she turned on the light. She got up out of the bed and looked in her purse for her cell phone.

"What's up Tracee?"

Tracee was Majestic's younger sister. They were two years apart and the best of friends. They shared so many things together, and they were always there to keep each other in check. Their mutual accountability had kept them on the straight and narrow for all these years. Tracee ended up finding love and getting married. She was still able to be there for Majestic. They were not going to let anything stand in the way of them being there for the other one.

"Majestic, how are you?"

"I will be better when I can finally get some sleep."

"My bad, I was just checking up on you to see if you were ready to go."

"I am ready. This will be my first vacation in a minute and I plan on enjoying myself."

"I am ready to go as well. This island is all that Patrick has been talking about the past month. So we are going to go there and put our stamp on things."

"I bet you are, with your nasty self." Majestic said as she laughed. She knows that Tracee and Patrick had taken being fruitful and multiplying to another level. They have been trying since day one of their marriage to have children. Tracee was always bragging about places and times they had expressed their passion for their marriage. They hadn't been successful in having children yet. It had been seven years and no luck. Tracee told Majestic that they were never going to stop trying and by their actions, they weren't going to. Majestic has grown used to Tracee talking about it.

"Majestic, we are going to be on an island getaway and we are definitely going to get away, just for moments at a time. Just long enough to, you know what we do." Tracee said as she started to laugh.

"If I didn't know any better, I wouldn't think you were a Christian at all."

"I am one and I am just a happily married one that is enjoying her partner for life. We can enjoy each other as much as we like and that is what I plan on doing. One day, you too will be able to be like me."

"Whatever, I could never catch you though. You counter is too far ahead for me. Wait, why am I entertaining this conversation with you? You didn't call me to talk about that did you?" Majestic asked, because she didn't feel like talking about passion tonight. She wanted to get some sleep because this was going to be the most sleep she would have had all at once, in a long time. Every moment on the phone was taking away from that.

"No, I really called to see if you have had any contact with Ryan?"

"No, I haven't emailed or anything. It has been four years. He was dating this island girl and they are probably married with little Ryans running around."

"How does that make Majestic feel?" Tracee asked, with sarcasm in her voice.

"I don't feel anyway about it. I haven't seen him in thirteen years because I am not counting the pictures that I have received. I haven't seen him in person and the feelings I had for him are long gone. What we had is dead and besides, we were only friends."

"True, you were only friends but you really liked him. The only thing that stopped you guys from being together was the fact that you were both going in opposite directions. Everything else lined up. Your ideas, interests, habits and walk with God was all in tune with each other. So don't sit on the phone acting like it is nothing."

"Tracee, please; we have both moved on. He was obviously not waiting on me and I wasn't waiting on him. We knew what we had was over so we just moved on with our lives."

"Majestic, so you are not going to even call or let him know we are coming? If he has a girlfriend or not means nothing because he is an old friend and we just want to check up on him."

Majestic knew Tracee was right. What is wrong with emailing him and letting him know that she was coming to the island. They are old friends and were close back in the day. The more she thought about it the more she wanted to do it. She was curious about how he was doing.

"We will see. I will bring his information with me and when we get to the island, I will contact him and see what happens."

"Now that sounds better. Make sure you bring some cute outfits in case he is single."

"I will leave that up to you. I will just borrow one of your outfits."

"I don't know about that. All of my cute outfits are still to risqué for you, grandma."

"I have some cute clothes that reveal a shoulder or two or sometimes a knee," Majestic said as they started to laugh. Majestic was known for being cute and conservative with her outfits. Tracee's outfits were a little sexier but not too overboard because they were still classy and could be worn without compromising her Christian witness.

"Exactly! Just make sure you have something cute and a little sexy because we will be on an island and I want to have at least a cute and sexy day where we hang out, just me and you, and have some fun."

"Ok, I will bring something just for you. You are trying your best to corrupt me."

"Not really. I just want you to let your hair down for once."

"Alright. I am going to bed now. Tell Patrick I said hi."

"What and give him a heart attack? I still have use for him. I don't want to kill him with your never-before-seen kindness for him. One day you guys are going to be good friends." Tracee said as she laughed at the idea of Majestic and Patrick being friends. For some reason, Majestic and Patrick bumped heads since day one. It was something about Patrick that irked Majestic and she hasn't been able to get past it.

"If it is God's will. Anyway, go and get some sleep or do what it is you do. I will see you guys on the plane tomorrow."

"Goodnight Majestic. I love you." Tracee says as she hung up the phone.

"I love you too," Majestic replied. She placed her cell phone on the bed next to her.

Majestic knew that Tracee was going to make sure that she has a good time on this trip. That was one thing about Tracee, she was fun and that she always made sure that others were having a good time. Now Majestic was happy because she was finally going to get some sleep. She had planned this night for awhile. She wanted to wake up refreshed and feeling great as she was leaving for vacation, finally. She knew she deserved one so she was looking forward to getting away and just refocusing herself. She had her focus on the gallery; now it was time to focus just on her and take it easy. For Majestic, that starts tonight. Majestic began to pray. She prayed that God would watch over her for this trip. She wanted to have a good time and to be safe. Above all, she wanted to meet someone. She had so many thoughts of love and how she wanted to share special moments with someone special. She has gone to romantic places in the past and had watched others spend time together and she couldn't help but feel a little jealous. Watching couples holding hands and snuggling was so hard on her. Seeing them kiss was really unbearable. She just wanted God to bless her with a mate. She was really a hopeless romantic that was at times very lonely. Not physically lonely, to where she wanted intimacy, but she was lonely emotionally. She wanted someone to talk to and share her life with. Majestic knew she desperately wanted someone to call her own. So she prayed for that and went on to pray for family and friends. When the prayer was over, she just sat there because she was slightly excited because this island was the perfect place to get away from it all and she looked forward to that. She turned off her light and let the darkness soothe her to sleep.

* * *

"Everyone, I just got through talking to the pilot and we are preparing to take off in a few minutes. Take the time to make sure you are wearing a seatbelt and all items are stowed. We are leaving in a few moments." Patrick said as he sat down next to Tracee.

"Well if you had been sitting in your seat already, you would have heard the stewardess say the exact same thing. I think maybe he was just sharing that information for you and you only," Majestic said without looking away from the window. She just shook her head because she was used to Patrick always trying to be in charge of a situation. He felt like he knew everything, and he was always trying to show out in front of everyone. He was a lawyer and he walked around like the world was his courtroom. She knew Tracee loved the fact that he took command of the courtroom during trials; Majestic couldn't take that from him. He was great in the courtroom but, in Majestic's opinion, terrible in real life. Majestic really didn't care for him that much, but he was her sister's husband so she had to have a small level of tolerance for him. He had a little head with a close hair cut, big ears and some round glasses that sat on the tip of his nose at all times. He thought he really looked cool by having them there, but Majestic was annoyed by it. Sometimes when he felt like he was making a point in conversations, he would push the glasses up to the regular position but then magically they would end up at the end of his nose again. He wasn't all that cute to Majestic. He had an extremely long neck that was funny to see in the winter because he could never find a turtleneck sweater that would cover his neck. The thought of that made Majestic smirk. He was about 6'5" with an average size body except for his legs, which were extremely skinny for his body type. So, to Majestic, he was the human giraffe and that was her inside joke. Now her sister Tracee was a gazelle. She rocked the long braids halfway down her back. The style complimented her because just like Majestic, she had thick eyebrows that were the focal point of her face with her hair being braided. She was caramel colored and very pretty. She had a thin frame but curves in all the right places. Tracee had always wanted to be taller so she could become a model but she stopped growing at 5'5", and that dream was lost. None-the-less, she was easy on the eyes and received compliments all the time. Her mom and dad, Renee and John Manning, were bison. They were round, dark brown and slow moving. They were always together and that was a lost part of relationships. They loved each other's company and didn't do anything that the other couldn't be a part of.

Her mom was African-American with a beautiful brown color and her dad was a dark-skinned Puerto Rican. She loved her parents because they showed her what true love looked like throughout their marriage. Majestic thinks back to her mom asking her if she was jealous of Tracee and Patrick's relationship, but the truth be told, she was really jealous of her mom and dad's relationship.

"If I can get half the love that they show each other, I would be totally happy," Majestic said to herself as the plane started down the runway. Majestic liked flying in her dad's private jet. She has had a good life. Her dad is a second-generation owner of a corporation that grows and processes coffee beans. Once they got the contract of a lifetime with "Coffee Heaven", the largest coffee distributor in the world, their family was set financially. She grew up with the finer things in life and had access to whatever she wanted; the private jet was one of them. She has always had money and never really wanted for anything. So it was no problem for her to pick what college she wanted and whatever career she chose because if push came to shove, she had money to fall back on. She was the only one who chose not to work in the family business. She had that independent streak in her and it was in everything about her. Tracee chose to go into the family business as the accounting manager. Their mom was the business manager. Her dad provided the funding in opening her gallery, and she knew she could never repay him.

"Well, that is our cue; we are going to the back of plane now to get more privacy. See you guys when we land." Tracee says as she grabs Patrick's hand and begins to pull him to the back of the plane.

"Gross," Majestic said, as she shook her head. She knew that Tracee and Patrick loved opportunities to enjoy the passion of marriage and flying thousands of feet above ground was no different.

"John, do you remember when we were like that?" Majestic's mom asked as she nudged her husband.

"Of course I remember those times Renee. I remember them like it was yesterday," he replied with a huge smile on his face.

"Now that is really gross. I hope it was a lot of yesterdays ago," Majestic said as she started to laugh.

"Majestic, I hate that you are by yourself for this vacation. I just feel bad for you. Everyone else has someone to share this time with and you don't." Her mom said, with a look of concern on her face.

"Don't worry about me, Mom. I have plenty to do while I am there."

"Like what?"

"Well, pictures."

"I know that Majestic, but what else?"

"I will sit at the beach, go on some tours and mingle with folks as I need to. Look, I am not going to ruin this vacation worrying about me being single."

"I know you won't, but I just want you to be happy; that is all." Renee said as she placed her hand on Majestic's shoulder.

"I am happy, Mom. I am a successful woman who has the greatest gift ever and that is two loving parents who have given me everything I could possibly need. I am happy because of you guys. I love you guys so much."

"We love you too baby. You can hang with us if you want. No need for you to be on that island walking around by yourself. We would love your company, so don't hesitate to be with us."

"Thanks Dad. I will keep that in mind." Majestic said, but she knew she didn't really want to be a third wheel with anyone.

"Now I am going to get me some rest." John said as he leaned his seat back, propped a pillow behind his head and closed his eyes to get some sleep.

"Move over, baby." Renee waited for Majestic to move over so she could sit next to her.

"What's up Mom?" Majestic asked, because she is so used to her mom reclining back with her dad to get some sleep. This was very unusual for her mom on any flight.

"Majestic, I have prayed and prayed that God would complete his plan for you."

"What do you mean Mom? I feel like his plan was to let me use my gallery to show the world the goodness of his love."

"I don't mean that Majestic. I mean his plan for you as a single woman."

That hit home for Majestic. She always prayed for a mate and it was a daily prayer. She never really thought that God was holding her back from being with someone because he wants her to complete a task. She has always had conversations with God and she was pretty certain that she had done all that was asked of her.

"You have been so faithful to God's plan for your life. I just hope that you have accomplished everything that he wants you to do while you are single. God has a view on relationships just like we do. I know and you know that life will change for you when you finally settle down. Your long hours at the gallery will go away. You will start to share your time with someone else. I know God has enjoyed your attention and obedience. He knows that once you give you heart away to someone that your time with God might decrease. God doesn't want to lose such precious moments that you have shared with him and him only."

"I don't think I would forsake God for anyone else. I take pride in the fact that I have lasted this long doing exactly what God would want me to do. I wouldn't want to jeopardize that at all. Hopefully I can find someone that shares my desire and purpose for our lives. If I can do that then I can make that transition an easy one."

"I know God has someone wonderful for you. You have been so true to your calling and in this day and age, you could have found a million reasons why you should have given yourself away but you didn't."

Majestic didn't have the heart to tell her mom that she had in fact given herself away before. Even though many relationships are affirmed by being intimate, she still felt terrible about breaking her promise to God. Majestic has heard many reasons her friends have given her on why they decided to share their bodies with someone else. She also had to endure reasons guys gave to entice her to share herself with them. All of it just made her sick to her stomach. She knew her body wasn't going to be something that she shared every time she felt like she really liked someone. Her body was very priceless to her and she could not even think about the idea of different men being able to get together and talk about an intimate experience they had with her. Them being able to talk about what they did and how they did it. She also knew there was going to be a great chance that she wasn't going to find a guy that has the same feelings and abstinence level that she has attained, but she was going to hope he was just like her.

"Mom, why are you so intent on me having someone?" Majestic asked, because as far back as she could remember, her mom had always asked about her love life. She would constantly inquire about it.

"Every mother wants her daughters to experience love on the highest level. I want you to get married and have children. To see you happy and sharing your life with someone you truly love is my goal. You have accomplished so much on your own starting with your gallery, your financial situation, and your walk with the Lord and these are all testaments to your accomplishments. I would love to see you sharing this with your soul mate, someone that would only enhance your accomplishments and be that loving support for you. Your father and I have shared all major accomplishments, disappointments, and ups and downs together. We drew strength from each other and we supported each other's decisions, wants and needs. I have loved every moment and I can only hope that you would be able to share moments too."

"I know, Mom. I sometimes wish I had someone to share special moments with as well, but I also think about all the guys I have dated and I am glad that none of them were the one. Many of them tried to make me out to be crazy for wanting to wait on intimacy. Most of them claimed to be men of God yet they acted just like men of this world. I know it is hard to do all that God wants of us, but at the same time, I at least want someone who is trying to do the things that God wants us to do. I don't want someone that follows only the rules that are convenient for them. Mom, am I asking too much? Am I asking for someone that is too good to be true?"

"Majestic, you are not asking for too much. Your Dad loves you so much that anyone short of Jesus would not be good enough for you. You are such a special woman that has chosen to be totally different from the rest. Many women wouldn't dare think to be the way you are. Here you are, being such a beautiful woman that can have anyone she wants. Instead you are waiting for a man that hopefully God has prepared, with only you in mind. That man is on a collision course with you and only God knows when the two of you will meet. Keep doing what you are doing and all will be well," her mom said as she ran her fingers through Majestic's hair. Her mom hadn't done that since she was a kid and that brought back memories of her mom assuring her that everything was going to be okay. She always had a knack for saying the right things.

"Well, all this talk about this wonderful future for me is getting me excited, so we need to stop before I start focusing on it too much. I really enjoyed our conversation. We definitely need to have more. I have given up family time for the gallery and just having a conversation with you reminded me of what I was missing out on. We need to do this more often."

"I think we should do this more often because I enjoyed it as well. Anytime you want to talk just let me know," Renee said, as she went back to her seat.

At times, Majestic needed that assurance from someone other than herself. She felt better knowing that someone appreciated what she was doing. She felt like there had to be someone out there that would be blown away by her accomplishments and ideas and would respect her body. She only wished that she had some way of knowing that person is due to come in her life because she felt strongly that no one from the past was that person. She just shuddered to think about her past relationships and how she could have even fathomed having a long-term relationship with any of them. She knew that God helped weed out the ones that weren't good enough for her. God had been watching and protecting her, and it's only a matter of time before he blesses her. She began to smile at the prospect of having someone to love and someone that would treat her like no other. She knew she would love that man like no one before. She would be the perfect wife and partner anyone could ever want. All she had to do now was just wait patiently on her mate. That was something she felt she could do. So as she looked out the window, she couldn't help but think that maybe she just passed over Mr. Right. Maybe he was down below working at his job, or cleaning his car. Maybe he was taking care of his yard or sitting in a library reading. Her mind began to flood with scenarios of what her future husband could be doing at this current moment. She knew that no matter how great the thought was of him, the truth of the matter was that they were apart or better yet they didn't really know if the other one really existed at all. It was one of those comforting yet sad thoughts that Majestic has gotten used to having.

"Control yourself, Majestic." She said, as she reclined and stared out the window, waiting to begin her vacation.

*　　*　　*

"Could you possibly look more like a tourist?" Tracee asked as she nudged Majestic's arm while she took a picture of the evening skyline.

"Could you have waited until I got the picture first before you asked me that?" Majestic replied as she retook the picture. She felt she was looking at one of the most beautiful sunsets she had ever seen. The sun was a tangerine color and it was slowly moving down the horizon, about to hide behind a plush green mountain. Majestic was waiting for the tip of the mountain to be at the halfway point of the descending sun. It was one of those classic post card pictures that she was adding to her growing collections of sunsets. Sunsets have been a very popular exhibit at her gallery and she knew that this would be a "money" shot.

"You know that the number one reason most tourists are robbed is because they have a tendency to look a lot like a tourist? Someone could be scoping you out right now," Patrick added in his usual fashion. Majestic hoped someone was scoping out the escaped giraffe and would come and take Patrick away.

"She is fine, Patrick." John interjected as he always did when he defends someone from Patrick.

"Get your pictures baby. I will be on the lookout for you."

"Thanks Dad." Majestic continued taking pictures. She loved the island already. As she looked down from the jet while they were flying over the island before land-ing, she realized that she had not seen beauty like this before. There is something about untouched nature that sends most photographers to a state of euphoria. It is the thought of capturing God's untouched gift to man that fueled her desire to capture more of it. The trees here just looked greener than back home. Flowers had more color to them. Mountains looked more majestic, and the sky just looked bluer than at home. At this current moment, she couldn't find anything wrong with the island, and that was a comforting thought.

"The guy at the hotel said the best restaurant on the entire island was right around the corner," Renee said, as she grabbed John's hand.

"Mom, I thought it was weird that he wouldn't describe the restaurant or tell us the name of it," Tracee said as she looked around.

"That was different," Majestic said as she continued to look for the next picture to capture.

"He said that there would be no doubt that you have found the restaurant when you see it," John added.

"I think that maybe he might be setting us up to be robbed. There is always the point man that sends the victims to a spot where they are out of their element and away from help," Patrick said as he grabbed Tracee by the waist as if he was protecting her. Majestic would nor-mally say something under her breath or shake her head at his comments, but at this moment she was focused on a sight that had her in a trance like a fly being enticed by a fly zapper.

"Oh my goodness, do you see what I see?" That was all that Majestic could ask.

"Ok, I guess we have found the restaurant," Renee said as she just stared.

"I see why he didn't say anything. It would have taken away from what we see now." Tracee added as she stopped.

Majestic was literally in a trance. Less than twenty yards away was the restaurant that the hotel worker was talking about. It was two stories high, shaped like a cube and surrounded by spotlights. There were at least eight of them that were shining on the outside walls of the restaurant. Most of the restaurant was made of glass. You could literally see inside the restaurant. You could see patrons sitting at tables on both levels of the restaurant. They could see the wait staff moving to and fro in their light-blue shirts, black vests and black pants.

"Do you see the sea animals in the walls? There is no way they have real animals swimming inside the walls." Patrick said as he began to walk faster.

"What a concept this restaurant has. I have never seen anything like it," John said, as he picked up his pace also.

"Wow," Tracee said as she looked at Majestic. "Are you going to take pictures or what?"

"Oh yeah." Majestic said as she snapped out of her daze. It was a state that she couldn't remember ever being in before.

"I can't believe you didn't think of that. I have never seen you in a trance before."

"I have never seen a restaurant with such life and energy as this one, but believe me, I am about to take pictures. I just want to get closer so I can get a better picture of the animals." Majestic said, as she fumbled for the right camera. She can't help but to be in awe of the restaurant. As they get closer they realized that the animals were 3D holograms. The outside of the building that wasn't glass displayed holograms. It was as if the wall was a movie screen, because the animals looked so life-like that you swore that they were being projected on the wall, but they weren't. The walls were able to display an image, and that was never seen before; it was definitely one of a kind.

"What a beautiful and unique view! Let's get inside and see how long the wait is going to be," Renee said, as she walked up to the entrance. She ran her hand along the wall to get a feel of the texture of it.

"Come on, shutterbug," Tracee said as she tried to encourage Majestic to stop taking pictures and join them. Majestic was trying to take as many pictures as she could. She knew that she won't be able to capture the full effect of seeing the animals in 3D, but she was taking pictures with all three cameras so she could decide which style of camera would come up with the best shot.

"I bet the wait is at least a few hours. There is no way that this place is ever empty. Everyone that has come to this island is probably trying to eat here," John said, as he held the door for everyone. "Majestic, it sure would be nice if you joined us."

"Coming Dad, I just wanted to make sure I got all the pictures that I could," Majestic said, as she took her last picture and walked quickly through the door.

"I understand, baby, but we are going to be here for four weeks. That will give you plenty of time to get that "money" shot."

Majestic always giggled when her dad called her pictures, *"The Money Shots."* He said that only she could take a picture of something and sell it to someone who could have taken the same picture themselves. As she was walking through the entrance, she could smell the different varieties of food, and it was intoxicating.

The inside was just as beautiful as the outside. The walls were made of glass, except now they had real sea animals in them. They had large turtles, and fish of all sizes and types. They had a large array of small to large sea creatures going about their business. They just swam to and fro throughout the walls. The floor was an off-white color with real shells in them of all types and colors. The ceiling was full of lights and there was a chandelier hanging over each table. The restaurant was so bright and vibrant that it just relaxed you and gave you a sense of excitement by just being there. This was one of the most elegant restaurants that Majestic had ever been in. She has been to a lot of them when she visited New York and at home in Las Vegas, but she thought she had seen them all until now.

"Hello. Welcome to the Heart of Velacious. This restaurant is literally where the heart would be of the island. We are so glad you chose to come here. How many will be dining with you tonight? The very beautiful hostess asked, and Majestic thought immediately of a peacock showcasing its beautiful feathers. The hostess had her own style and flair and that made her beautiful.

"There are five of us and we would like your best table." Patrick said as he took the lead.

"We like to think that all of our tables are our best. Would you like to dine on the inside or eat outside on the beach?

"The beach sounds wonderful, right Patrick?" Tracee asked, as she winked at him. Majestic had seen that wink before and it normally meant them setting up a time for passion.

"No, let's eat on the inside, since this is our first time," Renee said as she waited on everyone's approval.

"Inside or outside, it doesn't matter because we just want the best table that you have," Patrick said as he held onto the idea that some of the tables were better than others. From what Majestic could see, all the tables were the same. The tables were glass with steel legs and they had six chairs at all of them. They had off-white table-cloths that hung about halfway down the sides. If he was referring to them having a good spot where the tables were, it didn't really matter. Majestic felt that no matter where they sat, every view would be good because what she saw now was spectacular at every angle.

"Let's eat inside. What is the wait time?" John asked before Patrick complicated the process.

"Let me see," The hostess said as she walked to a flat screen monitor that was hanging on the wall behind the podium at the hostess stand. She began to touch the screen.

"Ok, we have a table on the second level. Right this way." She led them through the restaurant. Majestic couldn't help but notice the visual appeal of the restaurant. She could see people looking over their menus, drinking and eating their food and basically everyone looked happy.

"This place is awesome," Tracee said as she walked behind Majestic.

"At least we are not the only one in awe of this place," Renee said, as she looked around at the other people. As they were walking up the stairs they noticed that fish was swimming in the glassy six-inch steps.

"How cool is that!" Tracee exclaimed as she stops to look at the fish.

"That is so awesome. Those fish in there are so pretty," Majestic stopped to take a look as well.

"Come on Tracee, you might cause an accident or something," Patrick said to get her moving again.

Majestic just rolled her eyes at Patrick. She thought that maybe Tracee had already caused an accident by giving her heart away to Patrick. Majestic doesn't know why everything he does bother her so much, but it does.

"Here is our best table." The hostess said as she smiled at Patrick. She had picked a table by the window and they could see the whole beach from their seats. "Your server will be Juanita, and she will be here shortly. Enjoy."

As the hostess walked away, everyone sat down and begin to take in the sights.

"Majestic. Look at the white sand on the beach." Tracee said excitedly.

"Wow. That sand looks so pretty. It looks better in person than it does on the website."

"You are right. It does look better in person. The whole concept about this place is just great," Renee said as she joined them in the view of the beach out the window.

"I can't wait to see what the menu is like," John said as he patted his round belly.

"I bet you can't Dad," Tracee and Majestic started to laugh. Their dad was known for his appetite, so they expected nothing less.

"Good evening everyone. I am Juanita and I will be honored to take care of your dining needs tonight. First, I would love to get to know everyone so if you don't mind telling me your names, which will start things off perfectly."

When Majestic saw Juanita she immediately thought of a puppy. She reminded Majestic of a cute little puppy with such sad eyes because she could sense that Juanita was trying to hide a little sadness.

"My name is Patrick and this is my wife Tracee." Patrick said in his normal 'me first' fashion.

"My name is John and this is my wife Renee."

"I'm Majestic."

"Such wonderful names and again, I am Juanita. So let's start off with drinks. Water is complimentary of course so you don't have to ask for that. You will notice that you have a small island in the middle of your table that has lemons, cherries, sugar, non-sugars, creamers and other items to enhance your water or whatever beverage you choose to drink. We have tea, hot or cold. You can have any flavor tea you like. We carry all types so ask and we have it. We do offer sodas of all types, diet and regular. We have wines of all ages, red or white. Our wine selection is about two hundred and thirty deep so your favorite choice we probably have as well. We do have alcohol - whisky, rums, gin, or vodka of all brands. So basically the sky is the limit and the choice is truly yours. So here are the drink menus." Juanita handed everyone a menu. It took them all a few minutes to decide on what they were going to order.

"I will have your mango-raspberry tea." Majestic said as she handed her menu back to Juanita.

"Let's see, I want a bottle of Martin-Tourre wine, red, preferably about forty years old."

"I will join him." Tracee adds.

"I just want regular green tea," Renee said.

"I want a coke for now," John said as he handed his menu to Juanita.

"What a wide variety of choices. Here are your dinner menus and feel free to take your time and decide what you want. Our entrées of the day are as follows. We have two different types of soup. The first one is a White bean and Tomato soup. This is an excellent light soup that is perfectly blended with the light texture of the white beans and the sweetness from the tomatoes. Presentation of that is awesome. The next one is a Spring Asparagus and Lemon soup. The chopped onions and hint of sour cream was enhanced by the unusual blend of lemon and asparagus. Both of them have been getting great comments all day. The main course of the day is Grilled Swordfish with blueberry salsa. That is some of the most flavorful fish you might have ever had and the salsa gives it a nice sweet kick. So think about it and let me know.

"There is no need for me to think about it. I am sold. I will have the White Bean and Tomato Soup and the Grilled Swordfish." Majestic said as she handed over her menu.

"I will too." Tracee adds.

"Looks like the ladies have spoken. I will have the same." Renee said as she handed her menu over to Juanita.

"That sounds good, but I really want a steak. I want a T-bone steak, medium well. Give me a side of mashed potatoes and mixed vegetables. Also, since I am going all out, can I have a glass of brandy?" John asked, as he winked at Renee. Juanita nodded her head.

"Well, I want to have the grilled chicken with pineapple sauce. Give me corn and greens as my sides." Patrick said to Juanita. He shook his head as if he made a great choice.

"Great, I will place that order and get your drinks and soup out to you." Juanita said as she collected the rest of the menus.

"Hey you didn't write anything down. Are you sure you are going to remember all that?' Majestic asked as she realized that Juanita didn't write down anything.

"No need. I have an excellent memory. I think it might be in the water." Juanita said as she tried to hold in a laugh. "I am going to place the order before I forget it."

"This place is the bomb." Tracee said as she looked around.

"I really love this island, period." Majestic added as she started to look at the pictures she had taken on her cameras.

"This place would make a killing in the United States." John said as he grabbed Renee's hand.

"I know what you mean," Patrick said as he did the same to Tracee.

Majestic wanted to get up and run out to the ocean and jump in. Patrick was going to be Patrick, no matter what. For the life of her, she could not figure out what her sister saw in him. Then again, she truly didn't want to know. Tracee is one of those individuals that you would see with a man and wonder how they even got together. Tracee was your classic beautiful woman, with all the right physical qualities and the inside to match. Yet you'd see Patrick and you'd think that he was well over his head. Tracee had never been big on looks. She has always wanted someone that made her happy and could stimulate her mind, and Patrick does that. Majestic was just happy for her; to each its own.

"Ok, here are your drinks." Juanita said as she served the drinks to everyone. "Your soup will be here shortly."

"Juanita is the owner around? I would love to meet him or her and tell them how remarkable this restaurant truly is!" Renee asked.

"Sure. I will get him." Juanita said as she walked away.

"How about that you guys, even the owner is accessible." Renee said as she sipped her tea.

"I can't wait to find out about the concept behind this restaurant," Tracee said, as she made a toast with Patrick.

Majestic took this time to look around the restaurant. She noticed that there were a few families there with their children, but for the most part there were couples. They all looked so happy. At this moment, Majestic felt a little sad because this island was so beautiful and it just breathed romance, but yet there wasn't going to be any romance for her. Majestic could only look around at other couples holding hands and having conversations with each other. She noticed how they were looking in each other's eyes and just being so into each other. They all had looks of contentment and love. Majestic wanted that look but most of all she wanted someone to look at her like that. She wanted someone to hang on her every word. She wanted to be treated the way she noticed the couples were treating each other. Majestic was really tired of being by herself but she never focused on it too much because that is when she would feel sorry for herself. She didn't like feeling sorry for herself because that was a sign of failure, and to Majestic, that wasn't an option. She still had time to find someone and fall in love, she just had to continue to be patient and let God work things out for her.

"Hello folks. Here are your soups. Who gets them?" The waiter asked.

"The soup is for the ladies." John says as he eyed the brandy.

"I guess this is for you then, sir?"

"You are correct." John says as he grabbed the glass and smelled the brandy.

"Enjoy." The waiter said as he walked away.

"The soup looks so delicious," Renee says as she grabbed her spoon. Her face lit up after she tasted it. "Boy, this is some good soup."

"Mom you are right," Tracee said as she tried to get Patrick to try some, but he wasn't comfortable with being fed.

"What do you think, Majestic?" Renee asks.

"It is excellent," Majestic said, as she quickly put another spoonful in her mouth. Just as she was finishing with that spoonful, her mouth dropped open and she fell into a trance again. No one else at the table noticed it at the moment but her eyes were fixed on someone. Majestic didn't know what to think or do because she had never been smitten by anyone before but right now her eyes were fixed on a man. As he got closer she realized it was Ryan. She couldn't believe it was him, because she didn't expect to see him until later in the vacation. She watched him walk up the stairs and her heart was beating fast as if she just got through with one of her workouts.

Boom-boom.

Boom-boom.

That was the sound her heart made as it began to pick up pace.

Boom-boom.

Boom-boom.

It was as if it was a movie scene. What Majestic pictured was everyone slowing down for him as he was walking and it was like a scene where the handsome guy shows up and everyone focuses on him.

Boom-boom.

Boom-boom.

He was walking in slow-motion and everything he did was enhanced by the slow motion of her vision of him. She remembered the pretty brown skin that was smooth and baby-like as it is now.

Boom-boom.

Boom-boom.

She remembered the curly hair shaped like a mini Afro that spoke of mixed heritage as it is now. She noticed how the red color of his shirt only enhanced the glow of his skin.

Boom-boom.

Boom-boom.

He was around the same height of 5'8" but he had gained a little weight. She noticed he had a slight muscular build to him.

Boom-boom.

Boom-boom.

The goatee he was sporting was only accenting his chiseled face. He still had a youthful look to him but his walk and mannerism spoke of maturity.

Boom-boom.

Boom-boom.

In that instant she knew Ryan grew from a lion cub into a strong, handsome male lion. Majestic tried to snap out of her trance but she couldn't.

Boom-boom.

Boom-boom.

In the eight seconds it took for him to get from the stairs to where he was now which is about three feet from her table, she was able to stare and size him up. Majestic wanted to look away and she tried but she was hooked at the sight of him.

Boom-boom.

Boom-boom.

Then to top it off she couldn't believe that she was even thinking on the level she did. She had never gone as far as she has to check out anyone before and she had no excuse for what she just did.

Boom-boom.

Boom-boom.

To make matters more complicated she noticed that Ryan was coming straight towards her table but yet she was unable to stop staring or lower the spoon from her mouth.

"Good evening beautiful people. I am Ryan Levens, and I am the owner. I heard you had something you would like for me to know." Ryan said as he made eye contact with everyone at the table. When he got to Majestic, he took a second and deeper look. She could tell that he seemed like he knew her but he wasn't sure.

"Majestic?" Ryan asked, as everyone looked at her. Majestic just stared at him. She still couldn't believe that he was standing before her and that he looked so good.

"Ryan?" Tracee said as she took a closer look at him.

"Majestic's friend Ryan?" Renee asked Tracee.

"Tracee Manning, how are you doing?" Ryan asked, as he gave her a hug. Majestic could see that Ryan was happy to see Tracee and she hoped he felt the same for her.

"I am good. I am Tracee Christopher now. This is my husband Patrick Christopher." Ryan shook Patrick's hand.

"Pleasure to meet you." Patrick said as he let go of Ryan's hand and immediately puts his arm around Tracee as to give the impression that she was all his.

"This is my mom and dad, Renee and John Manning."

Ryan walked over and gave Renee a hug and shook John's hand. All the while, Majestic just sat there speechless and unable to move. She hasn't seen Ryan in thirteen years and she had forgotten how handsome he was. In her opinion he aged very well. She began to feel as if she should be kicking herself for letting him go. Her heart was still beating fast and she could feel some old feelings trying to resurface. Ryan walked over to Majestic and stood over her.

"My Beautiful." Ryan said, which triggered a flood of memories for Majestic. In the six months prior to him leaving, they would go out together. They were basically friends but they knew they had feelings for each other so there was always as certain level of flirting going on. One thing they would do was greet each other with Ryan saying, "My Beautiful," and Majestic would say…

"My Handsome." She said as she let him lean down to give her a hug. She wanted to get up and give him a big hug but her legs betrayed her. Her mind told her body what to do but her body wasn't listening. So she just sat there stiff as a board. She could only give him a half-hearted hug. It was one of those fake hugs you give a total stranger that hugs you. It looked like she didn't even want to touch him but in her mind, Majestic knew she felt the exact opposite but her body wouldn't listen to her mind.

"It is such a surprise to see you!" Ryan said as he felt the awkwardness of Majestic not standing up so he walked back around to where Juanita was standing.

"I thought you came out here to do volunteer work?" Tracee asked, because she remembered Majestic telling her that a long time ago.

"I still do but the restaurant fell into my lap. So I just went with the flow because I knew that God changed my course for a reason so I listened and followed."

"Well this restaurant is wonderful. We just wanted to know a little behind the concept of it," Renee said as she sipped her tea.

"I was worried for a second. I thought maybe I had to apologize for Juanita's poor attitude or something,"

Ryan says as he nudged Juanita, who just smiled. "Well, this restaurant was a vision of my parents. They wanted this restaurant to be a bright and vibrant place. One that was so bright that darkness had no place here. You see, my parents believed that with no darkness there would be no gloom. There would be no reason for anyone to be here in a bad mood. So if you noticed, there truly are no dark spots in the whole restaurant. If couples come and they want something a little cozier or if they wanted privacy we have tables on the beach for a more intimate feel but they also made the restaurant so desirable that people would forsake privacy just to eat inside. They wanted this place to accent such a beautiful island. They also wanted this to be a place for the islanders to earn money and help their families. Since there are not many moneymaking avenues here on the island, many natives break their neck to work here because we pay them above average. I believe that if you pay people well to do their job then they will do all that they can to keep that job. My parents were big on helping others and they went out of their way to instill that in me. So that is the cut-to-the-chase version of the restaurant."

Majestic heard him talking but she didn't feel like she actually caught a word that he said. She was still spellbound by him. She felt like he was the most handsome man she had ever seen. He had her in a trance, and that had never happened before.

"Well I am impressed. Where are your parents at now? Are your parents retired and they left all of this to you?" Renee asked.

"Not really. My parents died last year in a car wreck so I became owner by default." Ryan said, without hesitation.

"I am sorry to hear that, especially after what you just told us," Renee said, with concern in her voice.

"Don't be sorry. God's plan for our lives is his plan alone. I know my parents are in a better restaurant right now, eating with our Lord and Savior Jesus Christ. So I am at ease."

"Wow. I must say that they had great vision and I am happy that they were able to see the restaurant become more than a vision," Tracee said to Ryan.

"Oh yeah, because the restaurant is only about three and a half years old, so my parents have seen it exactly the way it is today."

"Have you guys ever thought about building one in the States? There is a great market for such a restaurant." Patrick asked trying to sound business savvy.

"No, we just wanted one. Once they saw what they had, they realized that one was enough. They wanted it to be another reason to come to this island. Just an added incentive to coming here; besides, building the restaurant had nothing to do with money, but just about their vision."

"Well, I wish we could have met them and were able to tell them what we are telling you now," John said as he broke his silence.

"You guys would have loved them. They were seasoned, just like you and Renee, but young at heart. I can't tell you how many times they were parasailing or just hanging out with the young couples that were visiting the island, which they befriended."

As Ryan was talking, a couple of waiters came up with their food.

"Oh, your entrées are here. I hope you love the grilled swordfish because that is one of my personal favorites. Well I am going to let you guys eat. As a matter of fact, Juanita their dinner is on me. That is just a small token of my appreciation for you choosing to come here tonight and for you being friends of mine from my past," Ryan said, as he smiled at Majestic.

"Well, thanks Ryan." John says as he extends his hand out.

"We really thank you," Patrick said, as he did the same.

"That is so nice of you!" Renee said as she looked at Majestic, who was still staring at Ryan. "Right, Majestic?"

Majestic finally snapped out of her daze.

"Oh yeah, thanks."

"No problem everyone. I hope you enjoy everything. I hope you guys come again during your visit here."

"We will." Tracee says as she sized up the fish on her plate.

"Ok, bye." Ryan said, as he walked off and went back down the stairs. Majestic was beginning to sweat. She had experienced something for the first time. She thought she had just gone through something she thought wasn't real. The whole concept of love at first sight was something she didn't believe in. She had men come at her and tell her they experienced some of the symptoms she just had and she didn't believe them. If they had indeed gone through what she felt, then she owed them an apology. It is funny because this was technically not her first time seeing Ryan but it was her first time in thirteen years.

"Baby what is up with you? You sat there like a bump on a log. You weren't cordial or engaging at all and that is so not like you. That is an old friend of yours and you acted like you didn't even know him," Renee said as she looked at Majestic with a confused look on her face.

"I don't know, Mom. I just spaced out for a minute," Majestic said, as she tried to hide the real reason why.

"You didn't take anything did you? No medicine at all?" John asked, as he showed equal concern.

"Oh no, I think my mind was just elsewhere, that's all. Don't be alarmed. Wow, this looks so good," Majestic said as she looked down at her food. She was hoping her diversion tactic worked.

"How is your fish, Tracee?"

"I tell you what; this fish is so good." Tracee replied as she continued to eat.

"The grilled chicken is excellent," Patrick added, as if someone asked him.

"Ryan has something special here. This steak is perfect, as is the rest of this restaurant. Ryan is truly honoring his parents' vision and that is good to see," John said as he cut his steak that seemed to be just so enticing. "I mean this steak is tender and juicy."

Majestic wasn't hearing a thing that anyone was saying. She was on Planet Majestic and Ryan was the President. Majestic was shaken and she knew she had better snap out of it. She attempted to finish off her soup when some leaked over the side of the spoon and landed in her lap.

"Great. I need to go to the restroom. I can't believe I just wasted soup on myself." Majestic says as she dabs the spot where the soup landed on her jeans.

"Girl you need to go to the restroom and put some hot water on it." Tracee said, as she flagged down a waiter walking by. "Excuse me, sir."

"Yes ma'am."

"Can you tell me where your restroom is located?" Majestic asked as she began to stand up. Good thing her jeans were dark blue so the spot wasn't noticeable.

"Sure. Go down the stairs and the restrooms are on the backside of the hostess stand."

"Thank you. Excuse me everyone, I will be right back."

Majestic wanted to kick herself. She couldn't believe that she was acting so out of character. First, she was staring at Ryan as if he was a large piece of gold and now she was wasting food in her lap. Majestic was so conscious on how she behaved in public that she would normally not bring any attention to herself and tonight she was doing the opposite of that. Good thing she didn't spill anything on herself when Ryan was at the table. She was happy that she had finished the soup that was on her spoon or no telling what would have happened. She was even thinking about how funny it would have been if she was drinking at the time and would have sprayed everyone with her drink at the sight of him. As she was descending down the stairs, she could see Ryan standing by the restrooms. He was talking to a couple of his staff members. Majestic did not want to run into him. She just treated him like she wasn't happy to see him. She wouldn't know what to say if he spoke to her. She wasn't even sure if any words would come out if he had spoken to her. So she knew she had to do some evasive action in order to avoid him. So once she was at the bottom of the stairs she went in the opposite direction towards the doors that led to the beach. She tried to walk at a fast pace but after a few feet she realized that the faster she walked, the more attention she drew to herself. So she slowed down to a normal pace. She made it to the doors that lead to the beach sitting area and they began to automatically open. Just as Majestic was walking out the door, Juanita walked up to her.

"Hey Majestic," Juanita said, scaring Majestic. Majestic jumped at the sound of Juanita's voice. "I didn't mean to scare you."

"Oh no problem. I was just looking for the restrooms." Majestic said as she tried to get out of this conversation.

"The restroom is on the backside of the hostess stand."

"Ok. I will see you back at the table then."

"Is everything ok up there?"

"Everything is fine. The food is great. Well, I'm off to the restroom."

"Ok." Juanita says as she turns to go back outside. She walked over to the bar and Majestic figured she was just getting a drink order for another table. So she wanted to quickly turn around and go to the restroom and beat Juanita back to the table.

"Hi Majestic," Ryan said, as he walked up to her. Majestic instantly felt her heart pick up a faster pace. She was now face to face with him. She knew she had to collect her composure and hold a conversation.

"Hey Ryan," Majestic said as she gave him a hug. This time she gave him a real hug to make up for the fake one she gave him a moment ago.

"Is there something I can help you with?" Ryan asked as he smiled his million-dollar smile. Majestic felt like melting at the sight of his smile.

"Yeah I am lost. I was looking for the restrooms." She didn't want to say she was lost but it was the first thing that came to her mind. There are a few situations where you would say something you didn't want to say, and for her this is one of them.

"No problem. The restrooms are right over there on the backside of the hostess stand." Ryan said, as he turned and pointed behind him. Majestic paid no attention to where he was pointing; she was just staring at his face. At this moment she was in awe of him.

"You still look very pretty, Majestic. I have wondered what you looked like, and now you are here before me and I am impressed."

"And you are still handsome, Ryan," Majestic said as she tried to hide her smile.

"I would have never thought in a million years that I would walk up the stairs and see you and your family. It was a pleasant surprise. I was very happy to see you."

"We didn't expect to see you either. I was going to email you and let you know that we were here."

"Well, the last time I talked to you was four years ago and all the info you had for me, I have changed. So if you had tried to contact me, you wouldn't have been able to. I changed that a long time ago."

"I am glad we ran into you then. That would have been so not cool to have been here and not been able to contact you."

"I would have been mad if I would have found out that you came to the island and we didn't even get a chance to get together."

"That would have been messed up."

"If you don't mind me asking, how long are you and your family going to be here?"

"We are going to be here four weeks."

"Four weeks? That is a long time. Is this a business trip or a family getaway?"

"Both. We are here for a family vacation but I brought my cameras so I can take pictures for my gallery back at home."

"Oh yeah, you have a gallery. Well, if you need a tour guide to show you around to some of the sights then I would be honored to do that for you. Well, I don't want to be rude. I didn't even ask you if you were married or if you had someone special with you. We haven't talked in years so I don't want to impose. Not that it would matter; I would still offer the tour regardless."

Majestic began to smile uncontrollably. Ryan had no idea how happy she was to hear him say that. This was the first time in years that she has actually been happy that she was single. She wanted to just yell out she was single but she wanted to keep her excitement in to not give away too much. She was finally getting more relaxed and now she was able to think more clearly.

"No, I am single. No husband or special someone. A tour sure does sound nice; I might just take you up on that. Is there a way for me to contact you?" Majestic was so shocked that she actually asked him that. There was no way she was going to let this moment pass without making sure they had a way to contact each other.

"Sure." Ryan says as he reached into his wallet and pulled out a business card. "Here is my business card. It has everything you need to get in touch with me."

"Great." Majestic says as she slipped it into her back pocket.

"Well, I am here every morning at 8 am. So feel free to stop by. The inside part of the restaurant is closed until sunset but the beach part is open. You can ask anyone for me."

"Ok, I will."

"Great, well I look forward to seeing you again Miss Lost."

"Me too, Mr. Tour Guide," Majestic said without skipping a beat. Those were cute little things they would do and she realized now that she missed that.

"I hope you enjoy your meal and don't forget to order dessert. See you later," Ryan said as he walked off. Majestic just watched him and started to sigh. She was definitely smitten by him and it was obvious. So she began to walk towards the restroom, which was her true destination in the first place. As she was making her way towards the restroom she couldn't help but to replay the conversation she just had with Ryan. She was smiling just thinking about it. Once she made it safely inside the restroom she started to do a happy dance. She had never felt like this and she was feeling like she was in high school and the popular jock finally noticed her and asked her out. She just couldn't stop dancing until another woman walked in and she quickly played it off. She had totally forgotten all about the spot on her jeans because she quickly went out the door and started to head back to her table. Once she made it to the stairs, there stood Tracee walking down.

"Are you ok? Patrick thought that maybe you got kidnapped or robbed."

"I am fine."

"We know you are fine. Juanita told us you were downstairs by the entrance to the beach talking to Ryan." Tracee says as she started to get that look like she caught Majestic in a lie.

"She did?" Majestic asked as she recalled Juanita being at the bar but that was before Ryan walked up. She figured that she was so into the conversation with Ryan that she didn't even see Juanita walk by them.

"She sure did. So what were you and Ryan talking about?"

Majestic didn't want to tell Tracee that she tried to avoid Ryan by going the opposite direction and that was when she ran into Juanita and then eventually had her conversation with Ryan. She didn't know what to say because she knows that Tracee will interrogate her no matter what.

"Nothing. He saw me downstairs and just came up to say hi."

"Oh he did? I recall him saying hi at the table. Majestic, why are you insisting on holding out on me?" Tracee asked as she started to smile. The sight of Tracee smiling made Majestic smile. "He tried to holla at you?

"Well, um maybe." Majestic said, grinning from ear to ear.

"What? You have got to tell me everything!" Tracee said as if Majestic had some juicy gossip.

"I will, but later. I am so hungry and I want to eat my food."

"Ok but I am not going to let you go to sleep until you tell me everything, word for word."

"Ok, Tracee." Majestic said, as she tried to hide her smile.

As they were making their way back to the table, Majestic realized that they have only been here a few hours and already she was enjoying this vacation. If the next four weeks will be anything like today, she knew she was going to have the time of her life and that was a thought that she relished.

*   *   *

Knock.

Knock.

"Who is it? Majestic asked but she knew who it was.

"Tracee."

Majestic knew that Tracee was not going to forget to ask Majestic what the conversation between her and Ryan was all about.

"I had to catch you before you went to bed. I come to get some juicy news about you and Ryan," Tracee said as she walked in the door and sat down on the bed. Majestic closed the door and sat down next to her.

"Ok, tell me everything," Tracee said as she sat up and gave Majestic her full attention.

"It's wasn't that good of a conversation. I am going to start from the beginning and that was when we were at the table and he walked up. Now I am going to be honest with you. We haven't sat down and talked like this since high school so be serious and don't interrupt me because you know how you ask a question and before I finish answering that one, you ask me another one. Ok?"

"Ok, ok," Tracee said, as she tried to get Majestic to talk about the conversation.

"Well when he walked up to the table I didn't know what to say. I watched him walk up the stairs and I was in a trance. I couldn't move or speak. I was just staring at him."

"You? The same person who let him go? How ironic is that?"

"Yes, me. I was spellbound." Majestic says as she started to smile. It was funny to her how the sight of Ryan made her feel.

"Girl, I can't blame you. That man is gorgeous," Tracee added.

"So his whole spiel he gave about his parents and the restaurant went right over my head. I heard bits and pieces but I was too focused on him. Anyway, well when he got through and left, I tried to get my composure back so I attempted to eat and that was when I wasted soup in my lap. Then I got up to go to the restroom and as I was walking down the stairs, I saw Ryan standing by the restrooms talking to some of his employees. I wanted to avoid him in the worst way."

"Why? What were you afraid of? Why not just walk by and see if he would stop you and talk to you?" Tracee asked.

"Well I am not as bold as you Tracee. I just felt funny seeing him like that. Everything was just so strange. I had no clue he was going to be there and I didn't expect to act the way I acted either. I just think it is something about him that makes me nervous."

"I remember when you guys first met and it took you all of two months before you finally went out with him."

"I know, right? Anyway, so I had seen him at the restrooms so I went the opposite way towards the beach."

"You are crazy."

"I was making my way to the beach area when Juanita comes from beach area and scared the mess out of me. I definitely didn't expect to see her down there. So we had a quick conversation and in me trying to get away from her, I turn around and Ryan walks up to me."

"Finally we get to the good part." Tracee says as she starts rubbing her hands together.

"It wasn't all that great of a conversation," Majestic said, as she tried to downplay the conversation. No matter what Tracee thought of the conversation, Majestic was glad it happened and that was all that mattered.

"Anyway, he walks up and says, 'hi.' We just go back and forth with small talk. He asked me how long we were going to be here."

"Ok, that is promising," Tracee added.

"I told him four weeks. Then he asked me if it was business or family vacation and I told him both."

"Ok, you make yourself out to be a workaholic. What if that would have turned him off? In a way, it was work that motivated you to not be with him in the first place."

"Wait. If I hadn't said that then he would have never offered to show me around or be my tour guide as he said it."

"Oh he did? Now that sounds very promising."

"Then he asked me if I was married or had someone special. I told him no and that was when he gave me his card and asked me to let him know if I wanted him to show me around."

"That's what I am talking about, Majestic hooking up with Ryan on her first night in paradise. You said yes I hope."

"In a way I did. I told him I would think on it."

"Ok Miss Turtle. Go slow as always and you are going to miss a golden opportunity. You are on a beautiful island. A handsome man you know and still have feelings for has approached you. You are single and have been for a long time, I might add. This is where you can enjoy life and do things you wouldn't normally do."

"What are you talking about? I know all of this but I am not going to go crazy. I am going to take it day by day and see what happens."

"Ok, well I am going to bed. What time are you meeting him tomorrow?" Tracee asked as she stood up and handed Ryan's card back to Majestic.

"What do you mean? I am not going to do that already. I don't want to seem desperate." Majestic says as she stands up.

"Give me that card back," Tracee said as she snatched the card out of Majestic's hand." I am going to call him. If you don't want me setting up the date for you, I would advise you to call him and set up a meeting time and place."

"No way. I am not doing that."

"Why not?"

"That is not my style and you know it."

"Majestic it's ok to ask a guy out. That is not forsaking your Christian values. That doesn't mean you are going to give yourself to him. It only means that you are interested in him and that is all. You are so concerned about your image and I understand that. Just don't lose an opportunity to enjoy yourself for the next four weeks. You owe it to yourself to do that. Call him. Tell him I made you call him or just let me do the talking for you, Ok?" Tracee asks as she looks to Majestic for the ok.

"Alright, you call him but don't make me seem sleazy." Majestic said, as she gave in. She knew that it wasn't hurting her Christian status or anything. She knew that she really wanted to go out with Ryan. She just wanted to play it off because she wanted to stay cool about it.

"Sleazy. You have done that already by getting his number. Just kidding, here goes nothing." Tracee says as she walks towards the phone. The phone suddenly begins to ring.

"Oh boy. You know that is Patrick calling here to make sure you wasn't robbed or kidnapped," Majestic said, as she started to laugh.

"Leave my man alone. He is only concerned, that is all. Besides he probably just wants me to tuck him in."

Majestic wanted to throw up at the sound of that. Patrick wasn't appealing to her at all but she was a little bit jealous at the level of love they have for each other.

Majestic can only hope to have a marriage that is full of love and passion like theirs.

"You guys are gross."

"Majestic we dated for a year and a half. We waited until we were married before we finally got intimate. We are only catching up." Tracee says as she picks up the phone.

"Hello."

Majestic just shook her head and smiled. If that was what it is like to love someone but wait until you are finally married before you become intimate. If the passion is intensified because of that then waiting is definitely worth it, in her opinion.

"No this is not Majestic, this is her sister Tracee. Who is this?"

Majestic was wondering who would call her. It was probably room service.

"Oh hey, Ryan," Tracee said, as she motioned for Majestic to come closer.

"How did he know where we would be staying?" Majestic asked, as she got closer to Tracee so Tracee could put the phone receiver between them so they both could listen to what he was saying.

"How did you get this number? Tracee asked as she waited on the answer. "Oh Mom filled out a comment card and put everyone's information on it. What was that?" Tracee asked as Majestic leaned in closer to try to catch what he was saying.

"Oh no, that is no problem. No need to apologize for that. Majestic? "No she is in the shower right now. I do want to thank you for the dinner tonight, everything was wonderful."

Majestic wanted to just snatch the phone from Tracee just so she could hear his voice.

"What are we doing tomorrow? Patrick and I are going to spend time at the beach and just be lazy. Our parents are going to check out the shops and relax at the hotel. Majestic isn't doing anything. As a matter of fact she told me she was hoping to take you up on that tour you offered." Tracee says as she winks at Majestic. Majestic wanted to fall to the floor and die. She was so nervous right now. What if she was coming on too strong and giving the wrong impression about herself? She knew Tracee would take the bolder approach so she shouldn't be surprised by how upfront Tracee is in answering Ryan.

"Ok perfect. I will tell her to be there at 11am. Ok Ryan. You take care. Bye." Tracee says as she hung up the phone. "Yes!" She shouts as she gives Majestic a high five. Majestic just stood there grinning.

"Well?" Majestic says as Tracee just stood there smiling as she stared at Majestic.

"Ok sis, I have hooked you up. He was excited when I told him you were going to call him. See you should feel extra special because he called you. He said meet him at the restaurant beach area at 11am," Tracee said as she walked towards the door. Majestic felt extremely happy that he called. That showed her that he might still have interest in her as well.

"Thanks Tracee."

"Anytime. I want you to enjoy yourself. You need a vacation and you need to just hang out with Ryan even if it is just for the next four weeks. Just relax and take it easy. I am going to tuck my husband in. Goodnight, and don't be late tomorrow." Tracee said as she gave Majestic a hug.

"I won't be late," Majestic said as she closed the door and did her happy dance again. This time she wasn't worried about anyone walking in on her. She was very excited about the prospect of hanging with Ryan. She remembered how much fun they use to have and how great his conversations were.

"Ok Majestic, get a hold of yourself." She said as she finally stopped dancing. She walked over to her suitcases and began to look for something to wear. She wanted to be cute but not overly cute. She didn't want to seem like she was trying too hard to get his attention even though she wanted his attention. Majestic found a nice pair of white shorts with a white tank top and a nice white short-sleeved button down shirt. Majestic would have never thought that on her first night there she would be planning to hang out with Ryan already. She was so excited and she hadn't felt like this before. She had never experienced excitement on this level. This was a first, and at this moment she welcomed it. Love has been the one avenue of her life where she had not achieved success. It was a dark cloud over her head and she so desperately wanted to lift. She also knew that she didn't want to get too excited because this was a vacation spot. She knows that he lives here and she lives in Las Vegas, so a relationship would be impossible. The only thing is within the next four weeks she will leave and he would still be here. She welcomed the excitement, but she also was cautious to not like him too strongly because that would only complicate things for her, and she loved the order and drama-free life she lived. She has plenty to think about with her gallery.

"Snap, I haven't even checked on the gallery," Majestic said as she logged in on her computer. Before Tracee came to the room she was trying to log on and check on things at home. She had remote access to the cameras throughout the gallery. When she logged on, she saw a nice little crowd mingling throughout the gallery. Some people were standing around looking at the pictures. Some people were talking and they seemed to be comparing pictures. The workers were engaging the customers as well as doing their normal routine. Everything seemed cool but she wanted to call just to make sure all is well. She grabbed her cell phone and dialed the gallery. She was watching the camera over the area where the phone was to see who would pick it up.

"Majestically Captured."

"Hey Joan, this is Majestic."

"Hey. How are you enjoying your vacation?"

"Um it's alright so far. Beautiful place and I have already taken some great pictures. I am just ready to get some sleep. I just thought I would call and see how things were at the gallery. I have never attempted to be gone as long as I will be gone this time. I just want to make sure things are ok," Majestic said as she tried to downplay what had happened so far. Her concern over her gallery was genuine and it trumped any other thought at the moment.

"Everything is good. You just make sure you try to relax and don't call us everyday. I've got your back and you know this. I have been here since day one, so rest assured. I am like a mini you, or a Caucasian version of you," Joan said as she started to laugh. Majestic knew she could trust Joan. Joan and Majestic had been friends since college. They were the best of friends. So when Majestic told her about the gallery, Joan said she would quit her job as a sales rep and help Majestic run the gallery so she became Majestic's right hand.

"I am not worried, Joan. I know you are handling things there. Did we make any money?" Majestic asked.

"Oh yes. The Touch of Color exhibit was on fire today. We sold ten of the twenty-five pictures today alone," Joan said. Majestic could hear the joy in her voice. When Joan says the exhibit was on fire that meant it drew a lot of attention. Selling almost half of an exhibit is excellent. Majestic was very happy to hear that.

"Great, so you are going to put out more of them tomorrow morning?" Majestic asked because she wanted to make sure she had more opportunities to capitalize on the exhibit's popularity at the moment.

"Yes we are. Is there any one in particular that you want out there?"

"Let's put out the ones with the mothers and the babies. Those should move easily," Majestic replied as she reviewed the photographs in her mind. The Touch of Color exhibit was basically a large black and white photo. Everything, of course, was black and white except for the focus of the pictures. In the case of the mother and her baby, the baby was the only thing in color, the focal point of the photos. By adding color to the babies, they were demonstrated to be the center of the mothers' attention. Majestic was very excited about that exhibit.

"Consider it done. Is there anything else?"

"No, that is it Joan. I will let you go. Have a good night."

"Majestic, promise me you will have fun."

"I will have fun. I will even take pictures to prove it."

"Ok. Bye Majestic."

"Bye Joan." Majestic said as she hung up the phone. She didn't want to tell Joan that she planned on having a lot of fun. She was happy that things were going well back at the gallery so now she could take a shower and get her some rest. She wanted to be ready for her tour tomorrow. She tried to think about what tomorrow would be like.

She hoped that whatever happens that at least they would be able to talk and catch up on lost time. Just like the first time they were together, they would eventually be going their separate ways. That was the only downer about them hanging out together. Majestic could sense some feelings resurfacing, and she was worried about that. She was worried about them hanging out together and beginning to feel the way they felt thirteen years ago. It is a little early to be thinking like that, but four weeks is a long time and that gives them plenty of time to catch up. Majestic only hoped that they would enjoy each other regardless, so she wasn't going to worry about anything else. This was a vacation and so she planned on getting away from the super-serious Majestic and she wanted to hang out with the fun Majestic. Tomorrow will be the start of fun times and that was what she had been waiting to do for a long time. So she planned on meeting Ryan and just talk about the past. They had some great and fun times together because there were no ties. They were only friends so they could hang out and go their separate ways with no problems. She was very excited and she couldn't wait for tomorrow to come.

2

Majestic had gotten to the restaurant early. She wanted to soak in the morning view of the ocean. She had gotten up extra early to workout; well at least that was going to be her story. In all fairness to the truth, she couldn't sleep due to her excitement about today. She just did her normal routine and when she was done working out, she showered, went downstairs to the coffee shop and got her an iced coffee with whipped cream. That has been her normal breakfast the past few years. She was never big on breakfast so the iced coffee did the trick. So she grabbed her camera bag and just walked the beach until she got to the restaurant. She loved the white sand and how it looked so pure. It looked as if she was walking on a bed of white rice. The sand looked so beautiful. She just wanted to bottle it up and take it with her to Las Vegas. Majestic made sure she took plenty of pictures and she was able to get some great shots of the water, which was so blue and clear. You could actually see down to the bottom of the water, and that was a first for her; it was captivating. Majestic wanted to just run and dive into the water. She wanted to feel the cool water run through her hair. Majestic could picture herself swimming to the bottom and picking up seashells. The whole idea was soothing to her mind and she really had to fight the urge to get in the water. She could look over the horizon and see nothing but blue sky and blue water. The whole view was surreal. This was one of those moments where nature reminded you of one of its purposes. The purpose it was displaying today was beauty. To see such a large body of water so calm was breathtaking. She had literally just stood by the seashore and just looked at the water. Majestic felt like praying because she was so blessed to be where she was at this moment. God was giving her the chance to enjoy his creation. He had calmed the waters of this ocean, just like he had calmed her life. She was on vacation and that was a big change for her. She had worked long hours with no time off for the past seven years. This was her first chance to step back and do nothing. All she had to do now was just relax and enjoy herself. She felt that the prayers she was saying this morning were special because for the first time in a long time she didn't make it a personal prayer. She prayed for everyone else and didn't ask for a thing. She didn't ask for a good time with Ryan or anything of that nature. Normally her morning prayers were about doing well in her gallery and finally meeting her mate. Today she was just thanking God for a new day and for the beauty that was before her. Even with her taking time to do all of that she was still an hour early. So she just decided to just sit at one of the beach tables and just look at the ocean some more. So she walked the few yards until she was at the Heart of Velacious Restaurant. She just walked up to the nearest empty table and sat down. She loved the view but in all actuality all the tables outside gave you a wonderful view of the ocean. Majestic knew she could wake up to this view everyday. What could be better than to stare nature in its face when it is this beautiful?

"Good morning Majestic. How are you today?' Juanita says as she walks up to Majestic.

"I am good. I am just soaking in this beautiful gift from God. How are you this morning?"

"I am good so far. A little tired, but I am good." Juanita says as she smiled but Majestic could still see the bags under eyes. She was pretty but you could tell she lived a hard life. She looked worn out and Majestic couldn't tell last night because Juanita had makeup on but this morning she had so little of it on that it was easy to see how she really looked. Last night, Juanita was a cute but sad puppy and today she was looking like an old tired dog.

"You should be, you just worked last night. Do you always work this much?" Majestic asked showing concern for her.

"Yes. I normally work the night shift and Ryan lets me work any extra hours I want in the morning. He gives me that option so normally I take him up on that."

"Don't work too hard though. Money isn't worth killing yourself," Majestic said, as if she ever took heed to that advice. People have been telling her that for years and yet she hadn't listened at all. So now she was trying to pass that advice on to Juanita even though she couldn't follow it herself.

"I know but when you have little ones to feed you try to do all you can."

"Oh, you have children! How old are they?"

"I have a son that is ten and daughter that is eight."

"Wow, I didn't think you were that old," Majestic said. She knew she just told a lie because in all actuality Juanita looked old enough for children older than that. Her skin showed a certain older quality to it but her eyes still spoke of youth.

"I am twenty six years old. I just started young," Juanita said as she looked away. Majestic could only imagine what she had been through in her twenty-six years. Majestic felt that at twenty-six she was just scratching the surface of adulthood. Juanita looked like her life had been a fight and Majestic could tell that it really bothered Juanita but she didn't want to harp on that too long.

"Well, I would love to see them before I leave," Majestic said to try to change the subject.

"No problem. I will see what I can do. Are you here to eat breakfast? Juanita asked. "I could get you a menu."

"Oh no, I came to talk to Ryan. Is he here?"

"Ryan, yes he is here. Let me go and get him. Would you like to order something while you wait?"

"No, I will just wait here," Majestic said as Juanita walked off to go and get Ryan.

She felt sad for Juanita because she was working two shifts to support her children. By the looks of it, her life was already hard on her. Majestic could not recall seeing a ring on her finger so she felt that maybe there was no man in her life. That was another reason why Majestic didn't want to be intimate with anyone again until she was married. There was no way she wanted to walk around with children out of wedlock unless she was divorced. She didn't want to have to go through the public scrutiny of having children with no husband. Majestic was too cautious about her public appearance to have that happen to her. She doesn't frown down on anyone for having children that way; she just knows she wasn't strong enough to handle that if it happened to her. There are plenty of strong Christian women that have children and are not married. Majestic looked up to them and still respected them. To see the single women with children accomplish so much, and sometimes with no help, shows how strong those good mothers are to make sure that their children are taken care of. Majestic knows she probably could be a single mother but she doesn't want to chance it at all.

"My Beautiful." Ryan says as he walks up to Majestic from out of the restaurant. He looked so handsome in his blue polo shirt and khaki shorts. Juanita followed behind him but she was no longer smiling. She just stopped at the bar. She was just looking intently trying to see what he was going to do.

"My Handsome." Majestic says as she ignores Juanita staring at her from the bar.

"Wow, you look so beautiful today and I saw you sitting here earlier but I didn't want to break your moment of peace. I am so happy you took my offer to let me show you around the island," Ryan said as he smiled at Majestic.

"Yeah, I was just looking at God's gift and I was blessed by just seeing it. Oh and I am glad you offered to be my tour guide."

"Cool, well are you ready to go or would you like more time to soak in this awesome view?" Ryan asked. As he started to smile, Majestic noticed he had dimples; she was fighting off another trance. She had forgotten the small simple things about him and every time she noticed something, it would trigger her feelings for him.

"I am ready. Do you need to tell someone or any-thing?" Majestic says as she looks back towards the bar, Juanita was gone but everyone else was busy working.

"No, I normally leave about this time and I come back in time for the restaurant to open for dinner. So let's go."

"You are bringing us food also. Are we going on a picnic?" Majestic asked as she noticed the large bag in Ryan's hand.

"Not today. I will explain this later."

Majestic just nodded because she was ready to go. This was the moment she had thought about the whole night and all of the morning. She didn't know where they were going or what they were going to do. All she cared about was the fact that she was with Ryan so everything else was secondary to that.

"Wait. You guys are having ballroom dancing tonight? Where?" Majestic asks as she walks by an empty table that had a flyer announcing the dance.

"We have it on the first floor. We clear the tables in the middle and we just dance in the middle of the dining room."

"I don't want to miss that. So it starts at 7pm."

"Yes it does. We do ask that the dress be formal or at least semi-formal. I hope you have something formal or dressy. We like the look of everyone dressed up. We don't turn anyone away but we just like for everyone to give it the ballroom feel. Have you ever ballroom danced before?" Ryan asked.

"Yes, I do have a formal dress. I am a princess and I would never leave home without a chance to show the world that I am one. Yes, I have taken ballroom dancing, tango, salsa and just about any other style. I love to dance!" Majestic said. She was glad that all the money she spent on dance lessons might finally pay off.

"Great, then I look forward to you and your family possibly showing up. Everyone normally has such a wonderful time. This is our third year doing it so we hope it is as good as the first two years. So if you are ready," Ryan said as he grabbed Majestic's elbow and gently pulled her so she would start walking. Then as soon as he grabbed it he quickly let it go. Majestic didn't mind him doing that she just wished he didn't let go.

"Majestic, I see how pretty you look today but I must warn you that I have a convertible and sometimes it is murder on a pretty woman's hair. I just thought I would give you a heads up about the wind because I would hate for you to be mad at me."

"Don't worry; I can just put it in a pony tail. Besides I love convertibles." Majestic said. This would be her first time in a convertible, believe it or not.

"Great. So did you get some rest last night? The Gila Hotel is very nice. I have stayed there a few nights."

"Yes I did get some rest. I didn't know what kind of tour you were going to take me on so just in case it was a hiking tour I wanted to be ready."

"Majestic, if you were planning on going on a hiking trip then I don't know how you were going to make it with those sandals on."

"How do you know the boots are not in my camera bag?"

"I just remember you as someone that takes pride in being cute at all times. My bad if I put you in a category."

"You would be surprised at what I would do now. Hiking is something I have always wanted to do." Majestic said as she laughed. She knew she didn't fool Ryan at all. Majestic has always been the girlie type so she didn't do many activities outside unless it was running.

"So where are we going? I had seen some cool shops and few other resorts on this map. I made sure that I circled the ones I wanted to see first in red and the other ones in blue." Majestic said as she pulled the map out of her camera bag.

"Majestic, I am shocked. I thought you wanted to see the island! Those gift shops and resort spots are not the island. The island is where islanders live and not work. I was going to take you where you will see the island in its purest form. Is that ok with you?" Ryan asked as he directed her to his red convertible Honda Accord.

"That sounds real good to me. I didn't know Honda Accords came in a convertible style," Majestic said as she looked the car over.

"I think this is the island version. There are all kinds of cars that are convertible here that a lot of visitors say is strange. Oh before we get in the car, do me a favor."

"Ok Ryan, what do you need?" Majestic asked, clueless on what he was going to ask.

"Call your family and tell them where we are going. I like for you to be totally safe and I want your folks to be at ease while you are with me. Besides one spot where we are going, there are no telephone lines or any way to communicate once we get there. I didn't want to spring that on you once we got there but I promise you we will be safe. The police guard that area 24/7 and I know a lot of people there. As a matter of fact, more than half my staff lives there."

"Ok," Majestic said as she pulls out her cell phone. She didn't know what to think at first. For one she has never had to tell her parents where she was going because they know that she can take care of herself and would never put herself in danger. Majestic did like the idea that Ryan cared enough to let someone know where they were just in case and that showed responsibility and accountability on his part; Majestic liked that.

"Tracee, hey this is Majestic. Yes, I am with Ryan. I just called to let you know where I am going just in case. Where are we going Ryan?"

"We are going to Heaven of Flowers and to Vera Courts."

"We are going to Heaven of Flowers and to Vera Courts. Ok, you got that. Whatever Tracee, you are crazy, I will see you later."

"Around 4pm," Ryan says before she got off the phone.

"Around 4pm, crazy. Bye. My sister is crazy," Majestic said as she put her cell phone in her camera bag.

"It was good to see Tracee again. Her husband Patrick seems to be really nice," Ryan said, as he opened the car door for Majestic. Majestic always liked the fact that he opened the door for her because she knew that he had a level of respect for women.

"You would change your mind once you get to know him, I promise you." Majestic said as she got in.

"I will take your word for it," Ryan said as he opened the trunk and placed the bag inside. He then opened his door and got in.

"Let's pray," Ryan said, as he looked Majestic in her eyes.

"Oh by all means let's pray," Majestic said as she grabbed Ryan's hand that was extended to her. She loved the feel of his hand as he gave her hand a nice squeeze. She felt a little tingle go up her arm. So once he was through praying she didn't want to let go of his hand but she knew he possibly needed it to drive. She watched him start the car up and they pulled out of the parking lot. He turned the radio on and he had a jazz CD playing, but he turned the volume down.

"So catch me up on you. What have you been up to?" Ryan asked as they begin to drive.

"Nothing really but running my gallery."

"What's the name of the gallery again?"

"Majestically Captured."

"I like that. Nice wordplay with that."

"Thank you."

"Is business doing better?"

"Well when we last talked, I was into my third year with the gallery and I was still struggling. It was extremely hard and at times I really wanted to give up. I had prayed to God so much during those times and I had my mom to vent to. Now things are going really well. I can't complain at all."

"Good, because I remember you mentioning it to me about how you were frustrated with struggling with it. So I am glad to hear that you got over that hurdle.

"Thank you. It was a battle and I wondered if it was ever going to get better."

"I know you had enough faith and that you knew God was going to see you through."

"Oh yeah. You should check out the website that we have. It is really nice. You might find something you want to put up in your home, office or restaurant."

"I am going to have to check that out then. I would love to support you." Ryan said as he winked at Majestic. She started to blush because she was happy to be with him. She didn't realize how much she missed him. As a matter of fact she didn't know she had repressed feelings for him but they were definitely there.

"Great, so you are thirty-four, successful, independent and not married. I look at someone as beautiful as you and I think, "Taken or married." I would have never thought that you would still be single. I thought that maybe someone would sweep you off your feet by now. Unless you were serious about being a workaholic and you haven't found time for someone else. I remember clearly you telling me how you were going to throw yourself into your gallery and get the most out of it as possible."

"Yes I am workaholic but the real reason why I am single is simply because I have not found anyone that was for me."

"Are you for real? All the people in Las Vegas, thousands of them and you couldn't find one that was suitable for you?"

"Ryan, for real. I have dated and none was what I was looking for," Majestic said as she tried to hold back the real reason why she is single. She wanted to just come out and say that it was because every man ran when they found out that they had no chance of hitting a home run.

"Well, I am sorry to hear that. I am glad, in a way, but sorry to hear that."

"So what's your story then?"

Majestic remembers clearly that he was dating someone four years ago. That was part of the reason why she didn't stay in touch as often as she wanted to. He was with someone else and Majestic knew she would get jealous over it so she just stopped having contact with Ryan. She looks over at his hand and she didn't see a ring on his ring finger so she felt better about riding with him. If he was single then there must be a good reason. Majestic definitely wanted to know why he was walking around a place like this and single. She was hoping he wasn't some kind of "Island player." She definitely didn't have time for games and so far Ryan had never shown any tendencies like that. He was probably the best man she has ever known. If he was anything like he was back then, she knew he had to be taken by now.

"Well, my story is more cut and dry than yours. I was to be married but my fiancée died." Ryan said as he looked at Majestic with a serious look in his eye.

"Oh my goodness Ryan, what happened?" Majestic asked, as she was afraid that everyone he loved ended up dead and that wasn't a good way to enter back into his life.

"She died in a car accident. Well, basically she was driving the car that my parents were in when they were killed."

"Oh wow. I'm sorry." Majestic said as her world just stopped moving. It must be the worst scenario of all to lose your fiancée and your parents at the same time. She couldn't truly fathom such a loss and the pain associated with it.

"It was a rainy night. It doesn't rain much here but when it does, it is either a light rain or a hurricane. Sometimes there is no in-between. Well anyway, my parents were flying back to Houston because they were going to a reunion of sorts with my Dad's old company. I couldn't go because there was a bad case of the flu going around so I was bedridden. My fiancée volunteered to take them to the airport. My parents told her to stay and take care of me but she insisted on doing it. Well they were driving along when another vehicle lost control and hit them head on. They all died instantly."

"How horrible because that is a terrible way to die."

"So I haven't dated since. Not by choice, but I just haven't met anyone that I thought I would like to get to know more deeply," Ryan said with a hint of sadness in his voice and Majestic could understand why. That had to be a tough time in his life.

"That is so sad Ryan. I can understand you wanting to take your time. Healing is sometimes a slow process."

"It is but I am better. I felt like Job, from the Old Testament. God was letting Satan take everything from me just to test my faith and I never gave in. I wouldn't curse God or put the blame on him. I knew all three of them well and I can understand why God was ready for them. But hey, let's not dwell on that. I don't want to ruin our time together with sad stories. We can relive these stories at a later time. Is that cool with you?" Ryan asked, as he smiled at Majestic. Majestic knew that as long as he kept smiling at her she would talk about anything he wanted to.

"If you are cool with that, then so am I. So where are we going first?"

"That is a surprise. You will know when you see it."

"What is up with everyone saying that here? The guy at the hotel said the same thing when he wouldn't describe your restaurant or tell us the name of it."

"Majestic, you act like the other tourists by being so impatient. No one likes surprises anymore. I promise you, you will love this place."

"And if I don't?"

"Then you are not a true photographer."

"Sounds like a challenge to me," Majestic said, as she started to remember the little things they did together that made their friendship fun.

"It is and you will lose this challenge. Ok, I don't make bets but lets just say that if you don't like the place then you and your family can eat free at my restaurant the rest of your time here."

"Why do you think I am with you now? This little ride with you is all about the free food, baby," Majestic said before she burst out laughing. She wasn't known for being funny but she knew she said a good one that time.

"How cold is that?"

"What if I like the place? What do you get?"

"I get the satisfaction of knowing that I did something right in your eyes. That would be plenty enough for me. I used to love making you happy and watch you smile. I didn't care about anything else back in the day. It was all about Majestic then and today it is all about her again."

Majestic couldn't help but think of how sweet that was. Ryan was definitely a smooth guy. He has shown qualities of being a true Christian and nothing in his actions or talk has shown anything different.

"Deal?" Ryan asks as he extends his hand out to Majestic.

"Deal." Majestic says as she shakes Ryan's hand.

So as they were driving Majestic started to look around at the scenery. Every time she was driving in her car back in Las Vegas she would always survey the land and try to find the perfect picture. Now, they were just passing by buildings and shops. Nothing was too different from home. She wanted only money shots and so far she hadn't seen one. She can understand why Ryan told her that this isn't truly the island because these are man-made buildings. Nothing speaks of the islands in none of the architecture or design of any of them. So she just sat there looking, enjoying being in the car with Ryan. She wouldn't have guessed in a million years that on her second day on the island, she would be on a date, so to say, but with Ryan. She was starting to get a funny feeling. A feeling, that at least for the moment, she was treasuring.

"Ok, well let's park here." Ryan said as he pulled his car into a dirt lot. There were a good number of cars already there so Majestic knew this wasn't some cozy little place. She couldn't hear much so she didn't know what to expect. She did know that a dirt lot wasn't going to win any challenge.

"Don't move." Ryan says as he jumps out of the car Dukes of Hazzard's style without opening the door. He walked around the back of the car and walks over to Majestic's side.

"Ok, your turn." Ryan says as he gestures for Majestic to do the same thing. Majestic just sat there because she would try it but she didn't want to in the sandals and the all white outfit she had on.

"I am just joking," Ryan said as he opened the door for her.

"Hey, I was going to show you what I was made of," Majestic said as she grabbed her camera bag from the back of the car.

"You are definitely going to need that. So let's go. We are going right through those bushes right there." Ryan says as he points to some wild looking weedy bushes. They were in front of what looked like a huge forest of some sort. She wasn't dressed to go in to a forest or on any kind of walk through bushes. The bushes made sort of an arch over a dirt path. Majestic thought maybe he was just teasing her but she was going to call his bluff if he was trying to make her chicken out.

"Ok. Let's do it," Majestic said as she followed Ryan across the street and to the bush overlapping path. She followed kind of close because the further they walked on the path the thicker the bushes got until it was kind of dark towards the end. It seemed like they met a dead end when he knocked on what seemed to be a wooden door.

All of a sudden the door swung open away from them and Majestic's mouth dropped. Before her was at least two football fields' length of beautiful flowers of all colors and types. The flowers were all in rows and there were at least fifty of them. Each row was a single color but it had different types of flowers on it. They were all neatly grown and they all seemed to be at the same stage of maturity. The size of the flowers and petals were bigger than anything she had seen before. The roses were huge as were the carnations and the rest of the flowers. They grew larger and fluffier than any flower she has received or seen before. With all the rows being different colors, as you stood at the entrance looking over the whole field, it looked like the largest flower rainbow in the world. Majestic just couldn't believe her eyes. She knew none of her flower exhibits stood a chance next to what she was looking at now. She didn't know what to do or say. She just started walking down one of the rows. She had left Ryan standing at the entrance. She felt like a child and she just wanted to run down the aisles and look at every row and every flower. The beauty of the place captivated her. She didn't pay any attention to any worker or any visitors there. She just grabbed the first camera in her bag and started to take pictures.

"I take it you like it?" Ryan says with an, 'I knew you would' tone.

"Ryan, you were so right. This place is off the charts. What is the name of this place?"

"Heaven of Flowers."

That name was exactly what it should be in her opinion. She had never witnessed anything like this. To see a field of this magnitude with all of these well-tended flowers was unbelievable.

"This place is incredible. Such beauty and the smell of fresh flowers are intoxicating. This place is like a dream. Look at all of these rows so uniform and spaced equally. Everything is perfect. How many people do they have working here? It must take a lot of people to keep this place so beautiful!" Majestic asked as she continued to take pictures.

"Just about five families, so I will say about fifty to sixty people."

"They take care of all of this. Which family owns it?"

"They all own it equally. That is one thing that I love about this place. To have such a wonderful concept and this has been with their families for decades and not once have there been any fighting for power or anything. You see nature has a way of balancing good and evil. Let's take these flowers for instance. They were made for good. Nothing about this rose here is bad. It sole purpose is for good. Now a weed on the other hand is made to do harm to anything good. Nature defines roles and I think in a way these families have learned from these flowers how to handle this place. No weed or greedy person has come between the families. That is God ordained. Try to grow something like this back in the States and watch what happens. Money and power might consume them but here, God runs the show."

"These families are all Christians?"

"Oh yeah, they are some good people. I found out about this place about ten years ago. I was looking for some flowers for my mom for Mother's Day. I asked some of the islanders if they knew of a place that I could get some flowers and they told me of this place. As I was here looking I met one of the families. They explained to me the concept behind the place. I was so impressed with their reasons behind this establishment. They are truly after God's heart. Just like you I was in awe of this place."

"What was the reason?" Majestic asks as she continues to take pictures.

"They wanted to have a place to grow flowers but also a place to grow love. They feel that flowers express more than beauty. They express love in so many ways. They said that a seed is so small and that represents the first time you meet someone. The relationship is very small and needs so much more to be able to grow. The soil you put the seed in is very important for the growth of that seed. Bad soil will not let a seed grow so it is important to have good soil so the seed can grow and be nurtured. Just like in a relationship if your foundation is good, the relationship will have a chance to grow. That foundation being God, then you will give the relationship a chance to grow and be nurtured. You must water and look after the seed through all stages of its life and that is no different in a relationship. You must water the relationship with Christian principles, trust and love through all the stages of the relationship. Once the seed becomes a flower, you can tell immediately the type of care that was given to the seed. In a relationship, the same can be said when it becomes a union in marriage. You can tell the type of relationship that was had by the end result of it. They believe that with their whole hearts. Plant seeds and beautiful flowers will come. Give love and a beautiful relationship will come. That is their reason behind this place."

"How awesome is this place? God is definitely at work here."

"You cannot look over this place and not understand that God put this place here as reminder that we should appreciate God's gifts to us. These flowers are so beautiful and even though they are a lot of work, they are worth every minute of the sacrifice," Ryan said, as he looked proudly over the place. Majestic knew that Ryan felt like he had done something special by bringing her here. She felt that he was correct on thinking that way.

Majestic just kept on walking through the rows. She was snapping picture after picture. She was making sure that she got close ups and far away shots. She was mixing up the type of pictures she took. At this moment she was in a photographer's dream. To have access to such an extraordinary place was such a blessing. Many people have come to this island and they have no clue about this place. They might have gone back home and talked about how beautiful the island was and they never even left the resort. Majestic is glad that Ryan understood what she wanted.

"Take your time and take as many shots as you need to. We are not in any rush," Ryan said, as he followed Majestic up and down the rows. He waited patiently as she stopped to take pictures. He watched her read up on the type of flower that was in a section on the information cards. Majestic was now in work mode and that was the only thing that kept her mind off of Ryan. She had her mind racing as she was trying to process the pictures she was taking and trying to figure out what the best exhibit would be for them. She knew she had four weeks to decide but she also knew that these pictures would be on her mind for the rest of the vacation.

"Oh what kind of flowers are those that are behind you?" Majestic asks as she noticed some dark blue flowers. She had not seen flowers that dark of a blue before.

"I am not sure," Ryan said, as he turned around to try and find the information card.

"Well, let me get a picture of you in front of them." Majestic says as she motioned for Ryan to turn around and face her. She wanted to focus only on Ryan and zoom in to his face but she wanted to get the flowers also so she took a full picture. So she had him stand in front of many sections taking pictures. She loved the way he didn't care about taking pictures. Most guys would act too cool to take pictures but Ryan just went with the flow and Majestic liked that.

"Let me get a few shots of you. The flowers will only enhance your beauty," Ryan said as he extended his hand out for the camera. Majestic loved taking pictures so this was right up her alley. She finds time to take pictures of herself, and her house is decorated with them. She ended up taking a lot of pictures because she would take a silly pose then a serious one. She would take a picture then think that was the last one but then she would notice some different flowers that she wanted to take a picture in front of.

"Hey, would you like to go up to that stand right there? That way you could get a large view of the field," Ryan asked as he pointed to a stand that was about 25 feet high. It was steel and it looked like it was made as a lookout point.

"That is a great idea; do you think they will let us go up there?" Majestic asked.

"It is no problem. Many people that come here don't know that it is here for them to get a large view of the field. In the event that they were looking for a certain type of flower and couldn't find it, they could go on the stand use the binoculars they have up there that you could use to view the entire garden."

"Let's do it then," Majestic said, as she showed her excitement by walking quickly to the stand. Ryan let her go up first because he could tell she was excited. Once they got to the top of the stand and stood up to look around they were blown away by the view. Majestic could see the sun shining over the field and the view was heavenly. To get a bird's eye view of the place was something she was going to cherish for a lifetime. To see the rows extending out so far and to see the colors ranging from whites on the far side to darks all the way on the other side was a pure thing of beauty. It was a living rainbow and it was worth waiting thirty-four years to finally see it. Majestic had traveled the world looking for pictures that needed no explanation and she knew that this was definitely one of them. To see colors as bright and uniform as she was seeing it now gave her a new appreciation for beauty and the hard work it took to perfect it.

"Even if I would have told you the name of this place, it still wouldn't have given justice to what you are seeing now. There is no way to describe this place. What words would you use? Is there a word great enough to describe beauty of this magnitude?"

"You are so right. I am shocked at what I see here. This is extraordinary and I am so thankful that you brought me here. This has made my day, my life!" Majestic said, as she began to take pictures. She wanted to capture as many pictures of this view as possible. She basically went through all her cameras and she used all her lenses as she was trying to get the perfect picture. She knew film was expensive but she had her own lab where she processed her own film so she could be generous with the picture taking. As she was taking the pictures she could just see the type of exhibit she was going to have for them. She wanted to make sure that everyone would feel the same way she felt when she first saw it.

"Ok, I think I have enough," Majestic said, as she turned around to Ryan.

"Are you sure?"

"Yes I am."

"Ok, let's go to another section of this place and let's get you some flowers that you can take with you."

"Are you serious? I can pick any flowers I want?" Majestic asked, as she climbed down the ladder to get off the stand.

"Oh yeah, any kind you see in here."

"You don't mind if we walk up and down the aisles again, do you?" Majestic asked like a kid asking their mom to buy them some candy.

"Of course not; to see you happy is my goal. Just lead the way."

"Come on then," Majestic said as she motioned for him to follow her. "I am going to tell you now; I am one of those shoppers that take forever."

"Bring it, because I can handle it. Besides, that was why we came early."

"You think you have me figured out?"

"Oh by no means do I think that. I just figured that you would want to bask in such a beautiful scene, that's all."

"Ryan, you are correct on that," Majestic said, as she turned from him as she smiled. She was so happy that they were connecting again as if they were never apart. This trip's beginning stages were like a dream and everything seemed so perfect.

"My mom would love this place. She is the one with the green thumb. She has a beautiful garden back in Las Vegas. She is already the envy of the neighborhood with her garden and if she was to add these flowers to it, there would be no competition."

"Cool, let's bring her here one day. I can even set up a meeting with some of the families so they can share flower growing secrets with each other."

"She would be on board for that. She would so love that," Majestic said as she picked up the pace because Ryan was walking up and down the rows with her as she made selections from the wide array of flowers. So she thought she would compromise.

"Ok, let me buy some flowers from what I have seen so far, and when we bring my family I will look over the other sections."

"Ok, that is fine with me. Get the flowers you want. Let's get one of these baskets down here," Ryan said, as he grabbed one of the hundreds of baskets that lined the bottom of each row.

"Just load it up with whatever you want."

"Ok, I just want these green tulips here and those yellow hibiscuses at the front over there; that should do it," Majestic said as she grabbed a handful of green tulips and a handful of yellow hibiscuses from the adjacent row.

"Ok, do you have everything you want?"

"I think I do," Majestic said, as she looked over her basket.

"Right this way then," Ryan led the way.

Majestic was already trying to visualize how she was going to arrange the flowers in her hotel room. She knew the flowers would be a nice touch.

Once they got to the register Majestic noticed a burnt orange colored flower, a shade or two lighter than a rust color, which looked similar to a rose. The same flower pattern and everything as the rose but that burnt orange color was very unique.

"What kind of flower is that?" Majestic asked as she points at the basket full of burnt orange colored flowers. The girl at the cashier looked around to see which ones Majestic was pointing at. She saw which ones it was and then she looked at Ryan and smiled. Majestic didn't know what to think now.

"What?" Majestic asked, as she felt like she was left out of an inside joke.

"Well, those flowers there are special. They are only grown on this island. There are special minerals in the soil that is compatible to the needs of the seed. That's why some people that buy those flowers make sure they buy some soil too. Some have tried to grow them in different types of soil but it won't grow. Something about this island that truly makes it possible."

"That is neat. So what are they called?" Majestic asked again.

"No one really knows the technical name for those flowers. The story is someone found them growing one day and thought so highly of them that they took the flower seeds and started to plant them everywhere. No one took the time to name them or even cared. Here on the island they are known as, 'The Engagement Flower.' The story is those flowers are purchased for an impending engagement just as a way to symbolize a newness of life. So they won't even sell those flowers unless the purchaser has proof that he or she is going to be engaged. It is impossible to know for sure but they try to hold the people to be honest so as not to decrease the value of the flower."

"So I guess I cannot have even one?" Majestic asked even though she knew the answer. Ryan and the girl behind the cash register both shook their heads no. "Can I at least take a picture of one?"

"By all means." The girl at the register said as she grabbed the basket and handed it to Ryan.

"Where do you want me to sit this?" Ryan asked as he grabbed the basket.

"Just sit it right there," Majestic said as she pointed to a spot about ten feet in front of him. She then took a few pictures of the arrangement.

"Ok, I think that is enough," Majestic said, as she let Ryan know that she was done taking pictures.

"Wait," Ryan said as he picked the basket up and handed it to the girl at the register. She puts the basket back where she got it from but she took one flower out, cut off the whole stem, leaving about three inches. She then handed the flower to Ryan.

"Do you mind taking the picture for us?" Ryan asked the girl behind the register.

"I don't mind at all."

"What picture?" Majestic said, as she was clueless to what is about to take place. She felt that obviously they had a conversation going on while Majestic was taking pictures of the flowers.

"I want us to take a picture together." Ryan said as he motioned for Majestic to come to him. Little did he know that at that moment she wanted to run into his arms and give him a big hug.

"Ok," Majestic said as she walked towards Ryan and hands the girl one of her cameras. She definitely wanted to take a picture with him. So as she got closer to him, she knew she was going to cherish this moment.

"Ok, stand here. I want us to take two pictures. Let's take one picture of me putting the flower in your hair and the second picture of us just posing together."

"Sure," Majestic said, as she was just happy that they were taking a picture together. As he leaned close to begin to put the flower over her right ear, Majestic closed her eyes and pretended that he would lean down and kiss her. No kiss happened, but she knew that was a cute picture none-the-less.

"Man, you are so beautiful." Ryan says as he just looks and admires her. "You are definitely a beautiful blessing from God."

"Thank you," Majestic said as she smiled. It has been a long time since she heard a compliment from someone she wanted it to come from. It was refreshing to hear it. Ryan then stood on her left side and looked at her.

"Is it ok if I put my arm around you?"

"Oh yeah," Majestic said, as she welcomed the touch of his arm at her side and his hand on her upper back.

"On the count of three I am going to take the picture. One, two, three." The girl said as she took the picture.

Majestic knew immediately that picture was going to be her background on her computer. Without a doubt she was putting that one on there tonight.

"Thank you so much," Majestic said as she grabbed her camera with her right hand and hands the flower back with her left.

"No problem. I hope you enjoy your flowers. Have a good day." The girl said as she motioned for them to leave.

"Wait, we haven't paid for them," Majestic said as she realized that they we leaving without paying for the flowers.

"Don't worry. I put them on my credit. I furnish the restaurant with flowers from here."

"That was a very sweet gesture."

"Don't mention it. Are you ready?"

"Yes." Majestic said as she looked at her flowers. They were so large and fluffy. She couldn't help but to smell them. She knew she was leaving a place that has touched her heart and there was no way she was ever going to forget this place. As she is following Ryan to his car, she got out her camera that has the pictures that they just took. Majestic found them and the picture with him leaning forward and putting the flower in her hair and Majestic with her eyes closed, inviting him to do it conveyed a vision of love. It looked like a cover to one of those romance novels. Majestic loved that one just as much as the other photo with them standing side by side. As she flipped back and forth between the two pictures, she sees the difference in the perception of the pictures. One picture conveyed a vision of love and the other one showed two friends taking a picture together. That was how drastic the contrast was of the pictures.

"Well now we are off to our second stop on the tour. I hope you realize that this tour is really going to take more than one day. Is that ok with you?"

"I am fine with that Ryan."

"Good because I envisioned going to a couple places on every trip. So it is according to you how many days

I get to show you around. I know your family wants to spend time with you as well."

"Oh don't worry about my family. They are all paired up somewhere. I was the one that they were worried about not having someone to hang around. So with saying that I am free any day you want to finish the rest of the tour," Majestic said without hesitation. She did not want to miss out on spending time with Ryan.

"Great, then we can plan something later. Let's hit the road to our next destination. Let me get that door for you," Ryan said as he walked in front of Majestic so he could open the door for her.

"Thank you sir."

"Don't mention it. If you want me to, I can raise the top on the convertible so the flowers won't blow away."

"You don't mind? I would appreciate that. I didn't think about that before we bought the flowers." Majestic was impressed with how Ryan was always thinking about her needs.

"I don't mind at all. I wouldn't treat my flowers like that and I sure wouldn't treat yours like that. Just watch your head as the top comes down. The last thing you want to have as a reminder of your vacation is a knot on your head. I hoped you enjoyed that place? That was the first place that came to mind when you reminded me you had a photography gallery. I knew I had to take you there."

"Well, I definitely appreciate that. I like the fact that you understand what a photographer likes." Majestic loved the fact that he was considerate.

"Hey I always try to do what I can to help others. Besides, I know where the tour buses take people. They take them to a museum, gift shops, a mall and more places where folks can spend all of their money. I am not big on the tourism scene on the island. I don't think you have noticed but I don't have any advertisement signs anywhere on the beach or near any hotels."

"No I haven't noticed. Why is that?"

"I don't fall into the in-crowd when it comes to businesses around here. I pay above average wages and I offer great benefits. Many businesses try to pay bottom dollar and they offer the very basic benefits, which ends up costing the employee an arm and a leg to pay. When I have a job opening, I am not going to lie; I have at least a hundred people applying for the job. It could be the dishwasher position and I have managers from other establishments applying. Everyone knows that I am fair and I take care of my employees. That rubs the other owners the wrong way I guess."

"I admire that Ryan. You are willing to go against the grain to stick to what you feel is right. That shows a lot about your character."

"Like I told you, my parents instilled that in me. Besides, I know that God would want me to treat his people with the utmost dignity and respect."

"That is true. I just can't believe you guys own a restaurant, but not just any restaurant. You own the best one I have ever seen. That place is so far ahead of the competition. I bet you guys are doing pretty well. You have a prime location and everything. You are right on the beach next to a large ten story hotel."

"We definitely were blessed with that spot. What is funny was that was going to be the same spot that we were going to build our shelter. We wanted them to be on the best spot on the beach. We were going to use the beach as part of our therapy for them, basically letting them see how God has blessed us daily. So they were supposed to wake up on the beach and spend time with God, doing their daily devotions to him."

"Speaking of devotion, I haven't noticed any churches or anything around here. I asked the hotel and they said they have a few shuttles that come and take tourists to a few churches in the area. What church do you go to?" Majestic asked, as she felt this was an important question to test where his walk truly is. She knows that it wouldn't make him less of a Christian but she wants a man that is definitely focused on learning about God and how to apply God's principles to his life.

"We hold church at my restaurant. There is a Pastor that holds one service on Sunday mornings for us on the beach and it is awesome. For the guy to be a Pastor he isn't a bad cook at all."

"The Pastor is the cook at your restaurant?"

"Yes, he is one of four cooks. I told you I pay well and folks will leave their profession to work there. He does it part time because he loves to cook. For this island to be so beautiful and full of life, living here will change your mind about that. For the islanders this is all they know so suffering has been passed down for generations. Getting a job is a great benefit but working for me is probably like winning the lottery in Las Vegas."

"I must say I am impressed. You have taken on such a huge task," Majestic said as she realized that it must be hard to do what is best for yourself and others in a situation where it is better suited to be selfish. Not too many business owners try to be unselfish.

"Ryan, I must admit that you are still an impressive person. Just the fact that you consider your workers to be just as important as you is an absolute proof of your caring heart. That is such a great thing and really not done by most owners."

"I know, but I just don't understand why owners are so quick to treat their employees so badly. Many don't care about their employees' well-being because they know they could replace them at moment's notice. I don't look at it that way. I look at the fact that without my employees I would still have a restaurant but no life in it. The employees are the blood that makes the restaurant move and have life. Without employees the restaurant would die. I understand that, and I believe that it is my duty to treat them as an important part of the restaurant."

"I bet they appreciate you for that. Who wouldn't want to work for you?" Majestic asked, as her respect level for Ryan began to grow.

"All I know is that the restaurant is a blessing from God to me and all the workers that has ever worked there.

"I bet. I can tell you get a lot of satisfaction from it."

"I do. I feel like when people come to my restaurant that they made a conscious choice to eat there and it is my duty to make sure that eating at my restaurant doesn't go down in their memory as a bad mistake. I take pride in people gushing over every aspect of the restaurant."

"I can imagine, because my family and I were in awe of the place. I was blown away by how visual the place was. Being a photographer I am very visual and sometimes I notice small details that some people miss. I could look around the restaurant and I could almost tell exactly what your parents had in mind when they began to decorate the place."

"They had the talent for that. I wasn't born with it but I learned from watching them. I use to sit in the restaurant and wonder why they did this or why they did that. Once I started reading the comment cards and watched how people reacted when they noticed something, it hit me right then. When my parents had their vision of the restaurant, it was so detailed that they knew that people would notice even the smallest details and would know why they did what they did. Can you imagine that?" Ryan said as he shook his head.

"I can. I pretty much know the reaction I am going to get when I put up an exhibit. I can almost guess, word for word, what the comments and reaction is going to be."

"Wow that is cool."

"It is cool." Majestic agreed; she was enjoying their conversation. It has been a minute since she hung out with a guy who she was totally interested in what he had to say. Not once has Ryan dropped a corny pick-up line, licked his lips excessively, or tried to sneak a peak at the features of her body. He has made eye contact, and she could tell by his body language and through his eyes that he had been answering her questions truthfully. He was actually more interesting than she remembered from their past interactions. He still has a servant's heart, and that is so attractive. Not only does he have the physical attributes but on the inside he was just as beautiful as on the outside.

"Ok, don't get alarmed, but we are getting close to the area I warned you about. Once we get around the bend, the island as you know it will change. Forget what you have seen so far because you are about to see the true island in its purest form."

"Ok."

Majestic didn't really know what to expect, but she was ready for anything. As they rounded a long curve the first thing she noticed were the power line poles lying on the side of the road. They were lying down for as far as she could see. She could faintly see apartments in the distance. The road they were driving on became a little bit bumpier before it eventually turned into a dirt road. A little ways up the road was some sort of police checkpoint. There were about ten police officers either standing guard with a rifle leaning on their chest pointing straight up in the air or they had their guns leaning against a wire gate that separated them from whatever was on the other side. Once the car came within twenty feet of the checkpoint, a couple of the police officers began to walk towards them. Majestic's heart was beating fast because she wasn't used to violence at all and this would have been an area that she would have avoided. One police officer motioned for them to keep on coming forward until he motioned for them to pull over to the side of the road in a space big enough for a car between two downed power line poles. All of a sudden the other police officers started to come towards them. The first thing that came to Majestic's mind was a pack of hyenas. It looked like they were coming towards their next meal. One police officer stayed and he was looking very intently at them. Majestic was scared and she looked at Ryan to see if he was as scared as she was. He put the car into park.

"Ok, let's get out." Ryan says as he is staring at the convoy of police officers coming their way.

"Ok." Majestic said as she slowly opened the car door. She was extremely scared. This had the look of a shakedown and she didn't know if they were going to ask for money or detain them for a while. She really had no idea what was going to happen. Now she was happy that Ryan had her call her family to let them know where they were going and what time they were supposed to come back. She didn't want to make any sudden moves, so she took her sweet time standing up. She grabbed her camera bag and kept it close to herself as she closed the door.

"What's the matter, Majestic? I was going to open the door for you." Ryan says as he walked over to her side of the car. She was glad that he was next to her because she was scared. The cops were approaching and they were smiling as if they were up to no good.

"Nothing, I just wanted to get out before they came." Majestic said as she kept an eye on the police officers that were now a few feet from her.

"You have nothing to be worried about, especially from them because they are just hungry." Ryan said as he walked up to the police officers and begins to give them all a handshake. The guys seemed real happy to see him and she could tell that they knew each other. That put Majestic at ease but it still didn't stop her heart from beating fast.

"They are just hungry? How do you know that?" Majestic asked.

"I know these guys. They always want something to eat," Ryan said, as he walked to the back of his car and opened the trunk. He pulled out the brown bag he had put in there earlier and handed it to the police officers. They gathered around the one that had the brown bag.

He put his hand in the bag and began to pull out food wrapped in aluminum foil. He handed a couple to each police officer. They all quickly tore off the foil and began to eat.

"Fish tacos are always a crowd favorite." Ryan said as he grabbed a box out of the car and closed the trunk. Majestic thought they must be the best fish tacos in the world because the guys began to eat them like no tomorrow.

"I wish I had one because they look like they are enjoying them. Besides I am getting hungry." Majestic said as her stomach began to growl quietly on cue.

"That is why we came here to eat," Ryan said as he followed the police officers. He motions with his head for Majestic to follow him. So she obliged him and began to follow. She didn't see anything that looked like a restaurant in the distance. All she could see was a run down apartment complex that had about eight buildings that were three levels high. They looked like that had about 30 apartments in each building. There were two white medium sized, one-story buildings and one had a medical symbol on it. If there was a restaurant hiding in this place then it must be good if he drove all the way just to eat here.

"Guys, this is my beautiful friend Majestic. Majestic these are the guys," Ryan said as they walked up to the gate that the police officers were guarding. It was the only way into where they were going. Majestic didn't know if it was to keep people in or keep them out. Whichever reason made her very nervous.

Some of the police officers waved, some smiled and a few begin to check her out.

"Hey, she is with me." Ryan said jokingly to the older police officer. All the police officers burst out laughing. Majestic knew that was a joke a few years in the making and she walked in on the end of it.

"How long are you going to be here?" One of the police officers asked Ryan when they finally made it to the guard shack located directly next to the gate.

"An hour or so," Ryan says as he placed the box on the ground and signed a clipboard that was handed to him by the police officer. "I expect a car wash with this visit. Don't forget the rims." Ryan jokes as he picks the box back up.

"Ok. Ramon, spit on the car and don't forget the rims." The police officer said as he begins to raise up the gate. Majestic just followed closely behind Ryan and she looked back to watch the police officer lower the gate. This was definitely unexpected.

"Ok, just to give you a heads up. This is what happens when the government forgets about you. This is an apartment complex that is not assisted in any way by the city or government. There are about fifteen of them and this is only the first one. The rest are behind here and they stretch for about a mile."

That was when Majestic noticed a broken sign leaning against a broken tree that displayed "Vera Courts."

"Where is everyone at now? It is so quiet." Majestic asked as she noticed how quiet it was. It looked almost desolate, like the place was abandoned.

"Most of the grown ups are at work at the resort area or sleep. The kids are probably at the next apartment complex because they have a nice size park there."

"Ok."

"Now these apartments are considered to be a refugee camp of sorts. There is a large group of volunteers, from the United States, that live here and they take care of the people here. They mainly take care of their medical needs and help with the upkeep of the facilities. Most of the people that live in these complexes are not really poor but just people that cannot afford land to build a house on. Most of my staff lives here."

"But you pay them well right? Why would they live here?" Majestic asked as she was watching her step while she was walking on the dirt road. She didn't want to step on any large rocks or anything like that. The place didn't look like any place someone would want to live if they made decent money.

"I do pay them well, but they would have to save up a lot of money to buy land. The housing situation here isn't like back in the United States. They don't have builders that buy land, build houses and then sell them. Yes they own the land but they will not touch it unless they are able to get rid of the property outright. They don't want to have anything to do with the house once it is up. They won't build a house unless you buy the land, and then you have to find a builder that isn't going to rob you blind. Then it takes months to basically bribe the officials for permits and licenses. So basically they are better off living here. Rent is cheap and they have a hospital on site, school and a cafeteria."

"That is terrible. How can they get away with that?"

"That is the government way."

"If that is so then why is there police officers guarding the gate?"

"Good question. That is the government's way of saying that they do care about the people here. Even though the residents here pay for the protection but the government gets all the credit."

Majestic just couldn't help but shake her head in disgust. How could the government treat its people like they don't care? Then she realized that this was how some areas of the United States are. There are areas where they have to live like third class citizens but this brings it home for her. This is supposed to be a vacation island and the area that means anything to the government is the part that makes them money.

"I hate to change your idea of this island but I was sure you could handle it. I see a lot of good in you, Majestic, and I know you have the understanding to see what really is going on," Ryan said as he walked up to the first white building.

"Can you open the door for me please?"

"I sure can," Majestic said, as she turned the knob and pushed the door open. Once the door was opened Majestic could smell food cooking. She then looked around and noticed that this was the cafeteria. It was totally empty now. There were about fifty tables in ten rows of five tables. On the far wall was the prep area for waiters and waitresses. There were hundreds of dishes stacked on top of one another and separated by plates, saucers, bowls, cup and glasses. On the wall on the right was a ton of Polaroid pictures hanging on the wall. Majestic was sure that was photos of people that lived here. On the left wall was the dishwashing area and it took up the whole wall. There was a railing you followed to get to the point to where you would drop the dishes off to be washed.

"Follow me to the kitchen." Ryan said as he made his way to the prep area. Once they got behind the counter he headed towards a door that was hidden from the front door. He used the box to push it open and it was there that the smell of food was coming from. Once she made it inside the kitchen, she immediately noticed that they had three large grills and one regular oven in there. There was two microwaves and five George Foreman grills. This was definitely the kitchen area. On one of the grills, Majestic noticed four chicken breasts being grilled but she didn't see anyone around. In the middle of the kitchen was a large island that looked like it held all the pots and pans and things of that nature in there because there were no overhead cabinets. She still didn't see a cook so as she followed Ryan into the room and around the other side of the kitchen island there was no one around. Once she got around the kitchen island she could see a panel of the wall was ajar. There was a doorknob on it and she figured that was where the cook was. All of a sudden a little boy came out of the panel and uses his leg to close the panel shut. He had a frustrated look on is face. His arms were full of spices. He had a dark tint with shiny smooth skin. He had a Mohawk on top of his head and the rest of his head was shaved clean. He was about four feet and five inches tall and very slender. He had on a red Houston Rocket's jersey and some black shorts with some black and red T-Mac basketball shoes on. He was real cute and he reminded Majestic of a young bear cub.

"I keep telling you that a frustrated cook is never a good cook." Ryan said as he put the box on the island as the boy looked up to see where the sound came from. His face lit up when he saw it was Ryan.

"Ryan!" The boy said as he quickly put the spices down on the island and gave Ryan a big hug. He looked over at Majestic and stretched his hand out to her.

"Hi, I am Sebastian and you must be Majestic."

"I am her and you are too cute!" Majestic said as she put down her camera bag and shook his hand.

"You were not lying at all Ryan. Not one bit, because she is fine."

"No she is beautiful. What did I tell you? Boys notice body parts and men notice the face," Ryan said as he shook his head.

"My bad," Sebastian said as he read the labels on the spices. "I cannot find the Italian seasoning anywhere. I asked them to put it back where it goes. I did not label the spice rack for nothing."

"It is right here. Remember I told you to label the top of the spice as well so you can always glance at the top and see the initials on it and know if it is the one you need," Ryan said as he pulled the Italian seasoning out of the middle of the spices. "Here are more hamburger patties in case you run out." Ryan said as he patted the box.

Majestic could tell that Ryan has spent time with Sebastian and he had probably been trying to teach him how to cook.

"So you are the one cooking. How old are you?" Majestic asked as she watched him season the chicken with the Italian seasoning.

"I am eleven."

"Ten. You won't be eleven for five months. Women love honesty," Ryan said as he nudged the back of Sebastian's head.

"And you can cook already. How long have you been cooking?"

"About two years." Sebastian said, as he flipped the meat over to add some seasoning on the other side.

"Did Ryan teach you?" Majestic asked, because she wasn't sure if Ryan could cook since owning a restaurant didn't necessarily mean he could cook.

"Yes, he and my aunt did," Sebastian responded as he opened up a cabinet in the island and pulls out a skillet. He then walked over to a bunch of assorted chopped vegetables and dropped them in. He poured some olive oil in the skillet and began to season the vegetables. He looked very confident in what he was doing.

"Your aunt? Who is your aunt?" Majestic had to say it before she realized that he might be talking about Ryan's deceased fiancée.

"That was my fiancée."

"They both showed me what to do and gave me a start. I help cook around here because there are so many people to feed and cooks are hard to find because everyone has to work. Some people work more than one job or shifts, like my mom does." Sebastian said as he checked the chicken on the grill before going back to check the vegetables.

"Your waitress from last night is his mom."

"Juanita? That is your mom? We were just talking about you this morning," Majestic said trying to hold in her shock. Now she can piece together that strange look that Juanita gave her when Ryan walked up to her this morning. She definitely didn't look happy because Ryan wanted to see Majestic, and it made sense now because his deceased fiancée is Juanita's sister. Majestic hoped that wouldn't complicate things.

"You met my mom?"

"Yes she was my waitress last night. She was awesome."

"Cool," Sebastian said as he turned his attention to cooking. He was doing a great job because the food smelt so good and Majestic was really hungry.

"That food wouldn't happen to be for us is it?" Majestic asked, as she seriously wanted to try his food.

"Yes it is," Sebastian says with confidence.

"He is cooking for us and a special someone," Ryan said as he walked out the room.

"Your sister?"

"No way, Majestic. She never gives me credit for my cooking. There is this girl in my class that I want to impress so I am cooking for her as well."

"Oh so this is like a double date."

"Yes."

Majestic was so impressed with the way he moved about the kitchen. He had a handle on how to cook the chicken breast and the vegetables. Everything was just about done and the smell was enticing.

"Ok here are the plates and I wrapped up our silver-ware in these napkins." Ryan said, as he returned from the prep area with four plates and four sets of silverware.

"Good let's put the food on there, then," Sebastian said as he placed a piece of chicken breast and a portion of vegetables on every plate. He took extra care in the presentation of the food.

"Can I help?" Majestic asked as she felt like she should help out in some way.

"No you can just stand there and be beautiful. This is your day so don't worry. Sebastian and I have everything covered. Well, you know what? You can open the door for us." Ryan said as he nodded towards the door they came in. Majestic opened the door and she listened for Ryan to tell her which way to go. She noticed that Ryan grabbed two plates of food and Sebastian grabbed the other two. In a way that touched her heart because Ryan was trying to teach Sebastian on how a man should behave and Sebastian seemed to be very eager to learn.

"Let's go out the door we came in and follow the side walk on your left to the beach." Ryan said as he followed closely behind Sebastian. Majestic followed his instructions and there at the end of the sidewalk was the beach. The first thing she noticed was that the sand wasn't as white as the beach's sand at the resort. Nor was the water as clear as the resort's. It was kind of depressing to see how the islanders were treated. They had about twenty-five wooden 5 X 5 tables on the beach with four folding chairs on each side. One table had a little girl sitting there by herself and once she noticed Sebastian she stood up and began to wave. She was extremely cute and had a large smile on her face. She reminded Majestic of a little cheetah. The closer they got to her, Majestic could see her freckles and cute little button nose. She was about Majestic's skin color and about the same height as Sebastian. The sight of that touched Majestic's heart. To see this little girl probably having her first crush on Sebastian is so sweet. Majestic noticed how cute she was with her braided hair. Majestic knew if Tracee was here she would have liked her because they slightly favored each other. She looked so excited to see Sebastian and Majestic knew exactly how she felt because she felt the same way for Ryan.

"Hi Erin," Sebastian said as he put the plates of food down quickly so he could give her a hug. It was one of those sweet innocent hugs, real soft as if they didn't really want to touch each other. Ryan puts his plates down and he gave her a hug also.

"Erin, this is my friend Majestic." Ryan said, as he moved out the way to let Majestic walk up.

"I want a hug like everyone else," Majestic said as Erin extended her hand out to her.

"Ok," Erin gave Majestic a nice big hug.

"Did you bring some change Ryan?" Sebastian asked as he held his hand out.

"I sure did. I would ask you what kind of drink you want, but all they have is Big Red," Ryan said with a, "What can I say" look on his face.

"Big Red is fine with me."

Ryan hands over a handful of quarters to Sebastian and he ran over to the soda machine and got four bottles of Big Red. He returned to the table quickly and tried to give the extra change back to Ryan.

"That is for you and Erin," Ryan said as he waved his hand at him.

"I can never get enough of Big Red soda. No matter how much I drink, I just want more," Erin says with a big smile on her face.

Majestic just thought she was the cutest little girl she has ever seen.

"Let's pray for our food so we can eat," Sebastian said as he blessed the food. Majestic was so impressed with his mannerisms. A ten year old praying is an awesome sight. Majestic remembered growing up in church and many ten-year old boys wouldn't pray out loud or anything.

"I love grilled chicken. I was so hungry waiting around for the food." Erin said with her cute little raspy voice.

"Me too Erin" Majestic says as she begins to enjoy her food.

"She is pretty just like you said Ryan," Erin said as her and Sebastian began to giggle.

"I see now that you guys cannot keep a secret. I thought you were better than this? After all the secrets I have kept for you guys over the years and now you turn on me. I won't forget this one," Ryan said as he took a sip of his Big Red.

"Hey, this the first person you have talked about since my aunt died. What do you expect us to do? This was so unexpected," Sebastian says as he shrugged his shoulders.

"Very unexpected," Erin agreed.

Majestic was just soaking it all in. She realized that Ryan was feeling the same way she was, but of course she had no way of knowing. At least she knew that there were still mutual feelings between them.

"How did you find out about me so fast? I just saw him last night," Majestic asked, because she knew that Ryan didn't just drive over here to tell them about her.

"When Ryan dropped my mom off from work last night, he stayed and ate dinner with us and told me how you guys met and how he knew you from a long time ago. I told Erin this morning when I saw her at breakfast."

"Do you always bring Juanita home?" Majestic asked, as she felt a hint of jealousy coming on. She has never been the jealous type but now it was trying to creep its way into her life and she didn't like it.

"No, just on certain occasions do I actually take her home. Normally, she would catch a ride on the shuttle that drops off and picks up all the workers that work at the resort area but she was late closing out her accounts, so I just gave her a ride home." Ryan explained as he ate.

Majestic didn't want to make too big of a deal out of it. She just hoped that it was nothing.

"How is the food everybody?" Sebastian asked as he looked at everyone's plate to see how much was eaten.

"Little buddy, this is very good." Ryan says as he gives Sebastian a high five.

"Little buddy, this is very good." Erin giggled. Majestic could see why Sebastian liked her because she was so cute.

"I am impressed. You did an excellent job." Majestic says as she finished off the vegetables that were seasoned and cooked perfectly.

"I have been cooking for awhile but grilled chicken is my favorite."

"I must say that this is very delicious. You are going to be an excellent chef one day." Majestic said as she continued eating.

"He is better than some of the other cooks here," Erin said as she sipped her Big Red.

"Why is there a cafeteria here? Don't the apartments have kitchens in them?"

"Some units don't have kitchens. Only the higher priced apartments have kitchens. Everyone cannot afford kitchens so they don't put in any appliances in that area. They put carpet down so it is made into a small room. So instead of having a kitchen it is considered another bedroom. Besides that cuts down on the electricity because I think everyone that doesn't have a kitchen pay around two hundred dollars a month. The residents do have to eat so that is where the cafeteria comes into play. The volunteers cook the food, as do some of the residents. They serve four meals a day," Ryan said.

"We have breakfast, lunch, dinner, and late dinner." Sebastian adds. "I like late dinner the best."

"Me too Sebastian, because it is like a big buffet." Erin said, showing her cute smile.

"Late dinner is where they take all the leftover food for the day and they serve it buffet style. That also helps the people that get off of work late because they can still have a meal. It is a good thing because everyone gets to eat their fair share."

"That sounds cool, but where does the food come from?" Majestic asked. She was intrigued by how things were done on the island. They definitely don't do this back at home.

"They get the bulk of it from the volunteer's budget and I supply the rest."

"Ryan that is so nice of you."

Majestic was definitely impressed with hearing that. She knew Ryan was great guy but the more she is reminded of it the more she hated that she let him get away.

"Yeah Ryan, that is so nice of you," Erin said as she mocked Majestic. Erin had a cute way of doing it and she had great timing.

"Erin if you weren't so cute, I don't know what I would do with you," Ryan said as he smiled at Erin. Majestic could see the bond that Ryan had with Erin and

Sebastian as well. He was such a great role model and probably to them, a father-figure.

"We look like a family. Ryan is the daddy. Majestic is the mommy. Sebastian is the son and I am the daughter," Erin said as she looked at everyone.

"We would make a pretty family," Majestic added. She never thought about having children because she knows how much attention they need, and she didn't know if she would ever have time to do that because of all the time she puts in at the gallery.

"I think so too," Ryan said, as he looked at Majestic with a smile on his face.

"I don't. I don't want Erin to be my sister," Sebastian said as he shook his head in disagreement.

"My bad, I forgot that someone liked someone else," Ryan says as he pointed at Sebastian with one hand and pointed at Erin with the other. Sebastian began to blush.

"He does like me and I like him too," Erin said, as she watched Sebastian blush.

"He is blushing. How cute is that?" Majestic said as she smiled at the thought of Sebastian and Erin liking each other. At their young age, it was so cute.

"She loves making him blush. I know that he likes Erin because he is always cooking special dishes for her," Ryan said as he drank his Big Red.

"He does make all my favorite foods. I like when he does that," Erin responded.

"I must say that you are turning into a great cook. In a few years I am going to put you in my restaurant." Ryan said as he looked at Sebastian the way a father proudly looks at his son.

"For real? I can't wait. I want to be the head chef and make a lot of money," Sebastian was getting excited.

"What about me? What can I do there?" Erin asked, as she felt left out.

"We can make you the hostess. That way you can greet everyone with your pretty smile and just be the lady that you are."

"I like that idea, Ryan. I think I can do that," Erin said as she looked at Majestic with her pretty smile.

Majestic looked at them, and she was in love with them already. They were just so cute and respectful. They hung on every word that Ryan said and that meant that they cherished him. Little did they know that they weren't the only one, because Majestic definitely felt the same way.

"I think you guys would be a perfect addition to the restaurant."

"You think so, Majestic?"

"I know so, Erin. With you at the front and Sebastian in the kitchen cooking, I think that you guys will make Ryan lots of money."

"Speaking of money, it is time to pay up. That will be ten dollars for your plate and ten dollars for Majestic's plate." Sebastian said as he held out his hand towards Ryan.

"Pay up. You know the routine," Erin said as she finished her food.

Ryan pulled out a white envelope from his back pocket. He opened it up and pulled out a twenty-dollar bill and handed it to Sebastian. "Thank you for such a wonderful lunch, and here is ten dollars for you, Erin. That is because you are so cute." Ryan pulled a ten-dollar bill out of the envelope and handed it to Erin. Her eyes lit up with joy at the sight of the money.

"Thank you Ryan!" Erin stared at the money in her hand.

"The food really was good. Keep it up." Majestic added as she finished off her Big Red.

"Thank you so much Ryan," Sebastian said. "You are the best."

Majestic was almost moved to tears when Sebastian stood up and walked over to Ryan and gave him a hug. Just to know that Ryan was mentoring him and watching over him was touching to see.

"Well, we must go. I have to get the place ready for ballroom dancing," Ryan said as he stood up.

"I hate that we can't go," Erin said as she pretended to be sad.

"Next time, I will make sure you come, but just do what you have to do. Everyone here pulls there own weight so do what you are suppose to do and everything will be fine."

"We will. It was nice meeting you Majestic." Sebastian says as he walks over to her and waited until Majestic stood up and gave her a hug. Erin got up and did the same thing.

"What can I say, they really like you," Ryan said as he noticed the show of affection.

"I like them too," Majestic said as she just wanted to squeeze them some more.

"Ok, I will see you in a few days. Don't forget about the box of hamburger patties I left in the kitchen. Later." Ryan said as he grabbed Majestic by her elbow and gently pulled her, just like he did earlier in the day. Majestic thought it was a sweet, subtle way to tell her to move.

"Bye." Erin gave them a big smile, just like before.

"They are so cute. Sebastian is the perfect little boy and Erin is just so precious."

"They are and they are really good children," Ryan said as he waved at them.

"I don't care for this situation they are in but I see that they are making the most of it."

"They do. It can get tough here but everyone around here takes care of each other."

"From the looks of it around here, you really have to. It isn't the most beautiful of places but at least they have close access to a beach," Majestic said as she took one more look at the beach.

"They do have access to the beach but so do the hurricanes every hurricane season. This part of the island is called, "Hurricane Alley". If a hurricane hits the island this is usually where it hits. I can't tell you how many times they have rebuilt these apartments. That is why the power lines are down. The government doesn't want to have to continue to pay to have them put back up because hurricanes come and they just knock them back down. All the power they have for these apartments are from a huge generator. They haven't had a hurricane come in here in a few years, but they are always on guard. As a matter of fact, I am one of the coordinators of the response team that comes here and tries to put up sandbags and things of that nature to help lighten the blow of a hurricane. I am CPR certified and I am working on my paramedic's course so I could help out in all capacities in case of an emergency."

"Wow. I am impressed. That is so cool that you do things like that. You really care about the islanders."

"I do. Take Sebastian for instance. I have known him since he was first born. I have watched him grow up and I have been the only constant male role-model in his life."

"What about his dad?" Majestic asked, because she could not see how any man would not want to be in Sebastian's life.

"He has never met him."

"Is he here on the island?"

"No. He was a tourist that was on vacation. He hooked up with Juanita when she was working for another restaurant in the resort area. She was only sixteen at the time. Well they got intimate and because of the experience she got pregnant and the man didn't know at the time when he left the island. She tried to contact him but all the contact information he left Juanita was bogus. Even the name he gave her was bogus so she was stuck with the child. I knew her because of her sister; and believe me; she was devastated. I thought had she learned her lesson, but a few years later she got pregnant by one of the islanders. This guy was a total knucklehead. He is locked up now for armed robbery. Needless to say both of her children don't know their fathers at all," Ryan said as he shook his head.

"Where is her daughter at now?" Majestic asks as she is wondering why the little girl isn't around.

"She is in foster care. They took her from Juanita because Juanita fell into drugs real hard after all of this drama. One day Juanita left her baby at a drug dealer's house and the baby was turned in. Juanita was arrested and at the time she was so depressed that she allowed her daughter to be put in foster care. The only reason why Sebastian isn't in foster care is because his aunt, my fiancée, adopted him. So when she died, I wanted to adopt him but he wanted to help his mother get on her feet. I promised him I would do all I could to make sure his mom was able to get back on her feet. So when the restaurant was finally built, I asked my parents to hire her and the rest is history. She hasn't had any setbacks with drugs but depression keeps getting to her. She hates the fact she gave her daughter up so she is trying to get her back."

Majestic didn't know what to say. She felt sorry for Sebastian and Juanita. Majestic couldn't fathom having the strength to make it through such a situation as this. Majestic has lived a drama-free life and she knows she would have folded up a long time ago if she had to face the trials that Juanita had gone through. Her respect level for Ryan had grown leaps and bounds in just a day. To see him go out of his way to help others was very admirable.

"Does she get to see her daughter at all?"

"Yes she gets one visit a month. I let her off, with pay, to go and spend time with her. That is the least I can do," Ryan said as they finally make it to the guard shack. As Ryan is saying his goodbyes to the police officer, Majestic is just soaking in what she has seen and learned. Living her sheltered life she has never done any kind of social work or any volunteer work. She never really had time to do anything because of her gallery, but she never even thought about doing anything. This trip here had planted a seed in her that she wants to see grow when she returned to Las Vegas. Just looking at Ryan engage and socialize with everyone has shown her that she has so much she can learn from Ryan. He was so outgoing and had a free spirit to talk to anyone. She doesn't view everyone in the same way. She was always in business mode and she had this wall built up that she must portray strength and independence. Majestic cannot remember the last time she let her hair down and just had a good time without worrying what anyone thought. She hoped that this experience would change her for the good.

"Bye guys," Majestic waved at the police officers that were waving at her.

She walked towards the car and waited for Ryan to catch up. She just loved the way he moved and that special strut he had when he walked. It wasn't over the top it was very subtle but it gave him that little extra something that was appealing to Majestic.

"You have a fan club," Ryan said, as he walked up to the car and opened the door for Majestic.

"A fan club?" Majestic asked, blushing.

"Hey Ryan and Majestic, wait up!" Sebastian yelled as he and Erin ran up to the car. "You left your camera bag in the kitchen."

"Thank you Sebastian." Majestic says as she grabs the bag from him. She wanted to kick herself because this is the first time, in a long time that she had left her camera bag somewhere.

"That was cool of you to bring that to us," Ryan said as he gave Sebastian and Erin a high five.

"No problem," Sebastian said as he smiled. Majestic could see the look he had in his eyes when he looked at Ryan. He looked to Ryan for approval and it was so heartwarming to see.

"Would you two like for me to take a picture of you?" Majestic asked as she took one of her cameras out of her camera bag.

"Please do," Erin said as she fixed her yellow dress. It went down to her knees and it made Erin look so sweet and innocent.

"Wait, do you have a towel or napkin? I want to wipe the sweat off of me," Sebastian asked Ryan as he began to wipe some sweat off with his hands.

"I think I do," Ryan replied as he opened the door and looked in his glove compartment. "Here you go."

Majestic watched Sebastian wipe the sweat off of Erin first then he began to wipe the sweat off of himself. Majestic knew he was a child version of a grown up Ryan.

Ok we are ready." Erin says as she grabbed Sebastian's hand. A large grin stretched across his face.

"Ok. That is going to be a cute picture," Majestic said as she took the picture of Sebastian and Erin.

"Ryan, get in the picture with them." She motions for Ryan to join them. Ryan moved into the center of Sebastian and Erin.

"Ryan, would you like for me to take a picture of all of you?" One of the police officers asked as the walked up to them.

"Yeah, that works," Ryan said, as Majestic hands the camera over to the police officer. She then stood next to Ryan and she knew this picture was going to be too cute.

"Thanks man," Ryan says as he took the camera from the officer.

"Ok, we must go, but I will see you in a few days."

"We will see you in a few days," Majestic chimes in.

"Cool. I can't wait. Bye guys. Thanks Majestic," Sebastian says as he and Erin walked away. Majestic watched them as they walked away.

"How cute is that? I can't help but to say that."

"That is special, no doubt about that." Ryan said as he waited for Majestic to sit down so he could close her car door.

Majestic sat down and finished watching Sebastian and Erin walk up to the gate, speak to all the officers, and then continued their journey back to the kitchen where Majestic left her bag.

"Ok, let's go back to our side of town." Ryan said as he plopped down in the driver's seat and started the car.

"Ok."

Majestic was just looking over the area and in a way, she was happy to be leaving. It was so depressing in comparison to the resort where she was staying. Just like Ryan said, this was the real island. This is what reality is like behind the walls of the resorts and attractions that are marketed on the website.

* * *

"My God Majestic, you look so lovely," Renee said as Majestic walked out of the elevator. Renee, John, Tracee and Patrick had been waiting in the lobby for her to come down so they could go to the ballroom dance at the Heart of Velacious. Renee had grown impatient so she was going to take the elevator upstairs to get Majestic. It took Majestic longer than expected to figure out which dress to wear. She chose the red elegant gown she bought in New York a few years ago. She hasn't worn it before, and she was happy that it still fit her perfectly. The dress was nice and semi-form fitting to her ankles with extra tiny sparkles, which was next to perfect. She topped it off with her red heels that were they envy of Tracee when she bought them. Majestic felt like a princess. She knew she had the right look for the moment. She wasn't vain but she did stare at herself for a few moments because she hadn't dressed up like this in a long time. She was proud of how good she looked. She only hoped that Ryan would feel the same.

"Thanks Mom." Majestic said as she gave Renee a hug. Majestic liked the dress her mom wore. It was dark blue and very classy and tasteful. Majestic admired how her mom was still so beautiful.

"You look beautiful as well, Mom."

"Let's go get the others so we can go." Renee said as she grabbed Majestic's hand and led her to the lobby area where everyone was waiting. Majestic noticed a large number of people were dressed up so she knew it was a big deal for everyone.

"Are you a model or what?" Tracee asked as she walked up to Majestic. Majestic knew that Tracee would be borderline sexy with her dress.

"You had your braids touched up?" Majestic asked, as she noticed the neatness and shine to them.

"I found this salon on the strip and they hooked me up. Now you, I would have never expected you to have your hair pinned up, looking all classy and sexy." Tracee said as she turned Majestic around so she could see the back of her hair. "I am glad you put on the red dress. I told Patrick you wouldn't but you did. Those cross dangling earrings are tight. You went all out for tonight!"

"Surprised you huh?" Majestic winked at Tracee.

"My daughters both look outstanding," John said as he walked up and gave Majestic a hug. He had on his favorite navy blue suit with the white pin stripes in it. Majestic knew her dad dressed nice all the time so she knew he would have something to put on.

"You look nice Majestic." Patrick said as he walked up and stood next to Tracee.

"You do as well," Majestic replied as she admired Patrick's three button tan suit. For once he didn't look like a lawyer.

"Great, so the shuttle is here, so let's go." John said as he motioned for them to start walking towards the front of the hotel. They just followed the crowd of folks that were leaving the hotel to get on the shuttle. As the shuttle began to move, Majestic started getting nervous. She couldn't wait to see Ryan again. Spending the day with him was so refreshing to her and she couldn't wait for them to hang out again. She was almost getting used to her heart beating fast at the thought of him so she welcomed it when it began to beat faster. Majestic made sure she looked over at the ocean as they were taking the short shuttle ride to the restaurant. She hadn't had a chance to get into the water yet but she knew it was only a matter of time before she would get to take a dip. Tonight the water was calm again, and it looked so peaceful. Majestic just closed her eyes and pictured herself in the water, just standing there, soaking up the last of the sunrays before the sun went down. She pictured herself swimming in the water. She hoped that Ryan would get in with her and they could possibly go snorkeling or parasailing. Majestic could see a few yachts in the distance and she would love to be able to get on one. She has never been on one and she knew that she was going to be here for a few weeks so she hoped she could fit that in her schedule.

"Here we are," John said, as the shuttle stopped and everyone began to get off the shuttle.

Majestic made sure she still had her camera and her tiny purse with her as the shuttle drove off.

"There is a long line," Patrick said as he strained to see the front of the line. The line was long; about one hundred people were ahead of them. Majestic hoped they would be able to get a good table.

"It doesn't look good for us at all. We will be sitting so far in the back that we won't even be able to see the floor," Tracee said, sounding a little disappointed.

"It will be ok. We will just make do with whatever table we get," Renee said as she tried to make the situation better.

"Majestic, call Ryan and get us in." Tracee said, as she stood next to Majestic.

"I am not going to do that. How does that look with me asking for a hook up? If I can wait out here then so can you."

"If you got the hook-up you might as well use the hook-up," Tracee said as she tried to convince Majestic to call Ryan. Majestic just didn't feel right calling him and asking him to let her cut the line.

"We are fine, Tracee," John said as he put his arm around her.

"Besides this is a good time for us to take pictures while we wait."

Majestic shook her head in agreement. All of a sudden about ten waiters came out of the front entrance to the restaurant dressed in all black. The first waiter stopped at the beginning of the line and every other waiter stopped at every tenth person. They seemed to be handing out tickets to everyone. Once the waiter was almost to them when Tracee tapped Majestic.

"Ask him to get Ryan for us."

Majestic just looked at Tracee and shook her head.

"You are impossible. I said I wasn't going to and I mean it."

"I will ask him then."

"Tracee, let's just wait it out," Renee said with a little sternness in her voice.

As the waiter walks up to them, he gets on a two-way radio.

"Majestic, right?" The waiter asks Majestic totally catching her off guard.

"Yes."

"You and your party can come with me."

"That is what I am talking about," Tracee said, as she grabbed Patrick's hand and began to follow the waiter.

"Mr. Ryan requested that you and your party get the VIP treatment. So if you don't mind following me in; I will show you to your table."

"How did he know that we were out here?" Majestic asked.

"I don't want to take away from Mr. Ryan being smooth, but he can see you from the restaurant. He has a pair of binoculars but don't tell him I told you."

"That is our little secret," Majestic said, as she smiled. Ryan was looking for her and went to extreme measures to make sure that she was well taken care of when she arrived. She liked the idea of Ryan looking forward to seeing her.

As the waiter escorted them away from the line, Majestic was looking at the faces of the people and she bet they were wondering what was so special about them. Majestic could only delight in the fact that for one night she was a cut above the rest in Ryan's eyes.

"Ok, once we get inside there is a table with white roses on it. That is your table. You will be instructed what to do from there. Enjoy your evening." The waiter said, as he opened the door and let them in. Once they were inside, they all gasped. The restaurant looked totally different inside. The tables were moved out the center but Majestic could have sworn that there was a ceiling over that spot last night. Now there were long poles of light hanging down from the second floor ceiling. The poles of light were about twenty feet long and they hung until they were about where the tables would have been, on the second level, if they weren't moved. You could sit at the table or look over the rail without the lights interrupting your view of the dance floor. You could now see straight up to the ceiling and the spot where they sat at on the second floor was gone.

"A retractable floor. Remarkable." John stood there, shaking his head.

Majestic looked around and saw white carnations everywhere. They had decorated the place with them and it was so breathtaking to behold. All the tables now had a flower arrangement in the middle of them instead of a condiment island. The tables were covered with long white tablecloths.

"My goodness!" Tracee exclaimed, as she looked around the area.

"They went all out," Patrick said with amazement.

This place looked less like a restaurant and more like something out of a fairytale.

"You must be Majestic," A very pretty woman said as she walked up to her. The first thing that came to Majestic was she reminded her of a tiger. This woman had the look of power, beauty, and grace. She had beautiful long red hair and some of the greenest eyes Majestic had ever seen. She was flawless with her tanned skin and long, fitted white dress.

"I am Summer, and I am the hostess for tonight. I was instructed that you and your guests are the VIPs for the night. So let me show you to your table. Right this way please." Summer said as she strutted in her dress.

"You go girl," Tracee said as she nudged Majestic on her arm.

"What are you looking at?" Tracee asked Patrick as she caught him eyeing Summer.

"Nothing." Patrick says as he tries not to be embarrassed for being caught looking at Summer's figure.

Majestic took a quick glance at the dance floor and she wondered if she had enough courage to go up there and dance. She had taken plenty of lessons and she figured she would go up there once it got crowded.

"Ok folks. Here is your table. Someone will be here shortly to take care of you."

"Thank you Summer," Majestic said as she eyed the table.

"My pleasure." Summer said as she strutted away.

Majestic tried to find the best seat at the table because she wanted a full view of the dance floor. So as she was scoping out the seats she noticed that at every spot was a card that had their names on it.

"Oh wow. I guess I am sitting here." John said as he picked up the card that had his name on it.

Everyone found their card and sat in their spot. Majestic loved her spot because she could see the whole floor and there was no table blocking their view. Their table was right next to the dance floor. She had Tracee next to her on her right and Patrick was next to Tracee. On her left were Renee and then John. They were sitting at the only table shaped like a U. Right in front of her spot was six long stemmed white roses and one white rose cut like the one she put in her hair at Heaven of Flowers earlier that day. Tracee and Renee both had two white roses.

"So classy," Renee said as she picked up her white roses and smelled them. Tracee followed suit.

"Ryan is smooth; I have to give him that," John said, as he smelled Renee's white roses.

Majestic picked up the cut white rose and put it over her right ear.

"Girl you look so pretty. Let me get a picture of you," Tracee said as she grabbed Majestic's camera and took a picture of her. Majestic took the camera from Tracee and began to take pictures of everyone.

"Hi, I am Marcos and I will take care of you this evening. If you need anything, just ask me. I will take pictures for you; get you extra drinks and anything else you would like. So let me start you off by giving you this complimentary glass of white wine. Its Feunes: aged fifty years and its distinctive sweetness is a one-of-a-kind touch to any celebration. Here are your glasses; and for you sir," Marcos said, as he stopped at John, "The very best brandy we have." He placed a glass of brandy in front of John.

"All of this is compliments of Mr. Ryan to his VIP guests," Marcos said as he walked away.

"I tell you what: Ryan sure knows how to treat his VIPs," John said as he sipped his brandy.

"I can't wait to tell him thanks for this," Renee said as she sipped her wine.

"I know you don't drink often but you can at least enjoy one glass of wine with us. Do it for the sake of being here and being reunited with Ryan," Tracee said as she raised her glass for a toast. Majestic didn't really drink at all but she wanted to at least just enjoy one glass because this was definitely a special occasion.

"Here's to family and may the time spent here be one of the most special moments of our lifetime," John said as everyone toasted each other. Majestic tasted the wine and it was sweet but oh so good. She took a couple of sips just to enjoy the sweetness. Suddenly, the people waiting outside entered the restaurant, led by the waiters that handed out tickets. Everyone came in and sat down, some folks went straight upstairs to get a bird's eye view of the dance floor. Majestic and her family just sat there relishing the scene because they had the only table with roses on it and the only table shaped like a U, so everyone else that noticed these things realized that it was something special about them. So once everyone sat down and was settled in by ordering their drinks, Summer walked up to the middle of the dance floor with a microphone in her hand.

"Good evening ladies and gentlemen. I am Summer and I am the hostess for the evening. Tonight is a special night for us. This is the third annual ballroom dance night. As you can see, everything is in place for this night to be the most elegant experience you may ever have. So we hope you enjoy the festivities as I bring you the man that has made all of this possible, Ryan Levens." Everyone applauded. Majestic immediately began to look around because she definitely wanted to see Ryan. She spotted him coming out of a door across the room from where they were sitting. He was on the other side of the dance floor. When she finally focused on the full view of him and saw him in black slacks with thin red pinstripes, a matching vest and a red long sleeved dress shirt, she was stunned. He was so handsome and he literally took her breath away. He waved to everyone and nodded in the direction of Majestic. He walked over to Summer and he kissed her on the cheek and handed over the microphone to him.

"Good evening, beautiful people. I am Ryan Levens your humble owner of such a wonderful place as this. I am extremely glad that you all got dressed up and came here tonight. Tonight is definitely a special night but before we get started, let me give you a quick history about this restaurant. This place was the vision of my mother and father. They were a loving couple that moved here from Houston, Texas."

"Yee haw!" Someone yelled from the back of the room.

"My fellow Texans are in the house." Ryan said without skipping a beat. "Like I said they moved from Texas with a grown son, me, in tow. My dad spoke of making a difference in other people's lives and I was all for it. I just knew that we were going to come here and work with the less fortunate and bring happiness to their lives. Four years ago he sat my mother and me down, and he told us that we had a new plan that was finally going to happen. He had finally sold all his stock he had in a company he started in Houston, Texas. He had finally reached the point financially where he could begin his dream to change other people's lives in his own way, and not the traditional way. We were excited and then he dropped the bombshell on us. He told us he was going to open a restaurant and I was like, "Huh?"

Everyone laughed, and even Majestic had to smirk at that.

"My father looked at me and said, 'Ryan, believe me when I say that this restaurant is going to do more for people than any volunteer organization could ever do. We could sit around and give them clothes, shelter and God's Word anytime. No, let's give them a job, the ability to make money and take care of their own needs. Let's give them stability so when the time comes to give them God's Word, they will have understood already how God has been there for them. Not only that; let's make sure the best restaurant in the world is filled with the love of God. Let no man or woman walk into this restaurant and not feel like they have experienced something like never before." So we did just that. We prayed and prayed and what came of that is what you see today. Now the ballroom dance came about as a grand opening scheme but we decided to do it once a year. Now my parents are deceased, but the restaurant lives on with them in mind. As we enter another year, let the light flow and the love endure."

Everyone in the restaurant stood up and applauded. Ryan allowed them to cheer for about fifteen seconds. He then quieted the audience.

"Now it is customary to have my parents open the ballroom dance with a special first dance from them.

They are no longer with us, but I refuse to break that tradition. I have someone in attendance tonight that I would be so honored if she would have this first dance with me. I have known her for over thirteen years and I was shocked when she walked into the restaurant last night. She is a dear friend of mine. Let me introduce her to everyone here, the very beautiful Majestic." Ryan said, as he looked over in Majestic's direction. Majestic's heart wanted to jump out of her chest. She could not believe that he was asking her to dance in front of everyone.

"Go up there, Majestic!" Tracee said excitedly as Ryan walked towards them. All Majestic wanted to do was to drink up her glass of wine to calm her nerves but she knew that wouldn't be a good look. So she took a deep breath and began to stand up.

"That's my girl," Renee said, smiling.

"Majestic, may I have this dance?" Ryan said into the microphone as he stood at her table. He then stretched out the microphone so she could reply. Majestic felt like nothing was going to come out but she finally got the courage to speak.

"Yes."

Everyone applauded as Ryan walked around the table to Majestic and he leaned close to her and whispered in her ear.

"My Beautiful."

Majestic blushed. She was nervous, but she was soaking in this whole scene. Everyone continued to cheer for them. Ryan grabbed her hand and kissed it, and then he gently led her to the middle of the floor. Majestic prayed that her legs would follow suit and that she wouldn't trip or stumble to ruin such an event.

Ryan pointed to the band in the corner of the room and they began to play some trumpet laden waltz music. Ryan and Majestic began to waltz to the music. Right off the bat Majestic could tell that Ryan knew how to ballroom dance because he knew all the cues from the music, when to turn or stop and when to switch directions. It looked like a choreographed dance but it wasn't. Majestic just focused on Ryan's face and as they danced they looked deep into each other's eyes. Every time he smiled, she melted. Majestic felt like this had to be a dream. How many times does a woman get to get dressed up in beautiful gown, be treated like a queen and then have the whole place watch and admire her dance. Majestic took a quick glance up and she noticed that people had stood up and were standing at the railing, on the second level, watching them. This was so surreal. Majestic would have never guessed that a night like this was in her future. Here she is dancing with her Prince Charming in front of a couple of hundred guests. At this moment she could not think of another time where she felt so special and she knew that she could only thank Ryan for that. He twirled her away from him and she made sure she put an extra twist before she stopped and looked at him. He then twirled her back towards him and they did it again.

Majestic knew everyone was clapping but she could not hear them, because she was focusing on the music. She knew this moment was perfect and she wanted it to stay that way. She wanted to make sure that her one and only time in the spotlight was perfect. This was so fairy-tale-like. It was just like being at a huge ball and having everyone watching her being honored. What she liked the most about this dance was that it was with someone she cared for so deeply. The love she already had for Ryan was flooding back to the surface. He was someone she had always wanted in her life. She chose her career over him and at this moment she felt like that was a mistake, so she wanted to take advantage of this dance. The music was ending, and at that moment she didn't want the music to end. She wanted to enjoy this dance all night. To have center stage, being a lonely soul that hadn't experienced true love, Majestic was now seeing the fruits of her labor. She would gladly go through the ups and downs of past relationships all over again just to experience a night like this again. She now understood why she went through such bad times with relationships; it was so that this moment could be so special for her. So as they were getting to the last notes and the cue was coming that the music was going to stop. Ryan made the special move that told Majestic that he was going to dip her. So as the dip began she remembered to not rest her full weight on his arms because there would be a great chance of Ryan dropping her. So she pulled close to him when he dipped her. She looked into his eyes and she was captivated by what has just taken place. She is about twelve inches from his face and she just stared into his eyes. All of a sudden she felt his hand behind her back begin to lift her up. She was moving closer to Ryan. He just stared into her eyes as she got closer to his face until her lips were mere inches from his. She closed her eyes and she hoped that this was the moment that they were going to kiss. As his lips pressed next to hers, he just kept them pressed together for a second then he began to slowly pull away. Majestic savored their lips touching and when he slowly raised her back up to her feet. Everyone was standing to their feet, cheering. Majestic was blown away because to her this was a very special night for her. She stood there soaking in the accolades from the crowd. It was a wonderful feeling and she couldn't have scripted the dance any better. Every thing happened the way she wanted it to happen. The kiss was short but sweet and it was good and perfect for the moment. Her heart begins to flutter at the prospect of renewing something that was not fully taken advantage of in the past. Majestic looked at Ryan and he smiled and winked at her and at this moment Majestic knew that this was more than a dance. She realized that this whole vacation was going to be more than just a vacation, and the thought of that ran chills through her body. Ryan motioned towards Summer to bring the microphone to him.

"The opening dance is complete and now the floor is open to all." Ryan said as he handed the microphone back to Summer. The band played some slow jazzy music. Everyone that wanted to dance began to walk up towards the floor. Majestic knew her time in the spotlight was over but it didn't take away from the fact that it happened.

"May I have another dance?" Ryan asked, as he smiled at Majestic.

"Yes you may."

Majestic was not going to pass up any chance to be with Ryan. They were still in the center of the floor and to her, she could easily block out everyone that was around them. She only wanted to look Ryan in his eyes and enjoy this night. They used to go out in the past but it was to the movies and out to eat. Now they were doing things of the heart, like dancing. To dance with someone special in your life is sharing precious moments together. This was a romantic touch that Majestic loved. She took different dance lessons because she always dreamt of one day dancing with someone she loved.

"Thank you for sharing the first dance with me. That meant a lot and besides, if you didn't I was going to pull you up there."

"There was no need to do that. I really enjoyed the dance and that was very sweet of you to ask me and besides if you had asked someone else, I would have killed you."

"There was no one I wanted to share that moment with more than you. I have always wanted to share a moment that was romantic with you. I know we crossed the line a few times but we weren't romantic with it. I always wanted to do romantic things with you but I didn't feel right crossing the line because we were friends."

"I did too Ryan. I wanted us to be together but I knew that we were wrong for being intimate. I felt bad about it so I really was ok with you coming here and then I went to college and moved to Las Vegas. I guess we never really spoke on it so we let an opportunity get by us."

"I won't let it happen again. I am glad you are here and I just want to spend time with you, and I mean every moment that I can."

"I would like that."

Majestic knew that she loved that. She was captured in the moment. In fact, she has enjoyed every moment of that day. Spending time with Ryan was heartwarming, and it made everything they did that much better. To top it off they were having their first romantic moment, and it was priceless. The whole scene was out of a movie, and it made the effect of it greater. Now Majestic just wanted to continue the night with spending time with Ryan and she hoped it was full of dancing. So she looked up into Ryan's face and he smiled and pulled her close so they could slow dance. Majestic rested her head on his shoulder and closed her eyes. She was happy and it was a feeling that she hadn't truly felt in years. There was happiness in other things but not in love. This was a happy love moment and wished that it was only the beginning. So as they danced she just basked in the fact that she was with Ryan. The one true love of her life that was back in her life and she felt that was where he should be. She wanted to make sure that for the rest of the vacation, she got the most out of spending time with him. She was going to take full advantage of this chance. She had four weeks to enjoy Ryan and she knew that was what she planned on doing. She was going to try to make up for lost time. Majestic wondered what life would have been like if she had followed Ryan and moved to the island. She would have been enjoying the wonderful island every day and she would have been with her soul mate. There would have been plenty of dancing and romantic days and the thought of that makes Majestic feel like she missed out on so much. She knew she couldn't get back the time, so she wanted to make sure that she enjoyed every moment she had with Ryan. God had brought them back together for a reason, and Majestic felt it was more than to share a romantic dance together. The true reason on why God did it will be revealed in time. Majestic didn't mind because if it meant spending more time with Ryan then she could wait on what God was doing for them. She looked around the dance floor and she saw plenty of couples dancing. Everyone was just having a wonderful time. So many expressions of love and happiness were on their faces. Majestic hoped that everyone felt the way she did. She wanted them to enjoy this moment as she had. She didn't mind sharing her special moment with them. She knew that there was plenty of love to go around for everyone. Now that love was making its way back into her life, she wondered if love was here to stay. Would love stop in for a brief moment and then leave again? If she had her say in the matter, love was not ever going to be able to get away from her. So she held on to Ryan and pulled him closer to her. She didn't want to let him go. She only wanted to dance the night away and feel the love that was growing in her heart. Her precious moment was here and she was going to take full advantage of it. Tonight is the night that Majestic knew would be the changing point for her. After tonight, love was going to be her focus and she welcomed all that came with it.

So as she hugged Ryan, she knew that the best of her days were in the future, and that thought sent chills down her back. To know that things were going to change for the better gave her a great feeling. So Majestic closed her eyes and moved to the music.

3

"Who are those two children with Ryan? I knew he was too good to be true." Tracee joked as she saw Ryan walk up with Sebastian and Erin.

"Something is wrong with you, Tracee," Majestic laughed as she stood up. Majestic was so happy to see them. She hadn't seen them since they all went shopping a few days ago. Majestic ran up and hugged Erin and Sebastian. She then gave Ryan a big kiss on his lips. She then grabs Sebastian and Erin by their hands and walked them to the table where she was sitting at with Renee, John, Patrick and Tracee.

"Everyone this handsome young man is Sebastian and this pretty young lady is Erin." Majestic said, once they made it to the table.

"Well, hi Sebastian and Erin. My name is John and this is my wife Renee," John extended his hand out to both of them. Sebastian and Erin shook his hand.

"I want a hug though," Renee said as she stood up and hugged both of them.

"She is cute like me. Hi Sebastian and Erin, my name is Tracee and this is my husband Patrick." Tracee stood up and gave them both a hug and Patrick just extended his hand out but he didn't say anything, and that didn't sit well with Majestic. It took everything in her to not say anything to him but she didn't want to ruin the breakfast by being mean.

"Ok Erin and Sebastian you can sit next to me and Ryan on this side of the table." Majestic said as she showed them the two seats she had for them. Previously, they put two tables together, and Renee, John, Tracee and Patrick sat on one side of the table and Majestic sat on the other side so that Ryan, Sebastian and Erin could sit next to her.

"Good morning everyone," Ryan said as he made his way around the table to give out hugs and handshakes. He sat next to Majestic and grabbed her hand under the table.

"I love your braids," Erin said to Tracee as she sat down and smiled. Her voice was so cute.

"Why thank you. I like yours too. You know what; we look like we could be sisters." Tracee said to Erin.

"I know."

"Majestic tells us that both of you guys are ten years old," Renee said, as she started a conversation.

"Yes ma'am. I am going to be eleven real soon." Sebastian says proudly.

"Wow. You are going to be getting old," John said jokingly.

"You are going to be getting old." Erin said with a laugh.

"Isn't she the cutest thing?" Majestic says as she hugged Erin who was sitting next to her.

"She always says that and we are the same age."

"She says that because she likes you Sebastian," Tracee added.

"I do like him. I think he is cute." Erin said as she smiled, which made Sebastian blush.

"She does that all the time. She knows that makes him blush," Ryan said as he nudged Erin.

"How does that make you feel when she does that?" Renee asks Sebastian.

"I don't mind because I like her too." Sebastian said as he looked away and blushed.

"See what you do to him? Don't feel bad, I do the same thing to Ryan." Majestic said as she looks at Ryan, who just shook his head in agreement.

"That is a pretty blue dress you have on, Erin," Tracee said as she motioned for Erin to stand up.

"I know. I really like it. Majestic bought it for me." Erin said, as she walked over to Tracee so she could see the dress.

"She bought it for you? That was nice of her." Renee said as she smiled at Majestic.

"We took them shopping the other day."

"She bought me these Jordans too." Sebastian said as he stood up so that everyone could see his shoes.

"We have more clothes at home that she bought us too." Erin said as she returned to her seat.

"I wanted to buy my new buddies something. I wanted you guys to have something to remember me by." Majestic said as she looked at them. Majestic knew those children had touched her in a profound way. She really enjoyed taking them shopping and just hanging out with them.

"I am sure they are going to remember you for a long time," Ryan said, as he placed his hands on Majestic's shoulders.

"I know I am. I am going to write you and everything," Erin said as she placed her hand on Majestic's hand.

"Me too," Sebastian says as not to be left out.

"I think you should send her an email, she will get it faster that way," Tracee said, trying to be thoughtful.

"We don't have a computer at home," Sebastian said with a hint of sadness in his voice.

"Or a phone either," Erin added.

"That is ok, writing is good," Renee said as she looks at Majestic. "I have a computer and a phone but I miss letters that come in the mail."

"Me too. I love letters especially when my mom and dad write me," Erin said, as she got excited.

"Your mom and dad write to you?" Renee asked.

"I normally get two or three letters each year. I think it is because I don't see them that they write me," Erin said, as if it was no big deal to her.

"Her mom and dad are in jail," Majestic said as she saw the shocked looks on everyone's faces.

"They did something really bad and they have to go away for a while," Erin said but she showed no emotion.

"Who takes care of you?" Tracee asked, showing concern.

"My granny, but she is blind."

"That has to be hard on you. So Erin you really take care of her then?" Renee asked, as she tried to make light of the situation.

"We both do."

"Sebastian helps me out. It gets hard at times."

"Erin, I sure do hate that," John said, as he finally joined in on the conversation.

"There is also a volunteer that helps them out as well," Ryan adds.

"How about your parents, Sebastian?" Tracee asked, as she prepared herself for more sad news.

"I don't know my dad, but my mom works here," Sebastian said as he pointed at the restaurant.

"She does? Who is she?" Tracee asked Ryan.

"Juanita is his mom. Your waitress you guys had on your first night here," Ryan added.

"Small world," John said.

"We loved her. She was so nice and pretty," Renee said as she looks at Sebastian.

"Hi Mom!" Sebastian said as everyone looks around at Juanita coming from the restaurant. She had a frantic look on her face.

"What are you doing here?" Juanita asked as she bypassed everyone and walked over to Sebastian.

"Ryan brought me here for breakfast," Sebastian said with a scared look on his face.

"What is wrong with you, Ryan? How could you do this to me?" Juanita says as tears begin to form in her eyes. Everyone at the table was shocked. No one knew what to say.

"What do you mean?" Ryan asked as he could tell that Juanita was upset.

Majestic didn't know what was going on. She hadn't really sat down and talked with Juanita so she didn't know how she felt about everything that was going on.

"You know what I mean. My sister died a year ago and this is how you act," Juanita said as the tears began to flow. All of Majestic's family looked right at her. Majestic never got around to telling them anything about the situation with Sebastian, Juanita and Ryan. Now it was too late.

"What am I doing wrong?" Ryan asked, with a confused look on his face.

"You have been running around here, with her, all up in front of everyone." Juanita said, as she pointed at Majestic. "Bringing her all up in the restaurant and people are asking me questions like I have the answers."

"Leave her out of this. I mean it," Ryan said as he began to show a little emotion. Majestic just sat there because as of this moment, this was their battle.

"Why? You are not leaving her out of this. My sister loved you, she loved you so much she died for you and I can't believe that you have enough nerve to have another woman all up in my face and hanging out with my son. A year ago she did you a favor and it cost her everything. She died and now you repay her by being with someone else," Juanita said, as she grabbed Sebastian and pulled him close to her.

"You wait a minute. I loved your sister and I gave her my all. I know she died. I know she died doing a favor for me. Don't forget I lost my parents too. I lost three of the most important people in my life at one time. I have suffered more than you and I have been able to cope. I am now ready to move on with my life. I can't live in the past, because that can only bring me pain. What happened to my parents and your sister is horrible.

I have to live with that for the rest of my life but tell me this. Why can't I move on? It has been a year and I have sat in my sadness and done nothing. I finally get reunited with someone that I care about and everyone thinks I am wrong. Your sister died a year ago, but I didn't. A part of me died but I am still alive and I feel like I have every right to move forward. I have done my part. I have taken care of all of her family. You and Sebastian don't have to want for anything. I promised you that and meant it. I never realized that I had to die that day too and no longer live now," Ryan said, as he walked towards Juanita. Majestic wanted to say something but she didn't know what to say. Juanita motioned for him to get away from her but Ryan kept on moving towards her.

"Look Juanita. A year ago, all we had got taken from us and we cried, but we cried together. We have suffered, but we suffered together. We grieved, but we grieved together. What was so different about this time? Why couldn't you just pull me aside and ask me what I was doing? I would have gladly told you the exact same thing I have told you but without raising my voice. I would have sat down and explained to you what I was going through. I sat down with Sebastian and talked to him about it."

"Me too," Erin chimed in.

Juanita tried to smile but couldn't. She walked up to Ryan and gave him a hug.

"I am sorry everybody," Juanita says as she left the table area and started walking down towards the beach.

"Juanita!" Ryan called after her.

"Mom!" Sebastian yelled.

"Let me talk to her," Majestic said as she got up from the table and caught up to Juanita.

"Juanita, wait up. Please."

Juanita turned around with tears in her eyes. She had a look, on her face, like she really didn't want to turn around but something in her made her do it.

"I am so sorry about your sister. Believe me I am. When Ryan told me what took place, I was sick to my stomach. I felt so bad." Majestic said, as they stood face to face. Juanita just shook her head. Majestic could see the pain and hurt in Juanita's eyes.

"My purpose for coming to this island was to get away from it all back at home and relax. I knew Ryan from a long time ago, and we were like best friends at the time. We didn't date each other because we knew we were going to be apart. So we just stayed friends even though we had feelings for each other. I never planned to come here, have these feelings resurface for him and bring hate and discontent to everyone around him. I don't wish for any of this stuff to happen. I just got reunited with my friend and that made me happy and that was all I was thinking about."

"I know you didn't want this to happen. It's not you; it's me. I am just upset with everything that is going on right now. I have the anniversary of my sister's death to deal with as well," Juanita said as she cried. "I am so alone without my sister. She was all the family I had left. She helped me with everything, from getting a job, schooling, my children, and I mean everything. When she died, I had no clue how to do anything on my own. She had always been there for me, and then suddenly she was gone. She helped me raise Sebastian and even adopted him because I couldn't fully take care of him. I feel like a big failure. I am not able to take care of my own children. She did that for me and now she was gone. I had no one to turn to except Ryan. Ryan immediately stepped in and he has been taking care of Sebastian and me. He has taken that role that my sister had."

"I am sure that Ryan will always take care of you. Nothing will change. If Ryan says something he will do it."

"You don't understand. I don't want him to leave. I don't want you to take him from me. What will I do if he leaves me?" Juanita said, as she cried uncontrollably. "Sebastian will be crushed and I can't handle that. I can live with my pain but I can't live with watching my son suffer. That would push me over the edge."

Majestic just stood there for a second, watching Juanita cry.

"Juanita, what makes you think that Ryan is going to leave you and Sebastian? He hasn't mentioned any-thing to me about leaving the island."

"He doesn't have to say anything. I remember the way he looked at my sister when she would enter a room. I remember watching them just interact with each other. The way he touched her, spoke of her and was always considerate of her. I know that look every time I see it. I have seen it so much that I couldn't get it confused with any other look. That's the same look I see when he looks at you."

Majestic had to break the eye contact with Juanita because she didn't know what to say. Majestic knows that look and she has loved it. Ryan would look so deep into her eyes that it made her feel like if the room were on fire, he wouldn't know it at all. Nothing would break his concentration, and that was a wonderful feeling. To have someone that into you was so refreshing, and Majestic loved it.

"I am sorry Juanita. I don't know what to say."

"You don't have to say anything. I can't picture Ryan with anyone else but my sister but truly that is me being selfish. It really is because my sister would want Ryan to be happy. She would want Ryan to move on with his life. She would want Ryan to meet someone new and get married. That is how wonderful my sister was," Juanita said as tears ran down her face. Majestic was now getting teary-eyed. She only knew Juanita's sister from Ryan and Sebastian but every story was one of a wonderful person. That made Majestic sad, because why did she deserve more than Juanita's sister? Someone that touched so many people in a profound way had to die in order for Majestic to experience happiness, and the thought of that opened up the floodgates and she began to cry. Majestic knew how blessed she had been over these past two and a half weeks and it all came at the expense of someone else.

"Juanita, I know I am not your sister. I can never be the woman that she was. All I know is that I am here and I care for Ryan. I care for Sebastian and I care for you. If I am to be a part of Ryan's life, I will make sure that nothing changes regarding the relationship that he has with you and Sebastian. There's not one thing that I would want you guys to do differently. I want happiness, but I don't want it at the expense of others getting hurt or being left out. You have my word on that," Majestic said, as the tears continued to flow down her face. Juanita walked up to Majestic and they hugged and they both cried uncontrollably. Majestic felt Juanita's pain. Juanita had been down and out since she was sixteen. She always had someone she could rely on, but unfortunately she had also lost them. Ryan is all she had left, the last crutch available, and Juanita was afraid that he was going to be taken away too.

"Juanita, let's work this thing out together. I am going to be here for about a week and a half. Let you, Ryan and me, and Sebastian talk things out. If I am going to be in Ryan's life in a big way, then let's decide our course of action so everyone is taken care of. If I am not going to be in his life then let me and you still keep in contact and help each other out. I look at it this way. If I get to be with Ryan, then we both win because I wouldn't change a thing. If I don't get Ryan we will both have still won because things will stay the same for you and I will still have experienced the greatest four weeks of my life. All I ask is let's work things out. No one is going to leave you and Sebastian alone. I will make that promise to you that as long as I am alive, you will have a friend in me."

"Thank you Majestic. If anyone deserves to be with Ryan, it is you. You are so like my sister in many ways. Both of you are pretty, sweet and care about others. I won't stand in the way of you and Ryan. That would be too selfish of me. Ryan deserves to move on. He has been by himself for the past year and I commend him for that. He lost a lot on that day and I am acting like I was the only one who lost someone. Now, I have to swallow my pride and apologize to your family. I am so embarrassed."

"You don't have to be embarrassed. You are doing what any good mother and sister would do. Who wouldn't fight for what was right? You have a little fight in you and that is a good thing," Majestic said as she placed her arm around Juanita and they began to walk back towards the restaurant. Majestic could see that everyone was waiting on them to come back to the table. Majestic could see a look of relief on Ryan's face. Sebastian ran up to his mom and gave her a big hug.

"I love you, Mom," Sebastian said, as Juanita wiped the tears from her eyes.

"I love you too Sebastian."

Majestic tried to fight back tears as she watched them embrace. The love of a mother and her son cannot be broken. Although they have been through a lot, love has endured.

All of a sudden, Erin ran up and hugged Majestic. Majestic hugged her so tight that she didn't want to let her go. Majestic began to cry again as she realized that she came to the island to look for love and she figured that she would only find romantic love. Instead, she realized she had found true love, and that this kind of love can be shared with everyone. Majestic prayed to God to help her find love and now she believed the blinders were falling off of her eyes. The love she had experienced wasn't a selfish love, but a love for others. In two weeks she had gone from living in her own world; now she was sharing herself with others and that was a feeling she enjoyed.

"Is everything ok?" Ryan asked as he walked up to Majestic.

"Oh yeah, we are fine." Majestic said as she continued to squeeze Erin.

"I am sorry Ryan. I overreacted," Juanita said as she walked over to Ryan and hugged him.

"I am sorry too. Let's keep our lines of communication open. You know you can talk to me about anything. Let's avoid circumstances like this. You are still my sister and I love you." Ryan says as he kissed Juanita on the cheek.

Majestic just smiled. She sees why Juanita didn't want to lose Ryan. He cared so much for her and the thought of losing that would be hard to swallow.

"Can we eat now?" Erin asked as she rubbed her stomach.

"I think we can," Majestic said as she grabbed Erin by the hand.

"Good, because I want some pancakes," Sebastian said as he walked back to the table.

"Join us, Juanita. I think it would be good if you did."

"Ryan, you know I am working this morning." Juanita tried to remind him of the restaurant's policy.

"I am your boss and I am telling you to take off for the day and enjoy breakfast with us." Ryan says as he puts his hands on Juanita's shoulders and begins to push her ever so slightly towards the table.

"Ok. I will."

"Yes!" Sebastian said as he ran over to the next table and grabbed a chair and placed it next to him for her.

"Mom, you can sit here."

"I am sorry everyone. I have caused a scene and ruined your breakfast."

"Don't you worry. I see that everything has worked itself out. Let's just eat and get to know each other," Renee said as she walked over to Juanita and patted her on the back.

"I feel so much better," Juanita said as she sat down.

"Juanita, we are having a barbecue at Ryan's place tonight, we would love for you to come," Majestic said as she sat down at the table.

"I am sure everyone would love your famous barbecue corn on the cob." Ryan adds.

"It's good," Sebastian said as he licked his lips.

"It's real good," Erin said as she licked her lips too.

"I would love to try it," Tracee said as she nudged Patrick in his side.

"Me too," Patrick said as he realized what Tracee was asking him to do.

"I will come."

"Yes, one big family!" Sebastian said as he gave Erin a high five.

Majestic just looked around the table. That last statement rung true for her. On one side of the table was her original family: mom, dad, sister and brother-in-law. On the other side of her table, she hoped they were her new family. She only wished that Ryan, Erin, Sebastian and Juanita could be her new family. Majestic was so happy with God right now. Just looking at everyone talking and having a good time quieted her once lonely heart.

* * *

"Wow. After such a beautiful morning of sunshine, who would have thought that it would be raining by the end of the day?" Majestic said as her and Ryan rocked back and forth on a large swing on Ryan's back porch. It was so calming to watch the rain fall. The sun was still trying to shine but the clouds kept on trying to get in the sun's way. The rain was making very beautiful rainbows and Majestic wished she hadn't used up all of her film in her camera. They all came over Ryan's house to barbecue and that was the only thing that was on her mind, so she only brought one camera. They managed to barbeque everything before it started to rain, so their outside barbeque turned into an indoor one. Nonetheless, they ate and were stuffed, so now everyone was just relaxing after feasting like kings and queens. Everyone was inside except for Ryan and Majestic who decided to have a nice romantic swing together.

"Welcome to Velacious Island. That is one of the things that make island life so hard to figure out at times. Just when you think that rain is nowhere in sight, you are sitting at the beach drenched. It is funny at times, but you do get used to it." Ryan says as he put his arm behind Majestic's head.

"Speaking of at the beach, what happened this morning totally caught me off guard, and I didn't know what to do."

"Me too Majestic, because I never saw it coming. I had no idea that Juanita was struggling with us hanging together. Just the look on her face said it all. I have never seen her like that."

"All I can say is that she was worried about losing you."

"Losing me? What does she mean by that?" Ryan asked, with a confused look on his face.

"She told me that her sister was the one that took care of her and basically helped her with everything in life. So when she died, she said that you took over that role. She was afraid that I was going to take you from her and then she would have no one to turn to for help."

"I told her at the funeral that under no circumstance would I ever leave her. I know how fragile she is. I watched her grow up from a teenager to where she is now. I have seen the mistakes she made and how she compounded them by making more mistakes. I know that she isn't ready to be turned loose and be off on her own. I know that her sister would want me to take care of Juanita and Sebastian and so that is what I plan on doing."

"That is the right thing to do." Majestic says as she grabs Ryan's hand and held it close to her heart.

"How do you feel about it?"

"About Juanita and Sebastian?"

"Yes."

"I have no problem with it. They are really your family and if I want to be with you then I have to accept your family as well. Look, I care for Sebastian and Juanita. I want to see them doing well, and I know the bond you have with them. It would be so selfish of me to take you from them or stop you from seeing them and being in their lives. I want what is best for us but I don't want that at the expense of hurting someone else. We can balance our lives together."

"I am glad you feel that way. I love Sebastian and Juanita. They are like family to me and I will never turn my back on them. I have grown so attached to them that I never think of them as anything but family. Like I told you, I watched Juanita grow into a woman and I have been there since day one with Sebastian. We do have a very strong bond and I wouldn't know what to do if they weren't in my life."

"I am glad you feel that way. They both need that attention and care that you give them. I will support you in all that you do for them and if it is ok with you, I would like to help out in any way possible. I don't care if it is money, time or whatever. I am here for you and I am here for them as well." Majestic said as she looked in Ryan's eyes. She wanted to make eye contact with him because she wanted him to know that she was serious about what she just said.

"You don't have to."

"I want to. If they are apart of your life, I want to share in that too."

"Ok, because we are a package deal."

"I am cool with that but I am not cool with this rain," Majestic said as she shook her head.

"Why not?"

"We were having a wonderful time in the sun and now we are sitting here watching the rain. Believe me, I like the rain but today I wanted to see the sun. I wanted to hang out with the family in your backyard. Seriously, I wanted to beat you in some basketball." Majestic said, as she burst out laughing. Majestic had never played any sports, so for her to say that was funny to her.

"I hate to interrupt you guys but we might need to head back to the hotel. There is a Tropical Storm watch out for the island. I want to be better safe than sorry," Renee said as she poked her head through the open sliding door.

"I fully understand. This weather out here can be very tricky," Ryan says as he grabbed Majestic's hand and walked her into the house.

"Majestic, we are going to go now. This weather has me a little scared. I need Patrick to keep me safe back at the hotel," Tracee said as she smiled at Patrick. Majestic cringed at the sound of that.

"I know. Mom told us you guys were heading back to the hotel."

"You are not coming?" Tracee asked.

"No, I am staying here."

"What? You are staying here? Ok. Wait, are you for real? Tracee asked with a shocked look on her face.

"I am just playing. I am coming with you guys. Ryan has to take Juanita, Sebastian and Erin back home."

"I was about to say," Tracee shook her head.

"Thank you Tracee and Patrick for hanging out with me today. I had a wonderful time with you guys," Ryan said as he shook Patrick's hand and gave Tracee a hug.

"No, thank you. We enjoyed ourselves," Patrick grabbed Tracee's hand quickly after she got through hugging Ryan. Majestic just looked at him and shook her head.

"Renee, John. Thanks for coming over to my house. I thoroughly enjoyed talking with you as well." Ryan said as he put an arm around Majestic.

"Thank you Ryan for everything. I just want to say that over these past two weeks, you have made this family vacation one that we will never forget. The way you have treated my family and my daughter, I can never thank you enough for that," John said as he looked at Ryan. Majestic knew that look; that was the look of total respect and admiration.

"It has been my pleasure. It has been awhile since I have sat down with anyone that reminded me so much of my parents. It was good to have you guys here and I am so happy that I had the chance to meet all of you. I am extremely happy that I have had a chance to see Majestic because I have missed her so." Ryan said as he kissed Majestic on her forehead.

"Ryan, you have been a real blessing to us. We came here to go on a family vacation, stay awhile and leave. We thought we were leaving our families to come here and instead we have found family. You are such a wonderful person and what you are doing for Juanita, Sebastian and Erin is something that must be noted. I know you don't look for anything in return but you will receive much because God is watching and I know He is smiling upon your actions."

"Thank you, Renee." Ryan released Majestic so that he could hug Renee.

"I will meet you outside," Majestic said to Renee and John as they walked out the front door.

"Ok, so I will see you tomorrow right?" Majestic asked, as she grabbed Ryan's hands.

"Oh yeah," Ryan said as he pulled Majestic close to him. They just stood there hugging each other. All of a sudden they heard thunder and lightning.

"Oh boy, I think it is going to storm. I think you'd better go now."

"I will see you tomorrow sweetheart." Majestic said as she leaned in for a kiss. Ryan kissed her, and she really wanted to stay but she knew better. It was best that they continued to do what was right. Being alone, at night, in Ryan's house was not the best circumstance for them. That was the same situation that took place years ago when they became intimate and Majestic didn't want to go through the guilt again. One thing Majestic loved about Ryan is that he respected her and her wishes.

"Go. Call me when you make it to your room." Ryan said as he walked Majestic to the front door and held it open for her.

"Man, it is raining out there."

"I told you there is no in-between. It either rains a lot or a little. Just make sure Patrick is careful with you. Can I pray for you real quick?"

"Ryan, you sure can." Majestic says as she grabbed his hands. As Ryan is praying, Majestic is happy to know that her and Ryan were sharing a moment with God together.

"Thank you." Majestic said as she got a quick kiss from him before she ran out into the rain. She didn't want to leave, but she fought her desires and decided to go back to the hotel. She knew that she wanted to stay. She wanted to stay and be in Ryan's arms but that would probably lead to so much more. That much more was something that Majestic didn't want to be a part of right now. She was going to try her best to wait. It was harder this time because she had true feelings for Ryan, but at the same time she still wanted to please God. One day she will be able to do both with no regrets. She looked forward to that day with great anticipation.

4

"I can't believe all of this rain," Majestic said as Ryan opened the door to the restaurant. "Nothing was going to stop me from coming to see you."

"I can't believe you came over here. This is an emergency situation and you should have stayed at the hotel. Hurricanes out here are nothing to play with. You could have been hurt just running over here." Ryan said as he hugged Majestic.

"I know but I wasn't so now I am here. I wanted to be with you."

"I know you do but this is not good. If you were to get hurt over here, I wouldn't know what to do. I would be the one to have to explain to your parents what happened and why you came over here," Ryan said, with a frustrated look on his face. Majestic could see that he was getting mad at her for coming to the restaurant. The island was under a hurricane warning and Ryan wanted her to stay at the hotel. She didn't want him mad at her but she wanted to be by his side so she braved the elements to come over.

"Ryan, I really wanted to come and I am not trying to make you mad at me," Majestic says as she started to feel bad for coming.

"I am mad because I care for you a whole lot. I have gone through pain just last year. I take this very seriously and I am not trying to relive any heartache like what took place last year. I will not let it happen again. So hear me out please, you are supposed to be packing your things up and finding shelter in the hotel. You were told that there is a chance that the hurricane could hit this island and believe me, if it does, a hurricane that size can do some major damage. I asked you to stay at the hotel because there you will be safer than you will here." Ryan says as he removed the hat and rain poncho Majestic had on. Majestic didn't care if Ryan wanted her to stay at the hotel or not. She knew she was coming to see him regardless. She found out he was at the restaurant so she put on some jeans and came right over. She was soaking wet, from head to toe due to the pouring rain.

"It has rained the past week. I only have three more days left until my vacation is over. I have waited and waited but this rain is not going to end and I want to spend my last days here with you," Majestic said as she took the towel that Ryan gave her and dried herself off.

"Majestic, you were better off at the hotel. My staff and I have been here taping up all the windows because that hurricane still has a chance of hitting the island."

"I guess I will help you guys then." Majestic says as she is trying to make her point that she wants to be there with Ryan.

"What good would that do? I don't want you walking around near any glass. I want you to listen to me for once. I am not comfortable with you being here right now. I am stressed enough over this hurricane. Not only this one but anytime a hurricane comes because of the great threat of damage that could happen here. I am not worried about myself but I am for you. I get nervous when it gets like this so excuse me if I am coming at you wrong. Majestic it is not safe here. I really wished you had stayed at the hotel. I bet Renee and John don't know you are here?"

"No they don't but Tracee does."

"Why won't you just listen to me? I would be at peace if you were at the hotel, with your family riding this thing out."

"I know you would, but I would rather ride this thing out with you," Majestic said as she hugged Ryan.

"You sure are pretty when you are stubborn," Ryan said as he shook his head.

"Why thank you, and you are not half bad yourself."

All of a sudden the wind began to blow very hard and the rain began to come down faster. The lights flickered off and on.

"I have found the weather radio, Ryan. Here are the batteries." Marcos said while handing over the batteries and weather radio to him.

"I will do that for you." Majestic said as she took the weather radio and batteries from Ryan. As long as she was here she was going to help out. She didn't want to be a burden but she didn't even consider the consequences before she left the hotel. She knew her desire to be next to Ryan took over any common sense she might have had about the danger she could have put herself in.

"People, we need flashlights. Can someone go into my office and get the box that has them in there? They all have new batteries in them. We need to finish taping as many windows as possible," Ryan says as he grabbed Majestic by her arm and pulled her away from the front door.

"I am happy you are here Majestic but I would be even happier if you were in the safety of the hotel. There are less windows and better places for shelter."

"You are killing me Ryan. I don't care; I want to be with you. Unless you are going to walk me over to the hotel yourself, then I suggest that we just continue to prep the restaurant for the hurricane," Majestic said, as she put the batteries in the weather radio and turned it on. Now she was getting upset because Ryan kept on trying to get rid of her. She thought it was cute at first but then she realized he was serious.

"Look, don't get an attitude with me. I am only looking out for your well-being. I have seen what these hurricanes can do and the damages they can cause. It is not a pretty thing when something that powerful comes on land because it shreds everything it touches and I mean it shreds them to pieces."

"I understand that Ryan. I weighed the cost when I walked out of that hotel and ran by the police officers that tried to stop me."

"What? Are you serious?" Ryan said with a serious look on his face.

"No, I just thought I would try to make you laugh." Majestic says as she closed the battery case and turned the radio on.

"Hey everybody, the radio is working. Come and listen to the report." Marcos said as about six people came running.

"This is all you have?" Majestic says referring to the six employees that came running up. She knew that Ryan had over fifty people on his staff and this was barely 10%.

"These are the only ones that don't have children. I wouldn't dare ask anyone with children to stay. I really didn't want these people to help but they insisted on being here so I let them stay."

"Oh, you let them stay, but you are trying to run me off."

"Not now Majestic. You know that is totally different. That has to do with different relationships and feelings." Ryan said as he tried to make his point.

"Let's listen guys." Marcos says as he tried to get everyone focused. Everyone crowded around the radio. Majestic began to get nervous because she was the only one in the restaurant that has never been in a hurricane so she had no clue what to expect. Just observing the serious looks on everyone's faces began to affect Majestic. She wondered if she made a mistake in coming over to the restaurant.

"I repeat, this is the Velacious Weather Emergency Broadcast with a very important announcement. Hurricane Sue is fifty miles due east of Velacious Island. Hurricane Sue is traveling in excess of eighty miles an hour. All residences are asked to find shelter immediately. Find cover in a bathroom or under stairs. Be advised to stay away from windows and if you can't find adequate shelter, find a hallway or even a closet. All resorts are closed and hotels should continue with their evacuation procedures of all guests. The airport will only be open for one more hour. Take your necessary evacuation steps now.

I repeat, this is the Velacious Weather Emergency Broadcast with a very important announcement. Hurricane Sue is fifty miles due east of Velacious Island. Hurricane Sue is traveling in excess of eighty miles an hour. All residences are asked to find shelter immediately. Find cover in a bathroom or under stairs. Be advised to stay away from windows and if you can't find adequate shelter, find a hallway or even a closet. All resorts are closed and hotels should continue with their evacuation procedures of all guests. The airport will only be open for one more hour. Take your necessary evacuation steps now.

Everyone just stood there quiet.

"Majestic you must leave now. Go to the hotel and get your family and leave the island." Ryan said as he pulled Majestic aside.

"Are you crazy? I am not leaving and I am definitely not leaving the island."

"You don't understand."

That was all Ryan could get out before the warning sirens went off.

"Those are the sirens warning us. We have to go." Marcos says as he looked at Ryan for instructions.

"Ok, everyone let's leave. Get your things and let's go." Ryan said, as everyone got ready to leave. Majestic could now see the seriousness in Ryan's face and demeanor. Everyone truly understood the danger except Majestic. For the first time since the idea came in her mind to come over, she figured she might be in over her head. It was as if she was on the outside looking in because she didn't expect all of this to happen once she got over here. She was expecting Ryan to be happy to see her and they would sit somewhere quietly and wait the hurricane out. She didn't expect running and yelling and everyone to be scared. She wasn't prepared for that and it showed now because she now realized that this was indeed an emergency.

"The police are at the door!" An employee yelled from the front door.

"Let them in," Ryan says as he walked towards the door.

Now it really got serious; Majestic thought this was all a bad dream. The police are here and she knows there is no good reason why the cops would come at a time like this. Only a dire emergency would call for them to come and that worried her. It worried her because this was supposed to be her fairytale. This was her fairytale vacation full of love and a forever after but now it is turning into something worse. Her fairytale vacation was now turning into a nightmare. Of all things, an act of nature, is threatening to ruin her vacation. She was so in love with nature for the past three weeks. Now she sees how quickly nature can turn on you. So she runs after Ryan to see what was going on. As they are making their way towards the front entrance, in comes two police officers and John. Now it was real to Majestic. Being from Las Vegas, weather like this doesn't happen so she doesn't really know how to approach it. Seeing her dad and the police officers has suddenly awakened Majestic to her nightmare.

"Majestic. Why are you not at the hotel? Tracee told me you were over here and I couldn't believe that you would leave the hotel in weather like this. We have to go. I am sorry but we are leaving this island. That hurricane has changed its course and it is headed this way." John says as he walks up to Majestic. This was the first time ever that Majestic didn't want to see her dad. "These officers are escorting us to our jet. It is time to go now."

Majestic turns and looks at Ryan who then walks up to her and he hugs her. She wanted Ryan to tell her to stay but he never said that. She wanted him to say no to her father and that he would take care of her. She wanted Ryan to assure everyone that she was better off with him than leaving the island. She wanted him to say so much but instead he just hugged her tight.

"You should go." Ryan whispered in Majestic's ear.

"I don't want to leave you. This is not how it is supposed to end. Those past three weeks was not leading up to this. No, this is not how it is supposed to end." Majestic says as shock begins to set in because now she was no longer in control of this situation. She thought she had control when Ryan gave in to her wishes and let her stay. Now she has lost all of that control and that scared her because she is facing the fact that she has to leave the island. There was so much she still wanted to say and do and now those opportunities are going away quickly and she is powerless to stop it.

"This is not the end."

"I am leaving the island. We never spoke about what we wanted to do for the future. What about us?"

"Baby we have to go. I am sorry." John said as he grabbed Majestic's arm.

"Let's go ma'am. There is no more time." The police officer says as he opened the door and motioned for her to come.

That was exactly how it felt to Majestic. "No more time," kept on replaying over in her ears. She was crushed that after all the happiness shared that the end to the fairytale was cut short. She didn't want to cry but she couldn't stop it. If this was going to be the last time she would see Ryan she at least wanted him to know she really cared about him.

"Don't let it end like this, please don't. Ryan, I love you." Majestic says as she jerks away from John and runs and hugs Ryan. Ryan gave her one last kiss.

"I love you too. I will call you, I promise. If it's the last thing…"

All of a sudden a second siren went off. A beeping sound went off from Ryan's front pocket of his jeans. He quickly gets it out and it was a small white pager like device and it was beeping.

"I need to get to Vera Courts now. Can anyone of you men come with me?" Ryan asks his employees and they all said yes.

"We are headed that way, you can follow our escort as far as you need to." The police officer says as he motions for everyone to leave. As if on cue the power goes completely out.

Majestic's heart really dropped now. The power had gone off and the sirens are blaring. This was a full-blown emergency and they were stuck in the middle of it. They were on different spectrums of it. She was leaving the island to avoid it and Ryan was about to be stuck right in the middle of it. She was almost ok with leaving because she knew that Ryan was going to go someplace safe and ride the hurricane out. Now she knows differently because she didn't expect Ryan to have to go out in the weather and especially not to Vera Courts. Not after he told her that place is a sitting target for hurricanes.

"What do you mean; you have to go to Vera Courts?" Majestic said as everyone walked towards the front door.

"Majestic, you know I am one of the coordinators of the response team. It's my responsibility to get over there; I signed up for it. Besides, Sebastian, Erin, Juanita and most of my staff are there. I need to be there for them."

"Please be careful. Tell Juanita, Sebastian and Erin I said I love them." Majestic says as she was pulled outside in the rain. The rain was coming down really hard now and the visibility was faint. She was getting soaked again but she didn't care. She wanted to stay and she didn't care about any hurricane that was coming. She wanted to just sit down, Indian style, right on the sidewalk and hold her ground. Hurricane or not, she wasn't leaving her man, but it seemed that was only a thought. She was pulled into a police van that was really a cargo van with a police logo on it. Inside the van were Renee, Patrick and Tracee, who were all in the first row huddled together. In the back two seats was their entire luggage. Majestic squeezed into the front row and John sat on some luggage in the second row.

"Let's hurry up please." Renee says as the officers got in their seats. "They said that the hurricane could be here within an hour and I don't want to take any chances with that."

Majestic felt like she wanted to throw up. She literally felt like her stomach was churning. This was not the ending she wanted. In no way was this vacation supposed to end with a hurricane coming and forcing her to leave at a moment's notice. Her ending she predicted was Ryan and her professing their love for one another, deciding to be together and doing whatever it took to make that happen. Instead she felt so weird to be leaving all of a sudden. This ending did not sit well with her at all. It was so strange and out of place since the whole three weeks prior had been perfect. She begins to cry quietly and she tried to keep the tears inside and not to make a sound, but it didn't happen. Renee noticed she was starting to cry so she leaned over and began to caress her head. Majestic needed any type of encouragement right now. She could only think about being pulled away from Ryan and not even being able to say a proper goodbye. She knew what she would eventually say but that was supposed to have been days away. She was ill prepared to leave at a moment's notice.

"I know you are sad, baby, but we had to leave. For the safety of everyone we had to go. I wish we didn't have to, but we had no choice." Renee said as she continued to caress Majestic's head. Even though she needed encouragement, Majestic knew nothing that anyone could say would truly help. The only person who could help her now was in a car behind them going to risk his life to help others. What did she expect him to do? Fight for her to stay and possibly be put at risk of danger? Go with her, leave the island and leave everything behind? So many questions and none of them seem to be the right one. Would anything have made this situation better? Majestic was feeling firsthand what love was all about. Not the pain she was feeling, but the sacrifice. The sacrifice that the person you care about means so much to you that the only thing that will bring you peace is to make sure they are ok. Ryan is sacrificing everything to go and help a community of people for no other reason than the fact that he cares so much about them. Any other wealthy, successful person would not sacrifice their life and the possibility of dying when they have so much. Ryan didn't think twice about putting his life in danger and that is what scared her the most. She knew he would die for others to live.

"There he goes," The police officer said who was on the passenger side, looking out the window. "Your friend just turned off to go to Vera Courts." The police officer looked back at Majestic who could only shake her head. She didn't know the fine details about last year when his parents and fiancée died. All she knew was the weather was bad and someone crossed over into their lane and killed them. A little over a year later, could that be his fate as well? Majestic doesn't know why she thought of that, but it didn't help her at all; it only made her feel worse. She doesn't know why she is thinking so negatively. Maybe it was because she cared so much for him that any thought of losing him is making her think bad thoughts. She wanted to fight the bad thoughts off as she cried harder.

"Majestic, it is going to be alright. God will watch over him. He is one of the chosen ones put here to help others. It is not his time to go. Everything will be alright. He is just going to watch over Sebastian and Erin and be there for them." Renee said as she hugged Majestic to try to console her. Majestic couldn't stop crying; she felt so hurt by what had taken place. For the first time in thirty-four years she was close to beginning the relationship she had always wanted. Now she didn't know if it would happen. Now things are back to being uncertain and without closure. That was something she didn't want to face again, but now that it happened again, she felt unprepared. She was prepared to say the speech she wrote to let Ryan know that she was ready to spend the rest of her life with him. Now the speech had to wait. The only thing she could hold on to was the fact that God was in control of this situation. That brought her comfort but she still wouldn't know the outcome until God revealed it, and that scared her the most.

"How much longer until we arrive at the airfield?" Tracee asked as she held on to Patrick. The wind was very strong and they could feel the van being pushed around on the road.

"About ten minutes. We have to quickly get your plane loaded and then you are off. The pilot has been notified right?" The police officer driving asked.

"Yes. He is ready to go." John said from the back seat.

Now it was really beginning to hit Majestic that she was about to leave. Majestic tried to recall good memories from the past three weeks to help her right now but nothing came to mind. All she kept on thinking about was the quick goodbye and many unanswered questions. No concrete answers to questions and no certainty of the future. All she knew was that the vacation was officially over and she couldn't help but wonder if the same went for her and Ryan.

*   *   *

"It has been two weeks since the level five hurricane hit Velacious Island." Majestic said to Joan as they watched the CNN report about the devastation. "I haven't heard a word from Ryan. I don't know if he is alive or hurt somewhere, buried under some destroyed building. I don't know anything and it is killing me. I just need to know if he is alive that is all I am asking for at this point."

"I can't believe that they still don't have power to over 50% of the island. That is so sad to watch all those people suffer."

"I have called his cell phone, his house phone and the restaurant's phone and all are still disconnected. I tried the Gila Hotel, where I stayed, and they are disconnected as well." Majestic said as she wiped the tears from her eyes. This was becoming second nature to her to just cry and hope that all was well.

"I sure hate to hear that. Wasn't the restaurant the last place you said you saw him?" Joan asks as she turned up the volume on the television.

"Sort of; he was in his car going to Vera Courts. That was the part of the island he was responsible for in case of an emergency. He wanted to get there so badly. That little boy Sebastian, Erin and Juanita all live there or did live there. The part that Ryan went to go and help secure was one of the areas that were hit the hardest. Hurricane Alley." Majestic said as she began to cry. She had cried so much over the past two weeks. On the flight leaving the island she was a wreck. She went to the back of the plane. She basically curled up into a ball and cried. She didn't want anyone to say anything to her. Majestic only wanted to be left alone. When the plane landed she nearly forgot most of her luggage because she was in such a hurry to get home and turn on CNN or the Weather Channel to see if there were any updates to what was taking place. She stayed up the whole night trying to follow what was going on. It took her three days before she was able to go to work. Even then all she had been able to do was check for updates. If it wasn't on television, then it was on her computer, and even then she was checking on her cell phone too. She knew the first week was going to be hard but she figured that as the days went by she would feel better, but that hadn't been the case. Everyday had been just as hard as the day before.

"Hurricane Alley? No the hurricane was called, "Hurricane Sue." Joan says as she points to the television screen that had the hurricane's name on it.

"No the place Ryan was going to was called, "Hurricane Alley." It was called that because that place was known for being hit by hurricanes. The part that makes me sad is that was also the part where the islanders lived. Sebastian, Erin, Juanita and most of Ryan's staff lived there. They lived right near the water with these huge apartment complexes. Any hurricane or tidal wave could come and tear it to pieces and by the looks of it, it did."

Majestic was beside herself. All she could picture was Erin and Sebastian, scared and crying, trapped somewhere probably calling her name. The thought of that really made her cry and she had to leave the front area and go upstairs to her office.

"I will handle things out here for you," Joan said as Majestic gave her the thumbs up and closed her office door. She just slumped down, right in front of her door.

She started to hit the back of her head on the door, over and over again.

"Why did I have to leave?

"Why did I have to leave?"

Majestic kept on saying that over and over as she continued to hit the back of her head on the door. Not knowing was the worst feeling in the world. She wished she was there; at least she would have answers and would have been able to cope a whole lot better than she is right now. Now she was in no shape to take care of herself or run a gallery. All of her days have been cut short as she tried to be strong and take care of her business. She left early from work everyday. Today she thought she would make it to the end of the day, but as of right now, that wouldn't be happening.

"Why can't I get a grip?"

"Why can't I get a grip?"

Majestic had to keep asking herself questions because that way she wouldn't cry because her mind was occupied. She had to find a way to be able to function. She knew she couldn't keep on doing this everyday.

"Peace of mind, God that is all I am asking for." Majestic said as she picked herself up off the floor. She walked to her desk and she touched the mouse so her computer's screensaver would go away. CNN's website was still up. The website was still running the same tape that they had already ran the previous two days. Majestic had that loop memorized so she knew what was going to happen next so she minimized the website. Immediately she saw the picture she had saved to her desktop. It was the picture where she first met Sebastian and Erin. They were standing outside of Vera Courts. Looking at the picture now it was definitely a family portrait to Majestic. She knows she would have loved to have Sebastian and Erin as her son and daughter. They were the sweetest children with the biggest hearts. They were so mature but they still had their childlike innocence. Now she was looking at Ryan and oh how she missed him so. The thought that she might not ever get to see him again hurt the most. Now she was really mad for time lost over the years. She enjoyed spending time with him because every moment was so special. She knew that she loved him and hated that she never really told him how much or deep her love was for him. She thought she would get around to it but it just never happened. She also never thought a hurricane would come and force her to leave the island. Before the hurricane, they had planned to spend her last day together talking about the choices they were going to have to make. The choices were to be together and merge their lives, or stay good friends and live their separate lives. Majestic knew what her choice was but she didn't know Ryan's. If it was his choice to not be with her, she felt she could live with that. At least she would know the reason why. She can't live with the fact that she might not ever know if he wanted to be with her or not. He was everything she wanted in a man; he was very sweet and caring to her the whole time. He showered her with love and took very good care of her. He treated her like she was special and he made her feel like no one else mattered. Looking at the picture now made her long for his touch. Even a simple hug from him would make her day. Anything was better than nothing at all. No calls, no emails, no nothing. Not that all of that would be possible anyway, since most of the island had no telecommunication capabilities at the moment. Still, that is what gave her the most hope, the fact that he couldn't communicate with her. So she felt like maybe he was still alive but couldn't let her know. Maybe he was somewhere in a shelter and safe. He probably had Sebastian, Erin and Juanita with him and they were all safe. They were trying to call her and they were just as worried as she was. They wanted to call her and they were waiting patiently just as she should. The thought of that had helped her spirits and she was able to gain some composure. She began to think back to the day that they took Sebastian and Erin shopping. They were so happy to go and Majestic felt so glad to have taken them. She knew she wanted to do something, but she couldn't think of what she should do. Shopping seemed to be a good start. It made her day when Erin told her that was the best day she ever had. Majestic must have smiled that whole night. That was what she missed most about not being able to know if they were ok. She just wanted to hear their voices and know that they were well. So as Majestic was about to close her computer down, an icon appeared at the bottom right corner of the screen. It was the new email alert. She quickly went to her email to check and see who sent it. She received an update from the Emergency Update Team. It was a free service she subscribed to that would update her on any new happenings. So she was nervous while opening it. She skimmed over it, looking for any words that showed a sign of hope. She found one promising piece of information. She read that the island would have 84% power by next week. That gave Majestic more hope, as she would at least be able to know something by next week, if not sooner. Her cell phone rang suddenly.

"Hey Tracee," Majestic said as she answered.

"Majestic, how are you today?"

"I am better. I am trying to take it day by day."

"That is all you can do. I take it you haven't heard anything."

"Nothing so far. I received an email."

"From Ryan?" Tracee asked as she started to get excited.

"I wish. I subscribed to the Emergency Team's website and they send me updates on how things are going. I got an email today saying that over 84% of the island is going to have power by next week."

"That is great Majestic; hopefully you will hear something then."

"I know. Believe me I know they will definitely have power up at the resorts and since his restaurant is over there, he should be able to have power restored. The government is going to make sure they have means to make money again, so they will do everything in their power to make sure that area is up and running again."

"Right. Ok then that is definitely some good news. Since you have received that news do you want to go to lunch?"

"No Tracee, I am swamped at work. I won't have time to leave." Majestic responded, as she looked around her office at all the pictures she had gotten developed. She knew that she has to start deciding which ones are going into an exhibit and which ones weren't. That was a long drawn-out process that takes at least a week or two. At the rate she has been working since she came back from her vacation, it would probably take a good month.

"I knew you were going to say that so that is why I am outside your office door."

Majestic got up and walked to her office door and opened it. There stood Tracee with lunch for her and Majestic.

"You are not going to keep avoiding everyone. You have to get back to living your life, Majestic." Tracee said as she walked in and set the food on the coffee table. Majestic closed her office door and walked to where Tracee was taking the food out of the bag.

"I know, I keep telling myself that," Majestic said as she sat on the couch next to the coffee table.

"You have to do more than just tell yourself, you have to make yourself believe that it is true," Tracee said as she handed Majestic her salad. She sat down next to Majestic.

"You have to do everything the way you normally did it before the vacation. Your body knows what you do when you feel good and when you don't. Your body will react certain ways when things happen in your life that is good and bad. That is why it is easy to get up early when you have something to do and you are excited about it. When you don't want to face what you have to do, you will feel crummy and tired. That is you right now, crummy and tired," Tracee said as she began to eat her salad. Majestic was trying to eat her salad but it has been so hard these last two weeks and right now was no different.

"I know. Every night when I go to bed, I pray that I am able to begin to be normal again. I go to bed and I toss and turn. When I finally get some sleep, I wake up and I feel bad and then I wonder why I feel bad. It is because I am still worried about the unknown. If I could just have any news, I would begin to feel much better. At this point, bad news would give me some comfort. At least I would know the answers to my questions. As of right now, I am thinking the worst," Majestic said as she played with her food.

"Why would you think the worst? Why can't you at least be positive?"

"I try not to think negatively, but I can't help it. I want to think that they are okay, but since I haven't had any sign, I just feel like all is lost."

"Majestic, as much faith as you have in God, why is it so hard to believe that everything is fine?"

"My faith isn't shaken because my mind believes without a doubt they are okay. That is why I haven't gone over the deep end. No, it's my heart that is the problem. My heart is hurting because it has experienced love for the first time and now, for the moment, it has been taken away. My heart isn't as strong as my mind. My heart has been protected and has never been unguarded like I had it for Ryan and even Sebastian and Erin. I acted as if I was going to be there everyday with them for the rest of their lives. I didn't focus on the fact that I was visiting them. I thought of it as we were a family and that brought me happiness. I know it has only been a few weeks of knowing them, but the fact that I put everything into spending time and getting to know them was what sped things up. After the second week of being there it was as if all the feelings I had for Ryan came rushing back and it was as if we had been dating for years. It was as if we never missed a beat. I wanted to be with him, I wanted to tell him that I loved him; I wanted to be his everything. I could not believe that I let someone like that get away."

"I know you had a good time, Majestic. Mom and I talked about that all the time. We were so happy that you were back with someone special. I knew Ryan was special when he went out of his way to see that you were happy and he treated you like you were the cream of the crop. What sold me on all you guys was the fact that I watched you treat Sebastian and Erin the exact same way. I never thought you had mother tendencies in you. You looked like a mother with those children. You cared for them, you looked after them and above all you loved on those children. If the last thing those children remember is the fact that someone, who they didn't know, showed them true love. It is so easy to love a family member or a friend you have known for a long time. It is extremely difficult to look a stranger in the eye and tell them that you care for them and really mean it. You did that Majestic. You looked Sebastian and Erin in the face and you basically told them no matter how long I have known you, I care for you. I was so proud of you. I have never seen you so into anyone like I seen you with Ryan. I knew you liked him, back in the day, but you never told me that you really had feelings for him. I mean you were wrapped up in him," Tracee said as she ate.

"I was wrapped up in him. I can still remember all of those years ago when I first laid eyes on him; I knew he was different than the rest. He was so handsome and the way he moved; all of his mannerisms were special and unique. To see the huge heart he has only made it easier to fall for him all over again. I forgot how wonderful he was to everyone he knew. Ryan was selfless in his approach to everything he did. Just think about some of the things he did for me. He took me to the Heaven of Flowers. He knew I had an eye for beauty and he made sure that I experienced the beauty of that place. He took me to meet Sebastian and Erin and we all know how that turned out. He took me horseback riding. He took me to a small private beach and it was there we shared our first kiss. He made me the queen of the ball and we shared that magical dance. He showcased me around the island and made me feel like I was his. He welcomed my family and spent time with you guys as if it was nothing. Who does all of that? What man would go out of his way to impress a woman who decided years ago that he wasn't worth being with? Ryan did it because he didn't care if I appreciated it or not. All he cared about was the fact he was doing it from his heart."

"Ryan is a great man, and I mean a great man of God. I know God has his hedge of protection around him."

"I believe he does too. I just wished my heart would sync with my mind. Every time I look at these pictures of me and Ryan I get sad." Majestic said as she stood up and walked over to her large table she had in her office where she had some pictures developed from over the vacation period. "I see happy times of me and him together. This is only a memory. I don't want any memories; I want the real thing. I want to make new ones and not have to live through the old ones. I want everyday to be a new mem-ory. I just want everyday to be special again."

"They will be. You just have to regain your faith that God is taking care of everything as we speak. Maybe God is trying to see how you will react now that you have found someone special. You had plenty of time for God before you found Ryan. Once you found him, did you start lacking in spending time with God?" Tracee asked, as she flipped through the stacks of pictures. Majestic just took a moment to reflect on what she said.

"If anything, I was spending more time with God because I was thanking him every chance I got. I was happy that I was finally able to experience the joy of having someone special in my life."

"Let's just say that the worst case scenario has happened and Ryan, Sebastian and Erin are not coming back, where do you go from here? Do you just give up?" Tracee asked as she puts the pictures back down on the table. "Look Majestic, we know that you are having a rough time with this. We all are just not at the level as you but we are hurt too. You are not doing anyone any good by being all in the dumps. You have to find strength to move forward. We are all here for you and will help you every step of the way but you have to want it for yourself. Be the Majestic we all know and love. You were always the strong one and I need to see that again. You have mom and dad worried sick about you. They asked me to come here to check on you. Give me something I can tell them that is positive. You know I am not going to lie to them, so you better make me believe right now that you are okay." Tracee said as she looked in Majestic's face.

"You are right. I have been acting like there is no tomorrow. I should be better than this. Tracee I needed that from you. I have been babying myself ever since I came back. I have just been feeling sorry for myself and that has hindered me from continuing to be the person that God has made me to be."

"That is better. Move forward. You can still check on the situation but don't let it control you. Keep praying and God will give you your answers when He feels like you are ready to accept them. Right now you won't accept anything that isn't good, and you know that. When you are ready is when God is going to let you know. I think I know what will help you. You said that Ryan would find ways to help others in the midst of sadness. Do as he did when his parents and fiancée died. He went forth and took over all that they were doing. He didn't let anything die with them. He took what he gained and he shared it with others so you need to do as Ryan would do. Take what you have gotten and share it with others. You told me what all you learned from hanging around Ryan, well let's see it."

"Thank you Tracee." Majestic said as she gave her a hug. Majestic knew she couldn't continue to act the way she has been acting but no one was there telling her not to. All of her friends have been treating her like a child when it came to this situation. Majestic knew she had to bounce back and get back on track, no matter how hard it was going to be.

"I am off. I have too much work to do back at the office. I will tell mom and dad that you are better and that you are going to call them real soon."

"I am better, and I will call them."

"Bye Majestic. I love you."

"Love you too Tracee. Bye." Majestic said as Tracee turned to walk out of the office. "You can leave the door open."

Tracee smiled and opened the door and walked out. Majestic turned back to the table and she began to look over all the photos she had to go through. It had to be done, and now was as good a time as any.

"Man, this is a lot of pictures," Majestic said as she turned and walked towards her door.

"Joan, I need you." Majestic said into hallway. She faintly heard Joan acknowledge her as she walked back towards the table. Majestic knew she was way behind schedule. She had already put the exhibit on her calendar on her webpage and customers have already RSVP'd to be there.

"Majestic, do you need me?"

"Yes I do. Can you help me with these?"

"What do you need?"

"I need for you to help me decide which ones are going to go into the exhibit."

"Are you sure? You have never asked me before. I thought you liked doing them on your own," Joan said as she reminded Majestic of her old methods.

"This is the new me. I would love to share the process with you. I can see that you want to help," Majestic said with a smile.

"Ok, I am flattered. Let's do it," Joan said as she walked over to the table. Majestic saw the excitement in Joan's eyes and that brought a smile to her heart. It reminded Majestic of herself a few weeks ago. She knew how much joy she got from putting the exhibits together. Ryan never kept happiness to himself; he always shared it, and now Majestic was eager to do the same thing.

"Are you ready, because it is a long process?"

"I am so excited but yes I am ready," Joan said as she gave Majestic a quick hug.

"Ok, this is what I normally do first."

* * *

"Mom, I am right down the street. I will be there in a few minutes. Bye"

Majestic could not believe how many times her mom has called her. She knew it was way more than the norm. Even though Majestic was running late, it still didn't warrant five phone calls. Majestic made a quick stop to her house to check the mail. She had always made a habit of checking the mail. She did that because she was hoping that one day she would receive some mail that would give her some sort of closure on the Ryan situation. It has been a month since she has come back from the island and over a week and a half since all power has been restored to the island. All calls to any number she has had for Ryan have all been disconnected. She even called the Gila Hotel to see if the restaurant was still open. All calls were forwarded to a hotline number because the hotel was still under construction because of damages that occurred because of the hurricane. As far as Majestic knows, the worst has happened or that Ryan has used this as way to end it with her. She remembers Ryan saying that he promised that he would call her and she hasn't received one. So this trip she took to her house was an empty one because there was no special mail for her. So she just changed clothes and now she was ready for the get-together that her mom and dad were having at their house. Her mom kept on telling Majestic how she had invited a bunch of friends and she had a few relatives coming into town to join them. Majestic thought that was cool because it gave her a chance to see family she hadn't seen in a long time. She hadn't done much since she got back but work. She had finally been able to get back on track and now she was getting ready to show the pictures from the island in a few weeks. She was very proud of that exhibit because she could tell by the way Joan acted when she saw the pictures that everyone was going to love them. Joan was always in line with how the customers would react. If Joan really loved an exhibit, it sold well. If she was lukewarm on an exhibit, the reaction was close to her response. So as Majestic was turning on her mom's street she noticed a lot of cars, so she had to park a few houses down the street. She parked her car and she started to walk towards the house. She finally makes it to the house and she could hear everyone in the backyard laughing and listening to music. Majestic went through the front door so she could drop off the gallon of tea that she brought in the kitchen. She passed through the house and noticed that everyone was outside. So she decided to just bring the tea with her as she goes through the sliding door that leads to the backyard. Everyone noticed that it was her and they all came to greet her. It took her at least a few minutes to greet all forty two people that were there. Majestic noticed that it was all of their closest friends and family. Majestic knew something was up but she didn't know what. So she eventually got around to setting the tea down and she walked over to Tracee, who was sitting next to Patrick at the large table they had in the back yard. It was a large U and it was so big that at least sixty people could sit at it.

"Hey Tracee." Majestic said as she gave her a hug. "Hi Patrick."

"Hi Majestic. How are you doing?" Patrick asked totally catching Majestic off-guard. She wasn't used to Patrick asking her that because everyone knew that they weren't always nice to each other. He seemed to be in good mood.

"I am good and you?"

"Great. I couldn't be better actually," Patrick said as he smiled and hugged Tracee.

"Ok, what's going on Tracee?" Majestic asks as she tried to shake off the fact that Patrick was being nice.

"You are about to find out," Tracee said as she nodded her head towards Patrick. Patrick stood up and Tracee joined him. Majestic just sat there wondering what was really going on.

"We would like to thank everyone for coming out. This is a very special day for us. Tracee and I wanted you all to be here to celebrate with us. After all of our attempts to expand our family, we were finally successful. We just want to let everyone know that we are pregnant!" Patrick said as he kissed Tracee.

Majestic was so shocked. She jumped up and gave Tracee a hug before everyone else came over.

"You didn't tell me! You are wrong for that," Majestic said as she hugged Tracee again. She looked over at Patrick and he had his arms stretched out wide for her to give him a hug. Majestic knew this was a special occasion so she gave him one.

"I am so happy for you. I am going to be an aunt!" Majestic said as she touched Tracee's stomach. So how far along are you?"

"I am two months."

"Good."

"I am finally going to be a grandmother. It is about time!" Renee said as she and John walked over to hug Tracee and Patrick.

Majestic sat back down and watched everyone come up and give their congratulations to Tracee and Patrick. She could feel a little hint of jealousy creep up. Nonetheless, she was extremely happy for Tracee. She knew that one day she would be an aunt so this is a good day for her and Tracee. So as everyone was sitting down again, Majestic noticed that everyone was staring at Tracee as if she was going to say something. Patrick had already sat down so Majestic didn't know what Tracee was going to say.

"I am not the only person that has some good news," Tracee said as she tried to pull Majestic up out of the chair.

"Tracee. I don't have any news." Majestic said as she was confused about what Tracee was talking about.

"Yes you do," Tracee insisted.

"No I don't."

Majestic really had no clue why Tracee was saying she had something to say.

"Why don't you get up and tell everyone about Ryan, Sebastian, Erin, Juanita and Reagan?"

Majestic just looked at Tracee shocked. She couldn't figure out why Tracee would bring up them at a time like this.

"Tracee, why would you play with me like that? I can't believe you would ask me to do that." Majestic said as she started to get mad. It would normally take a lot to make her mad but she didn't like that fact that Tracee was asking her to tell everyone about Ryan after all she had been through. Tracee knew her pain about the whole situation so Majestic was hurt that Tracee was asking her to speak on it now.

"Tracee, you have hurt me, and I mean really badly. I just can't believe you would ask me to speak of Ryan right now," Majestic said as she fought back tears.

"It's okay. Tell them about me."

Majestic heard a familiar voice and so she turned around to see who it was. A few feet behind her stood Ryan, Sebastian, Erin, Juanita and a little girl that looked like a child version of Juanita. Majestic's mouth dropped wide open and she jumped up from her seat and jumped into Ryan's arms. She began to cry uncontrollably. She cried like never before. She was so happy to see Ryan alive that she couldn't help her emotions. She just kept on squeezing him really tight. All of the nights she stayed up worrying that he was dead were over. All the thoughts of wondering if she was ever going to see him again were over. All the thoughts of wondering if she was ever going to hug him again were over. All the thoughts of if she was ever going to kiss him again are about to be over. Majestic began to kiss Ryan on the lips over and over again, and then she started to hug him again. She totally forgot where she was and all who were there. She could only focus on the fact that Ryan was alive and standing in her arms and for that she was happy.

"My Beautiful," Ryan said as Majestic stopped hugging him and looked in his eyes.

"Say it again," Majestic asked because she had missed him saying that so much.

"My Beautiful, I missed you," Ryan said, as tears began to form in his eyes and the sight of that only made Majestic cry harder. Majestic just stared at him the best way she could with her eyes full of tears. For Ryan to be so happy to see her, that he was moved to tears melted her heart. No longer would she doubt if Ryan cared about her. A public display of emotions in front of total strangers had cleared up all doubt.

"We want a hug too," Sebastian said as he held his arm out.

"Yeah, what about us?" Erin chimed in.

Majestic looked at them and really couldn't stop her emotions now. She had prayed that they were okay. She wanted them to be alive. She couldn't imagine them having to suffer or worst: them being dead. Majestic couldn't think something so harsh could happen to two beautiful children.

"I am so happy to see you guys. I was so worried. I love you and you know that, right?" Majestic asked them because she never told them before, but she wanted them to know that she cared for them deeply.

"I love you too," Sebastian said as he gave Majestic a kiss on her cheek.

"I love you too. We are divas forever," Erin said as she kissed Majestic on her other cheek. Majestic just let the tears flow down her face when Erin said that they were divas forever. That was the little saying they made up when they were shopping together. Every time they tried on a cute outfit they would say, "Look at us, we are divas forever." So to hear Erin say it only brought back sweet memories.

Majestic was so happy because now a huge weight has been lifted off of her shoulders. All the worrying, crying, stressing, and weeping was now over. She knew they were alive. She now knows they missed and cared about her. She knows all of this because they were here now. She stood up and gave Juanita a hug.

"Juanita, I am so happy to see you. I am glad you are okay."

"Yes I made it and I am glad to be alive. I am so thankful that I got to see you."

"Who is this? Is this your daughter?" Majestic asked as she wiped the tears off her face.

"Yes, this is Reagan."

"You are so pretty," Majestic said as she gave Reagan a handshake. Reagan began to smile and she looked so much like Juanita.

"She looks just like you. She is beautiful." Majestic said as she took a step back to look at them. She wanted to just scream up to the heavens, "Thank you!!!" over and over again. The pain she was feeling was going away.

"Majestic, why don't all of you go into the house and talk? There is plenty to catch up on. We will all be here when you guys get through." Renee said as she brought Majestic a box of tissue.

"Ok, let's go in here," Majestic said as she grabbed Ryan's hand and led all of them into the living room. She had to look down at Ryan's hand to make sure it was real. How she longed to hold his hand and now she was and she wasn't going to let go.

"Everyone have a seat. Wait, let me sit here and I want you guys around me. I know that sounds crazy but I have been worried sick about you and now that you are here I want you as close to me as possible," Majestic said as she sat in the middle of the couch. Ryan sat on her right side and Juanita sat on her left. Sebastian, Erin and Reagan sat on the floor in front of her.

"I was so worried about you guys, and I mean extremely worried. I was worried day and night for all of you. I didn't know what to think. Last I remember was that terrible wind and rain. I was watching the news and it seemed like no one made it alive. I saw pictures of Vera Courts and I just knew that there was no way anyone could have survived that. I didn't want you guys to be gone. I was so scared that I was never going to see you again. I had no way of contacting any of you. I was so scared that something terrible had happened to you. I mean I cried so much. I cried everyday for you. I couldn't sleep or eat. I was a total mess and I am so happy to see you guys now," Majestic said as she fought back tears. She was so happy that they were all alive. It was like a dream for her because just thirty minutes ago she was under the impression that she would never see them again. Now they were right in front of her, and that began to soothe her heart.

"We are okay. We were very scared though," Juanita said as she put a hand on Majestic's shoulder.

"We wanted to call you but we couldn't because no phones were working. We had power but no way to call anyone," Ryan added.

"Ok, there are so many questions I have and I really don't know where to begin. Let me start here. How did you find me? I have never given you my address because we always emailed each other." Majestic asked Ryan since she never got around to giving him any info. Every time she thought about it and planned on doing it, she would get sidetracked and never got around to giving it to him. She had plans on giving it to him on their last night together but their last night never happened. That was part of the reason why she was so sick about being at home. She had never given him one piece of information on how to find her. So she really wanted to know how they found her.

"Renee gave me her information on the comment card she filled out at the restaurant. For her and John, she gave the address to her house right here, and for you, Tracee and Patrick, she put your room numbers from the hotel."

"Good thing for Ryan is that we give the comment cards to a secondary company that sends out promotional items and discount vouchers for us. Everyone that fills out a card receives something from us throughout the year. The company keeps the names and addresses in a database for us."

"Thank God for that," Majestic said as she looked up at the ceiling. Sebastian and Erin started to laugh at Majestic for doing that.

"So we were able to access that database and we pulled up Renee's address and number. We gave her a call and so now we are here." Ryan said as he kissed Majestic's hand.

"How long ago was this?" Majestic asked because since they are now here in front of her, she wanted to know how come they didn't come sooner.

"The company wasn't able to get the full list until their system was up 100% so we didn't get the number until yesterday morning." Juanita says as she looks at Ryan for confirmation.

"Why didn't my mom call me or give you my number?" Majestic asked because she wished she would have known this sooner.

"She wanted it to be a surprise for you," Erin said as she smiled her pretty smile at Majestic.

"It was a surprise, a very big one. This is the best surprise ever. I just wish I would have known that you guys were at least okay. I was so worried about all of you."

"Even Reagan?" Sebastian asks Majestic referring to the fact that Majestic never met her.

"Yes, even Reagan. I didn't know her but I still wanted her to be safe. Just as safe as you guys were or that I hoped you guys were. Now that I know you are safe, what happened with the hurricane? I saw the damage on CNN and I just kept on thinking the worst. Seeing all that devastation left me no room to think positively. Then you guys had no power for weeks, so tell me what happened and start when you let them take me from you," Majestic tells Ryan as she elbows him in the side.

"Ouch. Ok, for one I didn't let them take you. I am smart enough to know better than to take a man's daughter from him. That would have been one day that John would have shown you how much he loved you. I don't even think those police officers would have been able to protect me."

"You are silly," Majestic said as she tried to picture her dad fighting Ryan. She knew he would too, and probably to the death.

"Anyway, once I turned to go to Vera Courts I was so sad. I didn't want you to go but I needed you to go. Just the fact that I knew that you were leaving the island and that you would be safe helped me focus on what I needed to do. So I began driving towards Vera Courts and the rain was just coming down. Good thing no other vehicles were on that road with us because I was driving in the middle of the road because I was scared that I would drive off the road. On both sides of the road are huge ditches and those ditches were filling up fast with rain. So I am dodging debris and all kinds of things when I finally make it to Vera Courts. I drive up and of course there are no police officers at the gate so I took a few minutes to try to raise the gate up but it was stuck or something. So we had no choice but to get out of the car and run. Anyway so me, Marcos and the rest of the guys are running trying to find everyone. We run straight to the cafeteria because that was the spot where the emergency team felt was the safest place from the hurricane. We get there and we knock on the door because they are told to barricade it so that the wind won't tear it off the frame because that can seriously hurt someone. So they let us in and it is packed in there. How many people do you think was in there?" Ryan asked Juanita.

"I believe close to three hundred people."

"Three hundred? That cafeteria wasn't that big," Majestic said as she recalled the cafeteria being so small for it to have to cater to so many residents in the apartment complex.

"Three hundred people give or take. So they had the list ready of people that were there and the people that weren't there. On that list of people that wasn't there was Juanita, Sebastian and Erin." Ryan said, as he looked at them as he said their names.

"I wasn't there either," Reagan said as he raised her hand.

"Of course you weren't, baby. You were safe at the Stewarts' house."

"You were safer than we were. I was so scared," Sebastian said as he looked at Reagan with a face that was saying, "You'd better be thankful."

"I know. I was so scared that I was crying." Erin adds.

"So my job then was to take the list and find out if any of those people were okay. So, me, Marcos, the guys from the restaurant and about ten men from the cafeteria ran out and we split up and we went to the doors of everyone that was missing. Most of the ones on the missing list were not able to move without help so they were stranded. So we rounded up everyone that wanted to go the safety of the cafeteria. There were many people that didn't want to go; they wanted to stay in their apartment."

"Like my granny." Erin said as she interrupted Ryan.

"Oh was she okay?" Majestic asked as she remembered that Erin's granny was blind.

"We are getting to it. Well I went to Erin's apartment and that was where I found these three plus granny."

"She didn't want to go. I was crying and pleading with her to go but she wouldn't." Juanita says as she rubbed Erin's head.

"Right, so I find them there and after literally fighting with granny I was able to get her to leave the apartment. I think it was me begging her and the roof on the next unit being torn off of the building that really helped her decide that it was best that she left the apartment."

"Oh my goodness," Majestic said as he put her hand to her mouth.

"It was real loud. It sounded like a big piece of Velcro being ripped apart and when it landed on the ground, I thought it was an earthquake," Sebastian said as he fashioned his hands like a roof top to show Majestic what it looked like when it fell. Erin just shook her head in agreement.

"Yeah so to speed things up, I picked up granny and I began to carry her. That wind was throwing us around. I made Erin and Sebastian hold on to my belt loops so they wouldn't get lost behind me because I tried my best to run."

"We were all holding on to some part of him." Juanita said as she started to laugh.

"His clothes had holes in it. I could see his underwear." Erin said, as she started to giggle.

"That is another story. Anyway, good thing she lived on the first floor so we made a quick turn and we were out in the open. I mean that wind was howling and the rain was coming down so hard. It took every ounce of my strength to keep on standing. I don't know how these two made it." Ryan says as he rubs Sebastian and Erin's heads.

"We are real strong," Sebastian said as he showed off his muscles.

"So we are out in the open and we are trying to go back to the cafeteria. It was just our luck that the roof that fell off of the other apartment was blocking our way."

"Oh man. What did you do then?" Majestic asked, as the story had many twists and turns.

"Here comes the cool part." Sebastian said, as he sat up on his knees. He was getting excited.

"We had to turn around and go back to the apartment. We couldn't go around that debris; it was too much and the wind was still tearing it apart so pieces were flying around."

"A piece almost hit Sebastian," Juanita said as she grabbed his hand.

"I was too quick though. I was like dodging pieces of the roof as it was flying all around." Sebastian says as he pretends like he was dodging it again.

"It was only one piece Sebastian," Erin says as she shook her head.

"It was only piece and he didn't really dodge it, it just flew past him. Anyway, so we turned around and went back to the apartment. I decided that we were not going to stay in that apartment. The whole building seemed like it would give away at any moment. So I told them I was going to get the car and we were going to leave. We wasn't safe if we stayed and wasn't safe if we left but that was the choice I made. So I ran to the car and remember I couldn't get the gate raised the first time so this time I just rammed through it with the car and I drove all the way up to the building. I ran in the house and I grabbed granny and put her in the car and they jumped in the back. We then began to drive and it was very hard to see and the car was all over the road because it was hard to control it because of the wind."

"We were all praying out loud the whole time we were in the car," Juanita added.

"Where did you guys go? Did you go back to the restaurant?" Majestic asked because she couldn't picture them just driving around in a hurricane.

"Oh no, we drove to my house and we rode it out there, and that was a very smart thing to do. I don't know why I didn't think of that at first." Ryan said as he shook his head in disgust.

"Wow, it seems like you all had a very scary experience. How bad was the damage to Vera Courts?"

"Very bad. Most of Vera Courts is gone. The hurricane touched down at one of the other apartment complexes near Vera Courts. So the damage was horrific for all fifteen complexes." Juanita said as she fought back tears.

"Were there a lot of deaths?" Majestic asked but she could tell that it must have been a lot because of the way Juanita was getting emotional talking about it.

"Hundreds. It was bad." Ryan said as he grabbed Juanita's hand to give her some support.

"Oh my. At least you guys made it," Majestic said as she tried to help console Juanita.

"My granny didn't," Erin said, with a sad look on her face.

"What?" Majestic asks with a concerned look on her face. "I thought she was in the car with all of you when you went to Ryan's place?"

"She was with us. She ended up having a heart attack so we took her to the hospital." Juanita said as she shook her head.

"She died at the hospital a few days later," Sebastian said as he hugged Erin who began to cry.

"Erin I am so sorry. I really am." Majestic said as she motioned for Erin to come to her. "It's ok to cry Erin. Let it out and you will begin to feel better. Crying sometimes helps me," Majestic says as she kissed Erin on the forehead. Majestic felt so sorry for Erin. She has gone through so much in her ten years. Both parents are in jail and now her grandmother is dead. Majestic knew that no child should have to experience what she has gone through.

"What's going to happen to her now?"

Majestic wanted to know. She didn't want her to have to go to a foster home.

"I don't know yet. I filed papers to adopt her so it will be a matter of time before I find out anything. They are so backed up with other children they are trying to place."

"I hope they let me. I don't want to go to a foster home." Erin said as she reached for a tissue from the box that Majestic put on the floor.

"I don't want you to go either. I already have my sister in one. I don't want you in one too," Sebastian said as he put his hand on Erin's shoulder. Majestic looked at Juanita because she wanted to see if she was hurt by Sebastian's last statement. He really didn't mean anything mean by it but Majestic knew it could be hard on Juanita because it was her choice.

"What did I tell you Sebastian? I am getting your sister back." Juanita corrected him and he had a look on his face that showed that he forgot.

"That is great news Juanita. I am happy for you," Majestic said as she felt like things would begin to get better for Juanita when her children surrounded her. That will keep her motivated to do right. "Since the apartments have gotten destroyed where are you guys going to stay?" Majestic asks Juanita.

"For the time being, we are staying at Ryan's place."

"That is awesome. That is much better than staying at those apartments. Besides, there is plenty of room at Ryan's house for all of you."

"That will definitely help me out until I get a job."

"Why would you need to get a job? Are you not going to be working at the restaurant anymore?" Majestic asked Juanita.

"There is no more restaurant."

"Ryan you are kidding?" Majestic said, as she was trying to see if Ryan was joking.

"The hurricane tore the restaurant to pieces. All of that glass didn't stand a chance. I went to go and check things out and it took me a minute to find where the restaurant was supposed to be, because all of the buildings on that row were destroyed. I couldn't salvage anything because of all the damage. I couldn't believe that it wasn't there anymore."

"Ryan that is so terrible. That was your parent's dream and I can't believe it is gone." Majestic felt terrible about that news. She loved that restaurant and all of the memories she had there were all gone.

"It looked like someone took some dynamite and just demolished the place, the whole area as a matter of fact. It was like a bad joke, you know like someone moved the restaurant and was hiding it from me. I was speechless when I pulled up. I actually knew it was the restaurant because of the large seashell in the front entrance was still there. It wasn't hidden or anything and that was the only proof I had to where the restaurant used to be."

"All that hard work you and your parents put into it and it is gone now. So all of the employees are going to have to find work now, and that is terrible," Majestic said as she thought about how well everyone was taken care of when they worked for Ryan but now they are going to go back to making the minimum working for someone else.

"I know. I lost the restaurant but I still feel sorry for those that used to work there and are now out of work. At a time like now where everyone needs a job, there is going to be a lot of people out of work."

Majestic was sick. She could only think back to how beautiful and unique the restaurant was. That place was one of a kind and now it is gone.

"Oh baby, I am so sorry about that. I really am because I know that place was special to your family. What are you going to do now?"

"The insurance company came out and they accessed the damage. My parents had great insurance on it and we paid a very high premium to have hurricane damage so my parents were very prepared if something like this happened."

"Ryan that is good to know. At least you will be able to get the money and build the restaurant back." Majestic said, as she felt that would be the best thing to do. She looked at Ryan to see if he agreed but he only looked away.

"I don't think I am building the restaurant again."

"What? Why not?"

"Majestic that was my parent's vision. They knew exactly what they wanted and how to get it done. I have no clue on how to do any of what they did. It would be extremely expensive to do the restaurant they way they did it because the price of everything has gone up. Everyone will be scrambling for supplies to build their buildings back up. Not to mention that since I have filed the claim on the restaurant, trying to get insurance to cover it again would cost me twice as much and I can't afford that. So this allows me to start over and that is what I plan on doing."

"So what are you going to do?" Majestic asked, because she was curious to know what he was going to do.

"I was thinking maybe I could move here and do what I should have done years ago, and that is being right by your side," Ryan says as he smiled.

"For real? You'd better not be lying." Majestic sat up straight, showing her excitement.

"I am serious. I want to be with you. I want us to be together because I don't want to experience losing you again. I remember how painful it was and now I know it would be twice as hard. So I want to be with you if you would have me?"

"Of course I would have you. I love you so much and I am not going to let this opportunity pass me by. You are all I want, so yes I will have you and I wouldn't want anything else. I want you to be with me so that is perfectly ok with me."

Majestic was so ecstatic that Ryan was going to move to Las Vegas. She felt bad that he had to lose everything in order for him to come, but she was happy that it was going to happen and that is a real dream coming true.

"But, there is a catch."

"I don't care what it is, as long as you are going to be here then I don't care."

"I come with baggage," Ryan said, as he pointed to Juanita, Sebastian, Erin and Reagan.

"I wouldn't have it any other way. Las Vegas is big enough for all of you."

"Yeah!" Erin and Sebastian shouted at the same time. Reagan joined in and Majestic felt like she didn't really know why everyone was yelling but she joined in anyway.

"Are you sure? I don't want to impose on you and Ryan. I can find work and stability in Velacious." Juanita said. Majestic thought that she probably felt like she was a burden.

"No Juanita that is no problem. I would love for you to come too. Besides I could use another sister."

"Me too," Juanita said as she gave Majestic a hug.

Majestic thought back to when she prayed to God about doing something for Sebastian and Erin. She thought about how nothing came to mind. God was preparing her heart and life for what was taking place now. She knew that she had to show herself ready to take on love at its fullest. She only wanted personal love shared between two people; instead, God gave her real love that is shared by all. She felt the tears swelling up in her eyes again. A few weeks ago she was so depressed and sad that she didn't ever think that she would be happy again. Now she was sitting here surrounded by her new family. She couldn't imagine how she had enjoyed life without them before. They brought so much joy and happiness to her.

"Don't cry, Majestic. We are going to be a family," Erin said as she handed Majestic a tissue. The sound of her sweet voice only made it harder to stop crying.

"I love you Erin. I love you all. I haven't even known you guys that long, but I when I tell you that I love you, I mean it. I was so alone before the vacation. I had no one to call my own. I was sad and I would pray to God that one day I would experience love. When I got to the island my only plan was to get pictures and sit at the beach. God's plan was for me to find you guys and begin a bond that will last forever. So I say that to say I am glad that you all are a part of my life and we have a long road ahead of us. We have to work on adoptions; we have to move everyone out here, find a house, and put you guys in school so you see we have our work cut out for us."

"I want a house with a big backyard," Sebastian said as he began to think about a house.

"I want a puppy," Reagan said as she started thinking about the house.

"No, six puppies," Erin said as she smiled at Ryan.

"One thing at a time; let's just work things out. We are still leaving in a week to go home and finish business on our end. We have a ton of stuff to take care of. We will discuss puppies and things of that nature later."

"You guys are leaving in a week?" Majestic said as she started to feel sad. She didn't want them to go away so soon. She just got them back, and now they would have to go.

"Oh yeah, we were allowed to take Erin and Reagan for a week. They want us back and we don't want to do anything to jeopardize the adoptions. So we have to go. Believe me; none of us want to go. You should see how the island looks and I don't want any part of that. It looks nothing like it did before."

"Well I am happy to see you guys and I will make the most of you all being here."

"Well, can we eat because I am starving?" Sebastian asked as he stood up and held his stomach.

"Yes, let's go." Majestic said as she stood up and pulls up Ryan.

"Majestic."

"Hey Tracee," Majestic said as Tracee stuck her head in through the open sliding door.

"Bring your family out here; everyone wants to get to know them, so stop hogging them," Tracee said as she stuck her tongue out. Majestic just smiled because this was truly a happy day for her. Her burden had been lifted. They were indeed alive and in due time they are all going to be by her side.

"Let's go, family," Majestic said, as she led the way through the sliding door. She let everyone go through but she stopped Ryan.

"I want you to know you have just made me the happiest I have been in years. I promise you I will do all

I can to make sure that your decision to come out here for me is well worth it. I want us to be together and I am committed to you forever."

"You can best believe that we are going to make this work. We are destined for this and we will see it through."

"I love you Ryan."

"I love you too."

Ryan says as Majestic kisses him. She has waited to hear him say that for a month now. That was the longest month of her life. All the time she was worried about them, they were safe. They were waiting on the chance to come and see her. They wanted her and now they want to be with her. Majestic knew that she was so blessed to be in the position she was in right now. All the crying and doubting God on what he was doing for her had her feeling bad. She knew better, but this was dealing with an issue of her heart and she didn't know how to handle it. Her heart had never been broken before. Ryan was the closest thing to love that she had felt, and that was thirteen years ago. Now that those feelings were back and she was focusing on them, it was hard for her not to wonder about the worst because something so good couldn't be meant for her. Nothing dealing with love that was good was meant for her, and that was how she truly felt. So many failures at love had her skeptical about it being true. Now that Ryan was back in her life and love was their focus, she had a new outlook on love and the goodness of it.

Majestic was nervous, and she hasn't been this nervous in years. She wanted this night to be a memorable night. Tonight was the night she was going to show her new exhibit. This exhibit was of the pictures of her vacation at Velacious Island. After all that had taken place there, she wanted this to be extra special. She had so many pictures to choose from and she really wanted to display all of them. Normally an exhibit would be twenty to twenty five pictures, but this time she made this exhibit her largest ever, because she had seventy-five pictures. In her estimate, these were the best of the best. Thanks to Joan being there, she was able to narrow her choices down. After all, she had over five thousand photos to choose from. She had taken so many pictures that it was next to impossible to display all of them. She feels good about the pictures that were chosen. She felt that they made a strong showing of the island and that everyone who showed up would be thoroughly impressed with them. She invited all of her family, friends and normal clients. She extended the invitation further to invite members of the media too. She knew that she might have some of the only professional pictures of the island the way it once was. The island was going through a major overhaul since the hurricane three months ago, so she probably had pictures that anyone who has visited the island before would want to cherish. She knows the memories she had gotten from visiting the island were priceless and she would pay anything to relive them again. So Majestic was hoping that she could instill that into everyone who came tonight. She had some very important guests that she really wanted to impress. Ryan, Sebastian, Erin, Juanita and Reagan were all coming in to see the exhibit and that was where her nervousness stemmed from. She wanted them to enjoy the exhibit especially because they were in it. She took extra special care to make sure she got the best shots of them in the exhibit. This was once their home and probably the only lasting image left, because all of their things were destroyed with Vera Courts. They lost everything from clothes, toys, pictures and any other thing they had. That was a sad situation for them. Majestic knew that had to be disheartening. They really didn't have much to begin with, but it was theirs and that was all that mattered. Majestic knew that she had to step in and do something about that. So Majestic has been sending them money to buy clothes and things of that nature. She really didn't need to because Ryan was still well off, but she wanted to contribute anyway because she cared dearly for them. So Majestic really wanted them to love the pictures as much as she loved them. All of the bragging she did to her family and friends was now going to be seen firsthand, so there is no way the exhibit should let them down. She wanted this night to be better than any other one she had hosted in the past. She has had some great exhibits in the past so she is hoping that this one exceeded them. This exhibit was more personal to her because this was where she felt like life began for her. She wasn't fully alive until she found love again and realized that it was what she needed. There was no way she was going to have any excuses why she couldn't enjoy love. No distance was going to stop her; no one could tell her anything different, and there was no way she was changing how she felt.

"Majestic, you look beautiful," Joan said as she walked up and stood behind Majestic as she was fixing her hair in the mirror. Majestic was just double-checking herself to make sure she looked her best. Majestic took a page out of Tracee's book and wore a dress that was different from her usual taste. This dress was all white and it went down a little below her knees. It wasn't tapered off at the bottom in a straight line; it was tapered like a jagged edge. The dress was semi-hugging her all the way down and it hung off of one of her shoulders. It was classy and a little sexy. Majestic felt it was very tasteful and something she didn't mind wearing for Ryan. She had straightened her curls out so her hair was all the way down to the bottom of her back. It was nice and straight and it had a nice shine to it. Majestic felt very beautiful and she was happy with how tonight was starting off.

"Joan you look beautiful as well," Majestic said, as Joan turned around to show off her white dress.

"Thank you. So what's the game plan now?" Joan asked as she stepped up to the mirror as Majestic walked away from it.

"Ok, so are people coming in already?" Majestic asked as she walked to her computer to check her emails.

"Yes, we have about thirty five people here already."

"We did rope off the area of our new exhibit right?"

"We did. We have the spotlights shining on the curtains where the new displays are. Everything is in place. I just got through checking it all so that was why I came up here." Joan says as she applies lipstick to her lips.

"Well, we are good to go," Majestic said as she shut down her computer.

"Can I tell you something Majestic?" Joan says as she walks over to Majestic's desk.

"You know you can Joan."

"I just want to thank you for letting me help you with the exhibit. You don't realize how much that meant to me. I have walked this gallery a thousand times and I just felt like I wanted to do an exhibit too. I want to get that rush you get when someone loves a picture and just has to have it. I want the satisfaction of knowing that I made it possible for them. I would love to help you more often and I hope that I am not overstepping my place."

Majestic could see the seriousness and the passion in Joan's eyes. It was there for Majestic when she first started doing the exhibits. She still gets the chills when an exhibit is displayed and she gets the overload of relief when people love it. She can understand Joan wanting to be a part of such an ordeal.

"Joan, there will be plenty of opportunities for you to have your own exhibits. When Ryan moves down here, my hours are going to be cut short. I won't spend countless hours here. I will finally have me someone and I want to be there for him. The reason why I didn't let anyone help is because I had nothing else to do besides work on exhibits. Besides, you never expressed to me the desire to want to help out so now that I know that, I will bombard you with ideas and ways to make new exhibits as well as upgrade the ones we have now. Are you ready for that?"

"I am ready. You will see, I can't wait to get started!" Joan said as she walked over to Majestic and gave her a hug.

"Let's pray. Then we can go down there and knock their socks off with our exhibit."

"You know it." Joan said as they held hands. Majestic prayed that the night be all about God and that His love would be seen and shared with all who saw the exhibit tonight. Majestic wanted the very essence of God's love to be felt and for her which would make this exhibit the best ever.

"Ladies, we are getting packed down here. Most of the guests are here and I just got a phone call from the limo driver and your special guests should be here in a minute."

"Has my family shown up yet?"

"Yes Majestic, your family is here and are mingling with the guests."

"Thank you Lorenzo. We are on our way down." Majestic said as she walked back towards the mirror for one last check.

"Is he talking about Ryan?"

"He is. I am so excited about him being here tonight."

"You should be. Ryan is a great guy and you deserve someone that will treat you right and love you with all his heart. I get that impression from Ryan and I am happy for you."

"Thank you Joan. I am happy that God has allowed us to be reunited but this time, I am not going to let him go. I have learned my lesson the first time. No repeats here. I am going to love Ryan with every ounce of energy that I have left in me. I will make up for lost time."

"Good. You have so much love in you just waiting to be shared. I know you will make the most of this relationship and I only hope the future is as wonderful as you are." Joan said as she smiled at Majestic. Majestic remembered that Joan had been there through the frustrations of Majestic's dating past. She has been an ear, at times, for Majestic as she vented about how terrible things were going for her when she was dating.

"Joan, I feel the same way because it has been a long time coming for me. I have watched you and Tracee enjoy your marriages and I have always wondered when it was going to be my turn. I feel like my turn is finally coming around, and that excites me. I do thank you for always being there for me. You have always been like a sister to me, and I know that this is my first time mentioning it but it is long overdue. You gave up a lot to join me here at the gallery. You have been here through the months when I couldn't pay you and you have watched us rebound in a major way. Through it all you never lost faith in me and my vision, and I do appreciate that."

"Majestic, it was easy because God spoke to me a long time ago. He told me that there would be a time when I will step out on faith and realize that money isn't everything. I left a moneymaking machine in sales, and I came here to make enough to live paycheck to paycheck. The funny thing about it was I was so happy and stress-free. I had been praying to God to help me with sleepless nights and worrying about my next sale. I told him that if

He would give me piece of mind, I would trade it all for that. Believe me, he did just that. Now that we are doing very well, and I am not living paycheck to paycheck; I can look back and be happy that I had listened when God spoke and I stepped out on faith to gain what was truly mine. So I say that to say I love being here, and I love working with you. We are sisters and I am so glad that what we share here is a blessing for all," Joan said as she wiped a lone tear from her eye. Majestic cherished Joan and respected her so much. Here was a woman that believed in Majestic when at times Majestic didn't believe in herself. Majestic realized what an amazing example Joan was of a true friend.

"Look at you. Don't make me cry Joan, because this is supposed to be a happy night. Now I have to check my makeup and make sure everything is fine," Majestic said, as she walked back over to the mirror.

"You look fine, Majestic," Joan said as she grabbed Majestic's arm and pulls her into the hallway outside of her office. There was a small ten-foot hallway outside of her office that led to a spiral staircase, which ended in the gallery. Once she got to the stairs, she could see the whole gallery; it was packed. She followed Joan down the staircase and began to greet everyone. Good thing for her she knew everyone by name, so it felt extra special to be surrounded by close friends and family on such a special moment as this. Her grand display nights were always something she took extra pride in. She made it into a great event that everyone that came would cherish the moments forever. So as Majestic was making her way through the crowd, she saw her family.

"Good evening, Mom and Dad," Majestic said as she kissed her mom and dad on the cheek.

"Good evening lady, of the hour," Renee said as she smiled at Majestic.

"Baby, you look stunning," John added.

"Thank you for the compliment and thank you for coming. I am so excited about this night; I just want everything to be perfect.

"So do we baby," Renee said as she grabbed Majestic's hand. "This night will be so special for us."

"I hope so," Majestic said as she lay her head on her mom's shoulder.

"Look who decided to be sexy tonight," Tracee said as she walked up with Patrick.

"Hey Tracee," Majestic gave her a hug.

"Majestic, everything looks good in here." Patrick said as he waited his turn for a hug.

"Thank you." Majestic gave him a hug.

"So are the symptoms still getting to you?" Majestic asked Tracee because the first few months had been rough on her with her pregnancy.

"I am getting better. I have my good and bad days," Tracee said as she smoothed down Majestic's hair. "Look at you. Girl, you went all out tonight. Your hair is so pretty."

"I wanted to do something different tonight."

"Well, you definitely did that and you pulled it off too."

"Thanks Tracee. I don't want to be rude but I have to finish mingling."

"Go, we will be around," Renee said as she held John's hand and walks away.

"We will see you later on." Tracee and Patrick walked away.

"See you guys later."

Majestic was happy that her family was here. They don't always make it out to all of her events, but tonight was a very special one so Majestic hounded them to come. She wanted to share this night with them and so they made her night better by showing up. She began to finish her rounds. She made sure she spoke to every person there. She always went out of her way to do that. She felt that everyone here was special to her, so she wanted to make sure that they felt the same way. She saw a large gathering where the new exhibit was to be shown. She moved out a large section of the gallery. There was normally a moveable wall that held exhibits on both sides of it. Majestic had the wall removed so they could add chairs in that area. Since the whole front section was just windows, it looked like a grand display from the street view. Even if people didn't get in to view the exhibit, they could still see it from the street. Since nights like this was by invitation only, she knew she would still attract a large crowd on the outside of the gallery. That usually gets her really excited because that meant that everyone was excited as well. A lot of her high paying customers were standing by the exhibit, and that was a good sight to see. Majestic was getting great comments from everyone here. They were all eager to see the photos and that was a good sign. Majestic never doubted her exhibits. She was extremely confident in her pictures so she knew that everyone would love them as well.

"Majestic, your guests are here," Lorenzo said, as he pointed outside the window to a black limo pulling up. Majestic paid college students to stand outside and snap pictures of all the guests as they arrived. About ten of them ran to the curb where the limo was pulling in.

"Thank you Lorenzo," Majestic said as she walked to the front entrance of the gallery. She wanted to see them as they got out of the limo. She hadn't seen them in two months since they went home to work on the adoption process and to get things in order. She was so ecstatic that they were here that she wanted to see their faces when they exited the limo. So as the limo pulled to a stop, Majestic was standing at the end of the red carpet by the front entrance. There were people walking down the sidewalk and driving by that stopped just to see who would get out of the limo. So as the driver walked over to open the door, Majestic was got excited. First out of the limo was Erin, and she looked like a little angel. She was so pretty in her little white dress with the bow in the front of it. Her hair was not in braids any more; it was combed into a cute style. She was so pretty and Majestic's heart was moved when she seen her. She watched her get out of the limo and she immediately began to smile. It was as if she knew what to do because as the college students began to snap pictures, she would stop and pose for them. She was like a little star. By the look of the smile on her face, Majestic knew she was enjoying the attention. Next, Sebastian exited the limo in his black suit with a white shirt and black tie. He looked so handsome. He had cut off his Mohawk and now his hair was just nicely cut into a fade. He was just as photogenic as Erin as he smiled. He also walked, stopped and posed. Majestic was so thrilled to see them play along. She was happy because they acted like they have been doing this their whole lives. So as they came closer to Majestic, she couldn't help herself as the tears formed in her eyes. Three months ago, these children lives were turned upside down and now they were living life to the fullest. She still remembers the apartments and the atmosphere of that place and how Sebastian and Erin didn't let that faze them at all. They continued to fight through it all and were turning into wonderful children. Erin saw Majestic standing at the end of the red carpet and she ran over to her and gave her a big hug.

"Hey Majestic."

"Hey Erin, you look so pretty."

"Thank you. You look pretty too." Erin said as she continued to smile. Majestic was really growing closer to Erin, and she was enjoying spending time with her. Over the past few months Majestic had been calling Erin and talking to her on the phone. They had become really close. Majestic was hoping that the adoption would go through as planned. She wanted Erin to be a part of what she and Ryan were eventually going to be. If they could be a family one day, that would be something so special. Seeing Erin happy now moved Majestic to tears. To watch a little girl grow up with both parents in jail for the next 20 years, which was a shock to Majestic when she found out that her parents killed a man over his wallet. Then, she had to take care of her blind grandmother who eventually died and now she was standing on this red carpet without a care in the world. God had blessed Erin with the resolve of an adult. She was so strong and for her to only be ten was a testament to how great God is. Erin stood next to Majestic and held her hand. Majestic loved the feel of her little hand. Erin was just staring at Sebastian waiting for him to get through taking his pictures. He finally gets done and walks up to Majestic and gives her a hug.

"Hey Sebastian, you look so handsome."

"He does look handsome." Erin said to make Sebastian blush and right on cue he begins to blush. It was the cutest thing to see and it was just so innocent.

"Thank you Majestic. You look nice." Ryan says as he fights off his urge to keep blushing.

"Thank you," Majestic said as she tried to gain her composure. Sebastian was touching her heart so much. Here was a young man, dealing with a mom that was struggling, his sister who was adopted by another family and his dad who didn't care about him at all. He had to take on responsibilities like helping to cook for his community and be the man of his house at the age of ten. Through all of that, he was still the perfect little gentleman and his ways were so grown. Majestic had always been impressed with his level of maturity and she knew that was a God-given talent bestowed upon him. To have Erin and Sebastian standing next to her right now blessed her so much that if nothing else went right the rest of the night, she would still have cherished that moment. With them standing next to her, she felt a warm feeling in her heart. Next out of the limo was Reagan, followed by Juanita and Marcos. Reagan was so cute with her little white dress with black flowers on it. She had two big bows in her hair and she looked so cute, as if out of a magazine. Juanita had on a long white gown that was smooth around her shape and she looked so pretty. She looked her age now because her face was made up and she looked like a model. Majestic was shocked to see Marcos. Marcos was the waiter that took care of them at the ballroom dance at the restaurant and he was also the one trying to help Ryan get the restaurant ready for the hurricane. She didn't know that Juanita and Marcos was a couple but she was extremely happy for them. Juanita needed some stability and help in her life and hopefully Marcos was the one to do it. He had on a black tuxedo and black bow tie. His long hair was slicked back in a ponytail and he looked rather suave. So they stopped to take a few photos together and then they walked up to Majestic.

"You guys all look wonderful. Reagan you are so cute. Juanita, you look like a model and Marcos you are very handsome." Majestic said as she gave them all a hug. She was happy that they were here. She wanted to share this moment with them as well because this exhibit was about her experiences on the island and they were witnesses to those experiences.

"You look pretty as well." Marcos said as he moved out of the way so Juanita and Reagan could stand next to Majestic.

"Thank you Majestic, and you look beautiful. Thank you for inviting us. The limo ride was great and now this. I feel so special." Juanita said as she showed her excitement.

"You should feel special because you are to me. You deserve nights like this."

"This is a happy moment for me," Juanita said as she wiped a tear out of her eye, and that was when Majestic noticed an engagement ring on her hand.

"You are engaged?"

"Yes. Marcos and I got engaged a month ago." Juanita says as she grabbed Marcos's hand. Marcos nodded in agreement.

"Well congratulations on that! I am very happy for both of you." Majestic was happy with that news. Juanita needed a stable man in her life, someone that loves her for her and Majestic hoped that Marcos was that man. After hearing how Sebastian and Reagan came to be, it was good that she was trying to do things the right way and that showed Majestic that Juanita was getting wiser.

"My marriage will help me with getting Reagan back as well. I needed a lifestyle change and I needed to show that I can be responsible. I think this will start me in that right direction."

"It will Juanita, and I am very proud of you. I know things will work out."

That was good news to Majestic. She wanted Juanita to gain custody of Reagan. She knows how that was part of the reason for Juanita's problems were her feelings of failure with her children. If Juanita can get her life in order then a change would truly come. Majestic was happy with the prospect of that. Suddenly Ryan stepped out of the limo and the world stood still. He wore black two-button suit, a white shirt and a white and black striped tie. Majestic couldn't believe how handsome he looked. He looked like something out of her dreams. He stopped to pose for a picture and Majestic was enjoying what she saw. He looked so debonair and smooth. He walked towards her and she wanted to run up to him and jump into his arms but at the same time she wanted him to enjoy the red carpet moment by himself. Here comes the man of her life and she knew that no red carpet moment will be as special as this one is. The closer he got to her the more she realized how blessed she was to have someone as special as Ryan in her life.

"My Beautiful." Ryan said as he gave Majestic a big kiss.

"My Handsome." Majestic said as she tried to stop smiling. This was the moment she had been waiting for. They were now here and so the exhibit could began.

* * *

Majestic had gone through the whole exhibit. She could tell by the looks on everyone's faces that they were impressed and intrigued by her pictures. But now her most favorite picture was here and she started to get excited because this was her best one, in her opinion, of every picture she had ever taken.

"Now this last picture was one that was taken at, "Heaven of Flowers" and I love this picture so much. This picture was taken as Ryan was putting a flower into my hair. I had my eyes closed and the look on my face was one of love. He wasn't just putting any flower in my ear but a special engagement flower that was only meant to be given at an engagement. So they let me take a picture with the flower in my ear and so I just wanted to share that picture with you now."

Majestic nodded at Joan and Joan begins to take the curtain down but there was no picture up there. Majestic was shocked that there was no picture up there. She looked at Joan in hopes of reading her face so she would know what to do next. She noticed Joan was smiling and Majestic couldn't figure out why. Majestic felt this was not a moment to be smiling because her favorite picture was gone and she felt a little embarrassed by the picture being missing.

"Joan?" Majestic asked as she felt like Joan owed her an explanation.

"I asked her not to show that one." Ryan said as he stood up. Majestic was confused now.

"Why Ryan? You know I loved that picture and as matter of fact that is my favorite picture." Majestic said as she was getting a little upset because this was her exhibit and she wanted that picture in it. Besides, she didn't understand why Joan would listen to him about that picture when she knew how much Majestic loved that picture.

"I understand that but that picture wasn't right."

"I am confused. What wasn't right about that picture?" Majestic asked as she was starting to feel funny about what was taking place. She thought Joan and Ryan loved the picture.

"Well, in that picture you had the engagement flower in your ear and we weren't engaged. You know how guarded they are about that flower and the importance of keeping it sacred."

"Ryan, it was only a picture." Majestic said, as she is really beginning to feel sick. She was not fully understanding why Ryan was doing this, and especially doing it now in front of everyone at the grand display of her exhibit.

"Exactly but all of that is about to change because we are going to make things right." Ryan says as Sebastian walks up with an engagement flower. Majestic just stood there because she didn't truly know what was going on. Joan walked up and gave him a pair of scissors so he could cut the stem off. Now Majestic was catching on, and her heart began beating fast. Ryan then takes the flower and he waits on Joan and everyone there to pull out their cameras and he puts the flower over Majestic's right ear. Just like before. Majestic closed her eyes but this time Ryan steps up and kisses her on the lips. Majestic felt a chill go through her body. She kept her eyes closed a few more seconds as she was just enjoying that precious moment. She opened her eyes and was expecting to see Ryan standing there but instead he was on one knee in front of her. Majestic's heart was beating really fast now, and Ryan hadn't said anything. She knew what all of this meant and for that she was excited. Ryan grabbed her hand and everyone was just snapping pictures the entire time; even the college students ran up and began to take pictures of them. Majestic knew it was an instant classic. Here Ryan is all dressed up and kneeling in front of Majestic as she is decked out in her dress. What a moment that she was experiencing right now. To have this moment happen now was a great joy to Majestic and how she has waited for this to happen.

"My Beautiful. I love you so. I have always loved you. I have prayed for the opportunity to stand before you and profess my love for you. I am here now to let you know that only death can stop me from loving you. This love I have has been growing and growing since the first moment you walked back into my life. Now my only focus is to love you everyday like it is our last day together."

Ryan says as he reaches into his pocket and pulls out an engagement ring. Majestic's eyes got big and she began to cry. She was so overwhelmed with happiness because this moment is what she has hoped for her entire life.

"Today, I want to ask you in front of your family and friends. I want to ask you to spend your forever with me. I promise on this day I will love you until I can't love you any more. I am here to ask you to marry me. So will you marry me?" Ryan asked as he smiled. Majestic had tears rolling down her face as she cried tears of joy.

"Yes."

Majestic responded as Ryan placed the ring on her finger. She pulls him up and gave him a big hug. She was so happy and so was everyone else there. They were all clapping and cheering for them. She began to kiss Ryan and she ignored all the noise. She could only think about how she has prayed for this day. She had longed for this day. She had wanted this day and now the day was here! She couldn't ask for a better way to be asked. She couldn't think of a better audience to be asked in front of. She couldn't ask for a better man to ask her. This was truly out of her dreams. She was crying and it was tears of happiness and a few tears of relief. She just stood there hugging him, crying as everyone was still taking pictures. Majestic hadn't even really looked at the ring. She only wanted to hug Ryan and not ever let him go. He had made Majestic the happiest she had been in years. Her heart was still beating fast, but she didn't care. All she cared about was the fact that the ring on her finger symbolized that someone loved her above all the other women in the world. This ring meant more than that to Majestic. It meant that her never ending quest to find true love was over and that she was about to start a new journey. So she stopped hugging Ryan so she could finally take a good look at the ring. It was a beautiful three carat diamond engagement ring. It sparkled so bright and Majestic had never seen anything so pretty before.

"Majestic, congratulations. That ring is beautiful!" Tracee said as she walked up to give Majestic a hug.

"Thank you. I love this ring!" Majestic said as she started to cry again. She was so overwhelmed with joy that she didn't know what else to do.

"You deserve it. I am so happy for you!" Tracee said as she wiped the tears from her eyes.

"Now we are not supposed to all be crying. Congratulations baby," Renee said, as she wiped her tears off her face. She walked up to Majestic and gave her a big hug. Majestic was just looking at her ring because she wanted to make sure it was still there. She was waiting on her alarm clock to go off and she would wake up with no ring on her finger. That was the kind of luck she thought she would have if this moment ever happened for her. So as everyone was coming up and congratulating her, she was constantly taking peeks at her finger. She was enjoying the attention from everyone. She normally would get attention from something she had done, but now she was getting attention because of something she received. So she took the time to hug everyone that congratulated her and she made sure she showed off the ring.

"Majestic, I am sorry that I couldn't tell you the plan that Ryan came up with. I had to go with the flow but I am going to tell you that I was so nervous the whole night. I knew you loved that one picture and I didn't want you to kill me because it wasn't up there." Joan said as she hugged Majestic.

"I was going to kill you. Only this ring has saved you from meeting your Maker."

"I wanted to see your surprised look on your face when the picture wasn't there and I wanted to see the look on your face when Ryan popped the question. Congratulations on your engagement Majestic, because you really deserve true happiness and now you have found it."

"Thank you Joan. I am glad that you were in on the surprise. I had no clue this was going to happen but it has made it that much more special."

"It was definitely special. I was glad to be in on it. Ryan had called up here a few days ago and made me promise to help him. I couldn't pass up the chance to see you become so happy. I got teary-eyed as we planned the whole thing because I knew how sweet and special this night was going to be. Hey, let me get to work. I see that Lorenzo is getting swamped by orders." Joan said as she walked off to help Lorenzo take orders for pictures. Just about everyone was standing in line so Majestic felt the exhibit was a success.

"Congratulations." Erin said as she ran up to Majestic and gave her a hug. "If I am adopted by Ryan, will this make you my mom?" Erin asks.

"I would be your stepmom. Your mom would still be your mother."

"I want to call you mom. I think it fits you better."

"Me too." Majestic said as she continued to hug Erin. Majestic couldn't fathom life without Erin. She knew she would do whatever it took to make sure that she loved Erin with all her heart. Majestic just felt like after all Erin had been through, she deserved to be spoiled for awhile, and she planned on doing that.

"Congratulations Majestic." Sebastian said as he hugged Majestic.

"Thank you Sebastian. Now I will be your aunt."

"Yes." Sebastian said as he did a fist pump. That gesture made Majestic happy because that meant that he was happy to have her in his life and that meant the world to her.

"Now it's my turn to congratulate you on your engagement," Juanita said as she and Marcos walked up to her.

"Yes, I guess so," Majestic said as she hugged them.

"I know that you and Ryan will be so happy together. I just want you to know that I truly want this for both of you. I mean it. Forget what happened with us in the past. Just know that I am past that and I am really happy for you. If anything, my sister is looking down on us and she is smiling. She would want the very best for Ryan and I strongly feel like you are that."

"Thanks, Juanita. That means a lot to me." Majestic said as she reflected on the conversation that took place three months earlier. She knew that Juanita took it hard when she found out that Ryan had feelings for Majestic. Majestic is glad that they were able to talk things out and now this night could be special with no regrets.

"Baby, I am so happy for you."

"Thanks Dad." Majestic hugged him.

"Come here Ryan." John says as he motioned for Ryan to come to him. Ryan was mingling with a few guests.

"I am so happy for both of you. Ryan, you are a father's dream. Since the first moment I met you, I have been impressed with you. You have shown me that you love my daughter with all your heart and for that I am very happy. It is hard for fathers to give their daughters away. I am more than honored to give her to you," John said as he gave Ryan a hug; Majestic was blown away. She had never seen her father act like this. He didn't do it for Patrick but he had taken a real liking to Ryan and that made Majestic really happy. "Majestic, you have waited on love for so long. You have been very patient and I am so proud of you. I have given my blessing for this marriage so let's focus on the wedding and I will take care of everything. You just plan it and let me know what I have to do," John said as he hugged Majestic.

She was so happy that her dad wanted this engagement to happen. She knows her dad only wanted the best for her, and Ryan was definitely that.

"Dad, that is such a sweet gesture from you to pay for the whole wedding."

"That is the least I can do. To know that my baby is going to finally be happy for the rest of her life is priceless."

"Thank you John. That means a lot to me," Ryan says as he shook John's hand.

"Don't mention it."

"What are you guys talking about?" Renee asked as she, Tracee and Patrick came over.

"I was just telling them that I am going to pay for the wedding," John informed Renee.

"What? You only paid for half of mine!" Tracee said, as she winked at Majestic.

"You are such a hater, Tracee." Majestic winked back at her.

"We can definitely do that," Renee replied while smiling at Majestic.

"I just want to add that I know you are going to make a wonderful son-in-law. My daughter has not been this happy in ages and we owe you for that."

"We really, really owe you for that. She was a mess before now," Tracee said, as everyone laughed. Majestic was glad that everyone was happy for her and that every-one approved of Ryan.

"Let's go celebrate. Dinner is on me," Patrick said, as everyone looked at him in surprise. "I am going to be better. I know that we haven't always gotten along, but with the baby coming, I want things to be right."

"Thank you Patrick, but it wasn't always you. It was mainly me sometimes," Majestic said, as she walked over to Patrick and gave him a hug.

"I told ya'll. I kept on saying that she was start-ing stuff with him," Tracee said as she tried to hold in her laughter.

"Whatever Tracee," Majestic said as she walked back over to Ryan.

"Great. Let's go then. Since this is your night Majestic, where would you like to go?"

"Let's go to Eden's Bay."

"Don't we have to have reservations for that place?" Tracee asked.

"We do but I am on their VIP list so we can call and they will have a table ready in an hour." Majestic replied as she looked at everyone for confirmation.

"VIP status? You roll like that huh?" Tracee gave Majestic a high-five.

"Cool. I will call them then." Patrick took out his cell phone to call the restaurant.

Majestic was on cloud nine. She had just gotten engaged and it still felt like a dream. She had always thought about what it would feel like to be engaged. Now she knows firsthand, and it was a good feeling. This feeling was better than being at Heaven of Flowers. Better than being on the beautiful beach. Better than eating at the "Heart of Velacious." Better than the dance she danced with Ryan. The thought of that gave her an idea.

"Excuse me everyone," Majestic said as she walked over to the college students who were patiently waiting to get paid by Joan for a night's work. They knew that she paid them after all the customers left. Majestic asked them to stack all of the chairs that used during the exhibit. The students used the chair cart to roll them to a closet behind the front area. Majestic went behind the counter where Joan was and she put in a CD of some slow love songs. She turned it up in the area where the exhibits were and not where Joan was because she was still handling customers. Majestic then walked back over to her family.

"Eden's Bay said they can have us ready in an hour," Patrick said to Majestic as she got closer to them.

"Great, then we have plenty of time."

"Time for what?" Ryan asked.

"Time for our engagement dance," Majestic says as she grabbed Ryan's hand and led him to the open area where the chairs were. She pulled him close and they began to slow dance.

Majestic wanted this dance to be nice and slow. She wanted to just hold him close to her. She was so at peace at this moment. Love had found her and it had made a place in her life. It was avoiding her for so long, and she didn't think she was ever going to find love again. She had failed so many times that it became discouraging. Now she has made a commitment to love, and that is a victory. Majestic was actually dancing to her favorite song. The song spoke of love found and at this moment she couldn't agree more. So they just danced to the music and let love set the mood.

"Ryan, thank you for this night. It was such a surprise but I am happy it happened this way. It was like a fairytale."

"I am glad you didn't get mad at me for having Joan hide that picture."

"I was mad for a second but once I figured out what was going on, I was cool then."

"Great. I am glad you said, "Yes" and I am glad you love the ring."

"I do love the ring. I love it a lot and believe me there was no way I was going to say no. Only a fool would say no."

"I am glad that you are not a fool then."

"Me too. I was one before but I won't be one again. No gallery, no nothing will separate me from you ever again. I could have experienced this a long time ago and I kick myself for that."

"Maybe, but it is better this way because you fully understand and appreciate it. You had to experience the bad before you realized what was really good."

"That is so true. I have had bad; but now I have good, and I love good."

"Good loves you too."

"Ryan what you said when you asked me to marry you was priceless. I just want to assure you that I feel the same way. I will do all I can to prove to you that I love you. I don't want a day to go by that you don't feel loved. If you ever feel like you haven't received enough love from me, let me know and I will make up for it."

"Me too Majestic. I can think back to how I used to think about how life would be if I married you. I would think about just holding you and just loving the fact that I was coming home to you. Now my dream is about to come true and that is a great thing to know," Ryan said as he smiled at Majestic.

"That was my dream as well. All I know is that since it has come true, lets make sure that we love each other to the fullest."

"I plan on doing that. I want you to know that my mom and dad would have loved you. They would have felt the same way I feel. I know because they saw the pain I had when I left years ago. My mom knew you had to be someone special because she had never seen me cry before. I told her that we chose our goals over our hearts. She said that if the chance came again, choosing your goals over love wasn't the best option. You can do that once and make it, but twice would kill the heart. When I saw you again that conversation popped back up in my head and I prayed that if there was a chance to be with you, I was going to take it."

"I wish I would have met them. I would have told them what a wonderful son they have and if it was okay if I took him away."

"My mom would have fought you. She was known for fighting for me."

"I would have put up a good fight. I have my mind made up, so there was no way I was leaving that island without you."

"I do recall you leaving me, and I mean in a hurry," Ryan said, as they laughed.

"I knew you'd come and find me. I was just making sure you truly loved me so that was a big test," Majestic said while laughing.

"Of course I was coming to find you. Do you not remember how you looked in that two-piece bathing suit? Believe me; I was coming to find you."

Majestic couldn't believe that she was blushing. She was definitely flattered that Ryan was complimenting her. She knows that when someone you love compliments you, it is the best compliment in the world and that was how she felt now. If any other man said they liked her in that two-piece bathing suit, she would have been offended. That is the beauty of love. It can make anything seem better when it comes from someone you love.

"You weren't half bad yourself. I know you caught me checking you out."

"Of course I did. I knew you were that was why I was flexing," Ryan said as they laughed.

"I love you, Ryan."

"I love you too, Majestic.

They continued to dance through the song and when the next song came on Majestic looked over at her family as they just stood there watching them dance. Majestic motioned for Sebastian and Erin to come over to her. They walked up smiling like they knew what she was going to say.

"Erin, I remember how depressed you were when you weren't able to go ballroom dancing. So here is your chance to dance and you have the perfect person to dance with." Majestic says as she points at Sebastian.

"You are right. Let's dance." Erin says as she extends her hands out to Sebastian but he shook his head no.

"I have to ask you, not you ask me." Sebastian tells Erin as he folds his arms across his chest.

"That is right. You have been taught well Sebastian. Treat her like the lady she is," Ryan said, as he smiled at Sebastian. Majestic could tell that Ryan was proud of the things he taught Sebastian.

"Erin, may I have this dance?"

"Yes you may," Erin said, as she walked over to Sebastian and put her hands on his shoulders. Sebastian puts his hands above her waist and they began to dance. Majestic thought that was the cutest thing she has ever seen. The college students thought so too because they began to take pictures of them. Majestic and Ryan just watched them dance for a minute. They looked so cute together. It was their first crush and it was all so innocent. They just loved being together and just hanging out. They weren't corrupted by temptation or anything like that. They just liked each other and that was so sweet to see. Suddenly, Tracee grabbed Patrick's hand and they walked out to the area and began to dance. John and Renee followed suit and not to be outdone, Juanita, Marcos and Reagan all began to dance together. Majestic just looked around at everyone and she could just feel the love. At this moment she realized that one act of true love affected everyone, and that was such a blessing. Majestic couldn't help but thank God for what she saw. Everyone she truly cared about was here now, and in one way or another, they were expressing love to someone close to them. Majestic never pictured such an event, but she was so glad that she was part of it. She prayed quietly that moments like this would come often. She then looked at Ryan and gave him a kiss. She couldn't tell him enough how much she truly loved him. Her heart thanked him for fixing it and showing it what love was all about. She was forever in debt to Ryan and she doesn't mind spending her entire life paying him back. Before she started dancing again, Majestic noticed that the last customer had walked out the door. She saw Joan motion for the college students to come to her. She handed them all an envelope and then she ran off to the closet behind the front desk. She came out with a camera and started to take pictures of everyone dancing. Majestic started dancing again with Ryan. She was so in love with Ryan, so in love with her family and above all, so in love with God. This night was priceless, and she knew she couldn't have planned it any better. She had crossed a point in her life that she didn't even think was as close. She knew that she loved Ryan and that he loved her, but they never talked about marriage. He didn't give her any hints that he was planning on asking her, so this was a shock to her. So as she is dancing with him she could not help but to hold him close to her. This was her future husband and the thought of that sent chills through her body. They will become husband and wife and she loved that prospect. Every woman dreams of the type of husband that she would have one day. Majestic felt so blessed because she now had the type of person that she had been asking God for. Ryan was exactly the person she wanted. Everything was perfect in Majestic's eyes, and for that she was overjoyed. This dance they were doing was just the beginning; it was the beginning of a lifetime of dancing together. So as the music played, Majestic let herself be lost in thought. She could picture herself at the altar with Ryan and them both saying, "I do." She could imagine them kissing and running off into a limo. As she imagined them driving away, her heart started to beat faster because that day could not come soon enough for her. She was so ready for the next step that she didn't even want to enjoy this moment fully. She was going to take it all in stride, and because of her love for Ryan she will wait, however long it takes, until they are married. In the meantime, she relished in the fact that tonight was the night that the world found out that Majestic was loved. There was someone that loved her so much that waiting for her was worth it. The thought of that made her very happy because on their wedding night she would give freely what was earned. To know that her wait would soon be over, in more than one way, made Majestic smile.

Majestic was ready for that but she knew she still had a ways to go so she redirected her focus back to the present. She looked deeply into Ryan's eyes. Majestic just wanted to see his face and look into his eyes. She loved the fact that before long, they would be joined together as husband and wife. That brought her a quiet joy that moved her to tears. Before Ryan could see the tears she placed her head on his shoulder quickly. Majestic didn't want Ryan to know that she was crying because it wasn't like she was sad and needed to be comforted. No, she was crying because her longing to be loved in a special way was now fulfilled. Majestic just let the music, and her happy heart lead her as she danced with Ryan.

*　　*　　*

Majestic stood at the baggage claim terminal, waiting on Ryan and Erin. She had gotten to the airport early because she was so excited. Today was the first day that Ryan and Erin were officially moving to Las Vegas. Ryan had gained custody of Erin through adoption and that was the last bit of business that he had left to wrap up on Velacious Island. It had been four months since he proposed to Majestic and now they were finally going to be living in the same city. Majestic had been very patient during the entire process because Ryan was away from her. Ever since the engagement, she wanted to be with Ryan, but she knew he had to go away. Today was the first day of the rest of their lives together. She knew that since Ryan and Erin were moving to Las Vegas, her plate was going to be very full. She had so much to do. She wanted everything to be perfect, as the wedding date was getting closer. The wedding was a little over three weeks away. They were ready to get married now and didn't want to wait any longer. They were planning on getting married on January 1st. That day symbolized the beginning of a new year and for them it would symbolize a new beginning together and they couldn't wait. She needed to get them from the airport and take them to the hotel where they were going to stay until the wedding. The plan was for them to move into Majestic's three-bedroom house once they were married. Everyone was asking Majestic why not just move him in now; she informed them that they wanted to do things the right way. Majestic remembered what happened when they were together a long time ago. They overstepped the boundary and they became intimate. Majestic cringed whenever she thought about it. Not because she didn't want to be intimate with Ryan, because she did. It was the fact that she promised God that she would wait. She told him that she was going to be different from the rest. Majestic thought she had total control when it came to temptation but on those three fateful nights, thirteen years ago, she knew that she didn't have control. Majestic knew that three weeks was very doable because she has made it for thirteen years. A few more weeks wasn't going to hurt anyone. She wanted the weeks to go by fast though. She was ready for the day when they would be husband and wife. She knew that she would be the happiest woman alive. Not just someone with a few of the qualities she is looking for, but all of them. Majestic was so happy that she didn't just settle for anyone or put her true idea of what her man should be aside because she couldn't find anyone that measured up to it. She is much happier because she was patient and she believed that God was going to send her someone to share life with her. That thought only brought a smile to her face. She remembered all the prayers where she was basically begging God to complete her life's mission to have a husband. There were many days and nights that she was upset that she was by herself. She couldn't understand why someone like her couldn't find anyone to be what she wanted them to be. Was she not worthy enough to change for? It is not like she was asking for too much. She only wanted the men she dated to be more like Christ instead of thinking that they were already there. She knew they weren't and that is why she wasn't standing here waiting on them right now; she was waiting for the one who was striving to be the man she wanted him to be. She wanted someone who was truly after God's heart in everything he did. She wanted a man who respected her and treated her like no other woman mattered; that man was Ryan. Majestic began to pace the area because she was so happy to be able to see them again. She could only picture the looks on their faces.

They weren't coming for a visit for a week or a weekend, but here to stay. Not only stay here, but to be one with Majestic, and the thought of that made her want to do a happy dance, but she didn't want to draw attention. So she just walked back and forth trying to calm herself down. She walked over to the monitor and reviewed all the incoming flights. Majestic checked the screen for Ryan and Erin's flight. She saw that the plane had arrived so it was only a matter of time before they were reunited. Majestic knew that she is going to make the most of her new life. She had already started to limit her hours at the gallery and prepared the house for its new members. She was way ahead of schedule, and that was a good thing. With the approaching wedding, there was no way she would have been able to do both at the same time. Planning a wedding is so time-consuming and Majestic had to devote most of her free time to it. She was able to get a lot accomplished; as far as she was concerned, everything was on point.

"Mommy!"

Majestic heard a little girl yelling for her mom as she kept on pacing back and forth. She noticed the conveyor belt began to move. That meant that Ryan and Erin should be arriving to the baggage claim area very soon.

"Mommy!"

Majestic was wondering who the little girl was that was calling for her mom and why her mom was ignoring her. Majestic looked in the direction she heard the little girl. Erin and Ryan walked up to her, holding hands. It was the cutest sight she had seen. Erin was smiling and she began to wave when Majestic looked at her.

"I was calling you," Erin said as she ran up and gave Majestic a big hug.

"I didn't hear you. I only heard this little girl calling for her mommy."

"That was me. I was calling you Mommy." Erin said as she pointed to herself.

"Oh, that was you!" Majestic smiled. That warmed her heart to hear Erin call her Mommy. That only showed Majestic the level of love that Erin had for her, and that made her feel very special.

"Yes that was me. I was trying to get used to it since you are now my new Mommy."

"I am glad you called me that. Next time I will answer you."

"My Beautiful," Ryan said as he gave Majestic a kiss.

"My Handsome," Majestic said, knowing she would never get tired of calling him that. "How was your flight?"

"It wasn't too bad. We slept the whole time." Ryan said as he stretched.

"We slept the whole time," Erin said as she grabbed Majestic's hand.

"Good for you guys. Rest is good," Majestic said as she looked down at Erin because she knew that Erin was going to repeat what she said in her own cute way.

"Rest is good," Erin said as she laughed. She knew that Majestic was waiting on her to repeat what she said and that was funny to her.

"Ok, let me get our luggage." Ryan said as he walked over to the conveyor belt to retrieve the luggage off of it.

Majestic watched him as he went to get the luggage; she felt so blessed. To have Erin and Ryan in her life was so special. Just last year at this same time she was dreading another Christmas with no family of her own. No husband and no children to speak of, and no one to do wonderful things for. Now she had a family that was about three weeks away from being made final. She knew that this coming Christmas would be great, but next year would be even greater because that Christmas would be their first together after the wedding. Just the thought of marriage made her heart race. She was so excited by the prospect of that.

"Let's go get a luggage cart and help Ryan with the luggage," Majestic said as she gently leads Erin towards the luggage cart stand.

"You mean Daddy," Erin replied as she skipped with Majestic.

"You are correct. Let's get a luggage cart for Daddy."

"Ok, let's do that."

Erin was such a blessing. She had the biggest heart and was so sweet. All of her movements were just so innocent. She was truly a child that wasn't affected by all the drama that had taken place in her life. She has lost both of her real parents to the jail system and hadn't skipped a beat. She had latched on to Ryan and now to Majestic, and it felt like they have been there for Erin her whole life. Majestic couldn't help but feel sorry for Erin's parents because they were missing out on a blessing. She wanted to make sure she treated Erin as her own by showering her with love and affection. There wasn't going to be a day that would go by without her telling Erin that she loved her. Majestic knew that Erin needed stability and that is what Ryan and Majestic gave her. She would not have to worry about a repeat of losing Ryan and Majestic as with her biological parents.

"I think this one is good." Erin said as she pulled the luggage cart out of the space it was in.

"Check the tires and make sure it has gas in it," Majestic said as she watched Erin pretend to check for gas and kicked the tires.

"It looks good to me."

"Good. Let's take it to Daddy so we can get our luggage."

"Ok." Erin said as she pushed the luggage cart. She was so excited and Majestic couldn't blame her. This was the beginning of a new life for her. No more rundown apartments. No more taking care of her family, and no more worries. No longer did she have to be reminded that her parents were in jail. She would now have the chance to be a child and grow up the most normal way as possible. She would have a support system to take care of her completely.

"I was wondering where you guys went."

"We didn't want you to hurt yourself carrying that luggage. I finally get you to move out here and I can't have you get hurt on the first day," Majestic said as they approached Ryan.

"Good looking out. Ok, let's put the luggage on here." Ryan said, as the three of them placed the luggage on the luggage cart.

"How does that look Erin? Did we get all of them?" Ryan asked as Erin looked around the area and began to count the luggage.

"Yes, we have them all."

"The SUV is this way," Majestic said as she led them to her SUV that was parked in the parking garage.

"I don't know about you ladies but I am very hun-gry." Ryan says as they are walking.

"Me too," Erin chimes in.

"Ok, my SUV is right over there," Majestic pointed.

Ryan loaded the entire luggage into the back while Erin jumped in the back seat. He closed the door and gave Majestic a hug.

"Are you sure you are ready for this?"

"Very much Ryan, because you know I have been waiting on this moment for a long time. We are about to spend the rest of our life together and I can't wait."

"Let's go then," Ryan said as he kissed her on the lips and walks over to the passenger side of SUV and got in. Majestic got in the driver's side and she looked behind her to see Erin sitting there, smiling. Majestic knew this was the beginning of something good.

6

Majestic rounded the corner and now she was in plain view of the whole church. Everyone stood up and began to take pictures of her. She was about to take the walk of a lifetime. This is the walk that most women dream and hope for. As she walked down the aisle, she could hear everyone gasping at how she looked. She chose a more elegant white wedding dress that wasn't as puffy as most wedding dresses. It was more form-fitting but it still had a long train. Majestic remembered to smile so she would look her best for every photo that was taken. She was very nervous but excited at the same time. She had practiced this walk so many times in her mind that she pretty much knew how many steps to get to the front. She had her routine down in her mind. She remembered:

Step, step, breathe and smile.

As she made it down the first aisle, Majestic looked at the faces of everyone that had shown up.

Step, step, breathe and smile.

There was everyone here from workers at the gallery, workers from her favorite restaurant and coffee shop.

Step, step, breathe and smile.

There were members from her church, friends, and family members there. It was basically everyone with whom Majestic wanted to share this moment.

Step, step, breathe and smile.

There was only one person she cared if they showed up and that was Ryan.

Step, step, breathe and smile.

Anyone else who showed up was just icing on the cake.

Step, step, breathe and smile.

As Majestic was making her way down the aisle, she looked ahead and she saw Ryan standing there, look-ing so handsome in his gray tuxedo. Next to Ryan were Marcos and Patrick, and on the other side of the Pastor stood Tracee and Juanita. Majestic saw her spot. That is the one spot she had dreamt about her whole life. It was the spot of the bride-to-be and it was her life's destina-tion. So as she passed by the rows, she could feel her heart beating faster and faster. Majestic could hear her heart beating, *boom-boom, boom-boom.*

She was overwhelmed with excitement so as she passed the last row and Ryan walked over to her she couldn't help but feel special.

Boom-boom, boom-boom.

Ryan walks up to Majestic and she could see tears in his eyes, and the sight of that brought tears to her eyes.

Boom-boom, boom-boom.

She knew that he was getting teary eyed over her.

Boom-boom, boom-boom.

So as they made eye contact, he smiled and Majestic wanted to fight the tears from falling but she couldn't.

Boom-boom, boom-boom.

Ryan grabbed Majestic's hand and they both faced the Pastor. So as the Pastor began the wedding ceremony, Majestic was trying to quiet her beating heart. She felt as if she was going to hyperventilate. She couldn't stop her excitement at all. She was so happy to be in love and was extremely happy to be getting married. Now, no one had anything on her. No longer would she meet someone and hate to have them ask about her status. Everyone would always ask her why someone as pretty as her had no one. Then everyone would quietly think that maybe she was the problem. She hated that feeling; now it was finally going to go away forever. She would now look forward to answering that question. Better yet, she was going to make sure that everyone saw the ring on her finger. It was going to be like a beacon of light to the whole world. The whole wide world would see the beautiful ring and the beaming smile that she will have on her face everyday. To be married is a rite of passage. It is telling everyone that you went down the road that some true relationships travel on. If you can stay the course and make it as far as marriage, then you are telling everyone that you believe in commitment. To want to share your life with someone else is the ultimate sacrifice. You must share even your most intimate secrets, and for some people that is not easily done. Your life is no longer about you and what you want. It is now about what you and your mate want and many are not willing to be unselfish when it comes to relationships. Majestic was willing to do whatever it took to make her marriage work. After all she went through, wished for and prayed for, there was no way she was going to let anything ruin all the time she put in to get to this point right now. No argument, no person, no drama was going to put a damper on this relationship.

Majestic was patiently waiting on her moment to say her vows. She had been thinking long and hard about her vows.

"Now we've come to the announcement of the vows. Both Ryan and Majestic have written their own vows and they would like to share them right now," The Pastor said, as he looked over at Ryan. Ryan turned and faced Majestic. He held both of her hands and looked in her eyes.

"I, Ryan, so lovingly take you Majestic to be my wife. I vow to be more than your husband. I vow to be your best friend, confidant, supporter, lover, and encourager. I vow to live up to your expectations of me as your husband. I will truly give unconditional love and I will forever be the one that loves you to the fullest. I vow to make everyday another chance to prove my love for you. God backs these vows I'm saying to you, so my words will ring true. This day my vow will unite us under a single goal and that is to share our love for each other. I vow to do all I have stated until I die." Ryan smiled at Majestic. Majestic knew it was her turn and she hoped she would not forget any part of her vow.

"I, Majestic, take you Ryan to be my soul mate. I vow to be your faithful and committed wife. I vow to love you and show you every chance I get. I vow to honor our love under God's rule and I promise to be trustworthy, loving, understanding and true. I vow to continue to love and support you in all that you do. I stand before my family and friends today to prove without a shadow of a doubt that I love you deeply and I want to spend the rest of our lives together. I vow to be more than words but action as well." Majestic as looked at the Pastor. The Pastor stepped forward and asked for the rings. Marcos handed over Majestic's ring to Ryan.

"Do you, Majestic; take Ryan to be your lawfully wedded husband?"

"I do." Majestic said, as Ryan slipped the ring unto Majestic's finger. As soon as the ring touched her skin, she began to cry. This was truly a moment that she had dreamt of. As the ring was sliding on her finger, Majestic knew it was almost finished. Majestic received her ring from Tracee.

"Ryan, do you take Majestic to be your lawfully wedded wife?"

"I do," Ryan said, as Majestic placed the ring on Ryan's finger. They both look over at the Pastor and he stretched his arms out.

"By the grace and love of God, I pronounce them husband and wife. You may kiss the bride."

Majestic gladly walked over to Ryan and they kissed. It was one of those storybook kisses where it felt like the room was spinning around them as they kissed. As soon as their lips touched, Majestic felt a wave of relief come over her. Majestic knew that she had done it. Majestic has now finished the ceremony and they are now officially husband and wife. She held him close because she wanted to experience this moment that much longer. Majestic wanted to kiss him like the old Big Red gum commercials where the couple kept on kissing and kissing. Majestic didn't care about the reception or the pictures. She knew that at this moment, they were officially together and that was captivating to her. They finally stopped kissing and they turned to face everyone that was now standing and clapping. Majestic started to cry; she was the happiest she had ever been. She was now married! She could now check that off her to-do list. She had accomplished a task that she didn't really think was possible. Now they held hands as they walked down the aisle; everyone was standing and were either crying or clapping. There seemed to be no in-between. Majestic realized that she wasn't the only one who was truly happy for her. She saw her mom and dad, and they were both crying; that only made Majestic cry more. She knew that her mom was so elated that Majestic was finally married. She also knew her dad was just as happy for her because he knew that Ryan would treat Majestic the way her dad would want him to. So as they made it to the front of the church, they turned around and went back up the aisle so they could meet the rest of the wedding party and take pictures. Majestic felt so good, and at that moment she looked up to the ceiling and winked to God. She knew that God knew her heart and her thoughts and so he would truly know why she was winking at him. Majestic thanked God for bringing into her life the love of a lifetime.

* * *

"Welcome home Mr. Levens." Majestic said, as she opened the door that led to the kitchen from the garage.

"I am glad to be home, Mrs. Levens." Ryan said as he stood there and looked at Majestic. "Ok, I am going to pick you up and carry you inside the house just like what they used to do back in the day," Ryan said, as he opened his arms for Majestic. Majestic jumped into his arms and Ryan carried her into the house. They walked from the kitchen, through the living room and down the hall that led to their bedroom. Ryan walks in and sets her on the bed.

"Thank you Mr.Levens. I sure do appreciate that because my feet are hurting from those shoes I was wearing." Majestic says as she begins to rub her feet.

"It was my pleasure." Ryan said, as he stood there looking at Majestic. Majestic smiled back at him; she felt a little awkward. This is the very first time that Ryan has been in her bedroom, which was now their bedroom. She knew that she had to get used to it since they are now married. This was their wedding night and this was a night that she knew was coming. She knew the customs about wedding nights, but normally the newlyweds are not nervous. They wouldn't be nervous because they would have already been intimate in the past so some of the luster would be taken off of this night. Ryan and Majestic didn't count what took place years ago as being intimate, just a moment of lust. Majestic knew she was nervous but she hoped it wouldn't ruin this night. Majestic was still looking forward to this night so she wanted everything to be just as perfect as the wedding and reception was. So Majestic just stared at Ryan as if she needed him to take charge. Ryan walked over to her and sat down next to Majestic on the bed.

"Well, I think everything went well. The wedding was perfect and you looked so beautiful coming down the aisle. The whole time that you were walking, I kept on telling myself that there is no way that beautiful woman wants to marry me. It was like out of my fantasy."

"Well it goes without saying what I thought when I saw you standing there. I was trying to stop my heart from beating a hole in my chest. I was so nervous and I just didn't want to trip or stumble. That would have ruined everything and not to mention, I would have been embarrassed."

"Maybe, but I would have still married you. I would have rushed to your rescue and made sure you were alright. I would have been embarrassed for you though."

"I bet you would be but not as much as I would have been."

"Well, you made it safely down the aisle and you made it through the whole ceremony. Sorry that you had to see me crying, but I was crying because I was so happy. I didn't think I would cry but it was something about seeing you coming down the aisle that got to me."

"I was doing well until I saw you. Just seeing you cry made me cry. I was so happy that you were emotional because I have always needed reassurance and what better way to be assured than seeing it first hand. I thought it was sweet that you were doing that."

Majestic had never seen any man get emotional because of her, and definitely not at the sight of her.

That was so heartwarming to know that Ryan loved her so much that he would get teary-eyed. She had always wished that someone would love her on that level. Now she had someone that indeed cared for her intensely and that made her feel good.

"Majestic I do want to say that I truly love you and this was definitely the one day I will remember for the rest of my life."

"I love you too Ryan. This is the greatest moment of my life. To have you as my husband is more than a dream that has come true, it's a prayer that came to be."

"Well, tonight is the big night."

"Indeed it is. How do you feel about it?" Majestic asked, because she was curious to know how Ryan felt.

"I feel good. I am looking forward to this night and I have for awhile."

"I have too but I am really nervous and you know that we have had this conversation before. I just want it to be as nice as this whole day has been."

"Majestic don't you worry. I promise that tonight will be the perfect end to this day."

"I believe you."

"Good. Let's just do as we planned. You can run the bath water and I will get the CD and the candles."

"Ok, let's do it." Majestic said, as she stood up and turned around so that her back was turned to Ryan. She held her hair up above her neckline. Ryan took the cue and unzipped her wedding dress all the way down to the bottom of her back. Majestic then let the dress fall down her shoulders, and as it slid down her body, she was surprised that she has done this in front of Ryan. Although they were married now, she was still a little shy to undress in front of him. As she stepped out of the dress and turned around to pick it up, Majestic saw Ryan looking at her. She felt good because now it was ok for him to look at her in any way that he wanted. She was his and she knew that she is going to enjoy being free during intimacy.

"I thought you were going to go and get a CD and some candles?" Majestic asked as she let her hair down and picked up her wedding dress.

"I am, but I am so happy that I can stare at you all I want and I don't have to feel bad."

"You can stare all you want but we have a special thing to get to so you need to go and get the CD and candles so we can get this show on the road."

"You are right. I will be right back." Ryan says as he turned around and walked out of the bedroom. Majestic hung up her wedding dress in her closet. She then went into the bathroom and walked over to the bathtub. She then turned the water on and added bubble bath into the water. Ryan walked into the bathroom with an arm full of large round candles. He placed them around the bathtub. Majestic watched as Ryan lit all the candles. When he was finished, Majestic walked up to him and started to undress him. Majestic and Ryan climbed into the bathtub. Majestic leaned back on Ryan's chest. They just sat there for about thirty minutes just reminiscing about the wedding and the reception. Majestic loved the fact that they were approaching this intimate situation slowly. They were just taking their time because they knew what was about to take place but they still approached it in a mature manner. This is what really helped calm her nerves because she anxiously waits the moment that they would be passionate. So for now, she just wanted to relax with him in the tub and let what happens, happen.

"I am glad that you have this large bathtub. We are definitely going to have to use this more often." Ryan says as he hugged Majestic.

"I am glad too. I don't see any problem with us doing this more often. Those candles you lit smell so good. They smell like vanilla scent."

"It is vanilla scent. That is my favorite."

"Good choice."

Majestic nodded at Ryan and he knew it was time to get out of the tub and do what was on both of their minds. So bathe and dry each other off and then they made their way into to the bedroom. Majestic felt so relaxed and so at ease that she didn't feel nervous at all. She was ready to experience passion for the first time in her life. Not that lust they experienced years ago but a loving passion that she waited to have on their wedding night. No longer will she have to think about the past. So as they hugged each other and began to caress each other, Majestic welcomed this new feeling that she was feeling. It was a feeling that was deep inside of her. She felt like only Ryan could help her with this feeling so she stops caressing him and she begins to kiss him very passionately. Majestic was now ready to enjoy a night of passion with Ryan so before they began to take it a step further, Majestic cleared her mind of all thoughts because she wanted to focus on what was about to take place. This act was going to be an act that she never wanted to forget. To enjoy your spouse, on your wedding night, as God ordained it to be, was even more comforting. So as they continue to kiss passionately, Majestic let Ryan take the lead but she knew that it didn't matter if he did or didn't. At this moment she was ready to do whatever it took to enjoy this night. So as the passion began to heat up and they were ready to consummate their marriage, Majestic was on cloud nine and she didn't want to come down. She wanted to subtly tell Ryan that she was ready and if on cue he adheres to her wishes.

* * *

As the sun began to shine into Majestic's bedroom, it caught her looking at her ring. Majestic has been looking at it for the past thirty minutes. She wanted to admire it. She had longed for this finger to be occupied and now that it was, she just wanted confirmation so she kept looking at it. She was now at a point in her life where love has placed a hold on it. Majestic hoped it was a vise grip and one that wasn't going to be broken. Majestic thought love had nothing to do with her as if they were enemies but now she knew better. Love comes at the right moment when you will most appreciate it. Love doesn't come often for some because it doesn't want to cheapen the effect when it finally comes and stays. Majestic had been a stranger to love, so this feeling was very deep. She couldn't imagine living life without it again. That thought made Majestic promise herself that she was going to do all that she could to be loved and to give love. She didn't want to go back to the old Majestic where loneliness had a home. Now love had occupancy and Majestic wanted it to be a lifetime contract with no way to break it. So as she rolled over onto her stomach and she held her hand up in the morning sunlight she was so very thankful. She looked over at Ryan who was sleeping peacefully. Majestic wanted to just lean over and kiss him but she had done it so many times already that she didn't want to press her luck because she didn't want to wake him up. After all of the activity from the night before, Majestic felt that she should be asleep as well, but her excited heart won't let her. This is the 1st day after the wedding and she found out that she was still excited after the wedding as she was before the wedding. Majestic lowered her hand and she reached out to Ryan and rubbed her hand along his face. She was so happy that he was the one with whom she would spend her entire life. God had answered her prayers, and he did it at the right time. Majestic reflected on all the prayers over the years where she asked God to let this be the day that she meets her husband. She was so glad that God didn't work on her time because she would have missed out on Ryan, and that thought sent a bad chill down her back. '*Thank God for patience*' was all that Majestic could think of at that moment. Majestic was twice as glad because Erin was also part of the deal. She had her ring, her marriage, her husband, and her daughter; they were all a family now.

Majestic knew that God had blessed her with love. Not just a selfish romantic love, but true love that could be shared with others. Majestic realized that to have Christian love was the deepest, strongest love someone could possibly have. Christ proved that on the cross. Majestic was very grateful that God had entrusted her with His love and she knew that from this day forward all will know what love is through her actions and her words. Now she knows that love is majestic.

Omega